I0745096

CHRISTOPHER BUSH

THE CASE OF THE CURIOUS CLIENT

With an introduction
by Curtis Evans

DEAN STREET PRESS

Published by Dean Street Press 2019

Copyright © 1947 Christopher Bush

Introduction copyright © 2019 Curtis Evans

All Rights Reserved

The right of Christopher Bush to be identified as the Author of the Work has been asserted by his estate in accordance with the Copyright, Designs and Patents Act 1988.

First published in 1947 by MacDonald & Co.

Cover by DSP

ISBN 978 1 912574 99 5

www.deanstreetpress.co.uk

CHRISTOPHER BUSH
THE CASE OF THE CURIOUS CLIENT

CHRISTOPHER BUSH was born Charlie Christmas Bush in Norfolk in 1885. His father was a farm labourer and his mother a milliner. In the early years of his childhood he lived with his aunt and uncle in London before returning to Norfolk aged seven, later winning a scholarship to Thetford Grammar School.

As an adult, Bush worked as a schoolmaster for 27 years, pausing only to fight in World War One, until retiring aged 46 in 1931 to be a full-time novelist. His first novel featuring the eccentric Ludovic Travers was published in 1926, and was followed by 62 additional Travers mysteries. These are all to be republished by Dean Street Press.

Christopher Bush fought again in World War Two, and was elected a member of the prestigious Detection Club. He died in 1973.

Ｔʜᴇ Ｌᴜᴅᴏᴠɪᴄ Ｔʀᴀᴠᴇʀꜱ Ｍʏꜱᴛᴇʀɪᴇꜱ
Available from Dean Street Press

The Plumley Inheritance
The Perfect Murder Case
Dead Man Twice
Murder at Fenwold
Dancing Death
Dead Man's Music
Cut Throat
The Case of the Unfortunate Village
The Case of the April Fools
The Case of the Three Strange Faces
The Case of the 100% Alibis
The Case of the Dead Shepherd
The Case of the Chinese Gong
The Case of the Monday Murders
The Case of the Bonfire Body
The Case of the Missing Minutes
The Case of the Hanging Rope
The Case of the Tudor Queen
The Case of the Leaning Man
The Case of the Green Felt Hat
The Case of the Flying Donkey
The Case of the Climbing Rat
The Case of the Murdered Major
The Case of the Kidnapped Colonel
The Case of the Fighting Soldier
The Case of the Magic Mirror
The Case of the Running Mouse
The Case of the Platinum Blonde
The Case of the Corporal's Leave
The Case of the Missing Men
The Case of the Second Chance
The Case of the Curious Client
The Case of the Haven Hotel
The Case of the Housekeeper's Hair
The Case of the Seven Bells
The Case of the Purloined Picture
The Case of the Happy Warrior
The Case of the Corner Cottage
The Case of the Fourth Detective
The Case of the Happy Medium

INTRODUCTION

LABOURING UNDER SUSPICION
CHRISTOPHER BUSH'S CRIME FICTION IN THE POSTWAR YEARS, 1946-1952

SEVEN YEARS after the end of the Second World War, Christopher Bush published, under his "Michael Home" pseudonym, *The Brackenford Story* (1952), a mainstream novel in which a onetime country house boots boy, having risen for some time now to the lofty position of butler, laments the passing of traditional English rural life in the new postwar order, as signified by the years in which the left-wing Labour party held sway in the United Kingdom (1945-51). The jacket description of the American edition of *The Brackenford Story* reads, in part:

> *The Brackenford Story* is the story of a changing England. William saw the political enemies of the Hall gradually successful, whittling away the privilege it stood for. He saw squire begin to sell his land, the taxes increase, the great Hall sold, the beautiful trees along the drive cut down. And then with a Second World War, nationalization, rationing, pre-fabricated houses and queuing. William recalled with gratitude the kindness of his masters and their sense of responsibility for others. He saw that the bad old days of Toryism were not so bad after all. And he never lost his sense of outrage at the loss of something he felt was worthy of preservation.

A few years earlier, in July 1949, Anthony Boucher, the postwar dean of American crime fiction reviewers and a highly socially conscious liberal (small "l"), wrote with genial bemusement of the conservatism of British crime writers like Christopher Bush, in his review of Bush's latest crime opus, *The Case of the Housekeeper's Hair* (1948), making topical mention of a certain anti-Utopian novel penned by a distinguished dying tubercular English writer, which had just been published in June. "However much George Orwell, in *Nineteen Eighty-Four*, may foresee the forcible suppression of 'crimethink' under 'Ingsoc,' English socialism in 1949 takes pleasure in exporting mystery novels which disapprove of the Government and everything about it," Boucher observed with wry irony. "Like most of his colleagues, Christopher Bush is tartly critical of the regime; and an understanding of his unreconstructed Tory attitude is necessary if you're to hope to understand the motivations of this novel."

In both the detective novels and mainstream fiction which Christopher Bush published between 1946 and 1952, Bush, like many other distinguished mystery writers of the Golden Age generation (including Agatha Christie, Dorothy L. Sayers, Georgette Heyer, John Dickson Carr, Edmund Crispin, E.R. Punshon, Henry Wade and John Street), indeed was critical of the Labor government and increasingly nostalgic about a past that grew ever more golden in blissful, if perhaps partially chimerical, remembrance. Yet keeping Bush's distinct anti-left bias in mind, fans of classic crime fiction will find between the covers of the author's crime novels from these years--*The Case of the Second Chance* (1946), *The Case of the Curious Client* (1947), *The Case of the Haven Hotel* (1948), *The Case of the Housekeeper's Hair* (1948), *The Case of the Seven Bells* (1949), *The Case of the Purloined Picture* (1949), *The Case of the Happy Warrior* (1950), *The Case of the Corner Cottage* (1951), *The Case of the Fourth Detective* (1951) and *The Case of the Happy Medium* (1952)--fascinating observation of postwar social malaise in the age of British imperial decay and domestic austerity, as well as details about the rise of rationing, restriction and regulation, the burgeoning black market and, withal, that ubiquitous flashily-dressed criminal figure from Forties and Fifties Britain: the spiv (dealer in illicit goods).

Puzzle-minded mystery readers also will find some corking good no-nonsense "fair play" mysteries. "Few writers can equal Christopher Bush in handling a complicated plot while giving the reader a fair chance to solve the riddle himself," avowed the American blurb to *The Case of the Corner Cottage*, while Anthony Boucher applauded Bush's belated return to the American fiction lists after the Second World War, declaring: "It's good to have Mr. Bush back after too long an absence . . . he presents the simon-pure jigsaw-puzzle detective story with unobtrusive competence." Concurrently in the United Kingdom, author Rupert Croft-Cooke, who himself wrote fine detective fiction as "Leo Bruce," pointedly praised Bush's "urbane and intelligent way of dealing with mystery which makes his work much more attractive than the stampeding sensationalism of some of his rivals."

In the pages which follow this introduction by all means attempt, dear readers, to match your keen wits against those of that ever-percipient gentleman sleuth, Ludovic Travers. Frequently in tandem with his old friend Superintendent George Wharton and with occasional input from his smart and sophisticated wife Bernice Haire, the former classical dancer, Ludo continues to hunt, in his capacity as a sort of special consultant to Scotland Yard (or "unofficial expert," as he puts it), more not-quite-canny-enough crooks. Additionally Ludo, a confirmed fan of American crime films like *The Blue Dahlia* (1946) and *Call Northside 777* (1948), comes to find himself in ownership of the Broad Street Detective Agency, perhaps the finest firm of private inquiry agents in London. In these old and new capacities in the postwar world Ludo confronts his greatest cornucopia of daring and dastardly crimes yet.

The Case of the Curious Client

IT WAS IN the southern English coastal town of Worthing, Sussex, that Charles Bentinck Budd, a Great War veteran and member of Oswald Mosley's notorious British Union of Fascists (BUF), won election, in the fall of 1933, to the town council, giving Worthing the dubious distinction of becoming the first locality in the United Kingdom to elect as a councillor a card-carrying adherent to the cause of fascism, a dangerous authoritarian ideology then sweeping like a devouring fire across Europe. Upon his election, Councillor Budd immediately created an uproar in town by wearing his regulation BUF black shirt to council meetings. (On account of this apparel, Mosley's followers were dubbed "Blackshirts.") "Fascism is the one thing that will save this country," he pronounced in a triumphant post-election interview with the *Worthing Journal.*

In January 1934 a public meeting at the Worthing Pavilion Theatre was addressed by Councillor Budd and the deputy leader of the BUF, William Joyce (the future infamous Nazi wartime radio propagandist Lord Haw-Haw, who was hanged for treason after the war). Over 900 people were in attendance at the meeting, including some 150 local members of the BUF. Worthing's mayor and Conservative Party leader praised the behavior of the Blackshirts at the gathering and reported that local employers had expressed their approbation to him as well. Mosley himself spoke at the Pavilion Theatre in the fall of that year, at a meeting packed with Sussex fascists and fellow travelers, with protection from jeering protestors provided by nineteen strapping members of Worthing's police force. Although Charles Budd left Worthing in 1935, he remained in the BUF. Under the wartime imposition of Defence Regulation 18B in May 1940, he was arrested without trial and interned, along with over 600 fascists from Sussex, on the ground that they endangered the safety of the British realm. Citizens of Sussex accounted for over three-fourths of native fascist internees in the UK during the war.

Christopher Bush had reason to be familiar with these troubling events in Worthing, the so-called "Munich of the South." After a family falling-out in 1932, Bush with his companion Marjorie Barclay had left his residence "Home Cottage" in his native village of Great Hockham, Norfolk and settled for the next two decades at "Little Horsepen," a two-story timber-framed Tudor house located on the main street of the village of Beckley, Sussex, about sixty miles from Worthing. A month after the imposition of Defence Regulation 18B, Bush was made Adjutant Commandant of Highfield, an internment camp outside the city of Southampton. Not for the decorated author of the Ludovic Travers mystery saga and a series of "Michael Home" wartime thrillers was sympathetic dalliance with fascist enemies of the British Empire, in contrast with the Mosley admiring press baron Lord Rothermere, founder of the *Daily Mail* and the *Daily Mirror*, whom Bush had lampooned in his classic 1932 detective novel *Cut Throat*.

Christopher Bush recalls these events in Worthing in the Thirties and Forties in *The Case of the Curious Client*, which was published in the UK in late 1947 by Macdonald and in the US in early 1948 by Macmillan. (Bush would remain with these publishers for the next two decades, the rest of his writing life.) In his immediately previous detective novel, *The Case of the Second Chance* (1947), his sleuth Ludovic "Ludo" Travers (who during the postwar years essentially becomes the author's alter ego), discusses his friendship with Jewish movie producer Benny Markstein, indicating that he himself has no truck with anti-Semites. In *The Case of the Curious Client*, however, Ludo topically finds himself investigating the violent slaying of the anti-Semitic Herbert Dorvan, who is not only the novel's titular client but also its first murder victim.

The novel opens on Guy Fawkes Day, November 5, 1945--the first time in seven years that the festive occasion was to be commemorated with bonfires. (Bush, who specifically mentions the return of the famed bonfire at Lewes, Sussex, had made murderous use of the occasion before in his fiction, in the 1936 Ludo Travers detective novel *The Case of the Bonfire Body*.) Pending his friend Superintendent George Wharton's retirement from Scotland Yard, Ludo with Wharton plans to take over and run the Broad Street Detective Agency of Bill Ellice, who first appeared in *The Case of the Running Mouse* (1944), set nearly three years earlier in February 1943. Ludo is present one morning when the firm's loyal middle-aged secretary, Miss Bertha Munney (whose relationship with Ludo resembles that between Ian Fleming's Miss Moneypenny and James Bond), brings him a call from a prospective client, Herbert Dorvan, who is visiting London.

"I think—I know—my life's in danger," the agitated man tells Ludo, who agrees to meet him that afternoon. When he arrives at Dorvan's hotel, however, he learns that his prospective client has suddenly taken flight for his current residence in the village of Midgley, near Porthaven, a town on the southern English coast. (Presumably Porthaven is close to Seaborough, where Travers assisted police in three cases in the Thirties: *The Case of the 100% Alibis*, 1934; *The Case of the Chinese Gong*, 1935; and *The Case of the Missing Minutes*, 1937). Dorvan has left a message at the hotel requesting that Ludo come down to his home in two days to meet him. Ludo, trying to determine just what affrighted the man, is barely able to catch sight of him departing in a flurry at Charing Cross station. Two days later, when Ludo compliantly calls on Dorvan at Midgley, he finds his curious client lying on the floor of his house, fatally shot in the head.

Assisting the police in the investigation of Herbert Dorvan's murder (George Wharton soon takes over the case), Ludo finds that Dorvan was formerly the owner of a London variety and stage employment agency and with his late brother Richard was co-heir to his father's East End furniture business. The latter concern had fallen victim to Jewish competition before the war and as a result Herbert Dorvan in a rage "had declared war, as it were, on Jews in general"—even to the self-defeating extent of placing a sign outside the office of his variety agency which read in bold letters, NO YIDS NEED APPLY. One person recalls to Ludo and Wharton that Dorvan "had a place at St Leonards [on the Sussex coast]. Used to spend all his weekends down there, and you know what a hotbed of Fascism all that South Coast was. Brighton and Worthing, for instance. All the way down in the train you'd see the slogans chalked on the walls." During this time Dorvan became associated with the BUF, contributing funds and speaking at meetings and becoming "recognized as one of the big men [in the organization] by those in the know."

Did Dorvan's wartime association with the BUF, for which he was interned for three years, have something to do with his postwar murder? What do Dorvan's three nephews--radio impressionist Gerry Bruff and half-brothers Sidney and Robert

Dorvan, respectively the owner of a swanky London nightclub, The Ginger Cat, and a recently released Japanese POW--know about the deathly matter? What is the strange role played in the affair by nightclub "croonerette" Netta Malone (aka Daisy Carbury), who seems with her charms to have bewitched one or more of the Dorvan men? Eventually Ludo learns the answers, with some help not only from Superintendent Wharton, but his alluring wife Bernice ("still on the right side of forty"), who at her husband's behest beards the denizens The Ginger Cat. "When I told her what was in the wind, she said it would be perfectly thrilling. Maybe she would have adventures like those in American detective novels," comments Ludo wryly of his sporting wife. "If Bernice liked to think that a London nightclub of the Ginger Cat class was peopled with molls and gunmen and black marketeers, who was I to disillusion her?" There is also in the tale some rather timely assistance from the Yard's young Sergeant Jewle, "a loose-limbed, awkward-looking six-footer" who makes his debut here. In future books Jewle will claim a prominent place in the Ludovic Travers mystery saga.

Curtis Evans

PART I

CHAPTER I
THE NEW CLIENT

IT WAS ONLY when I began looking through my newspapers that morning that I realised it was Guy Fawkes Day. My old friend and colleague George—Superintendent, to you—Wharton will always have it that I am grossly extravagant in taking both *Times* and *Telegraph*, but then George is a great one for looking after the pence, and he is also no solver of crosswords. But, as I said, both my papers referred to November the Fifth. There was the old pre-war kind of gossip about the Bonfire Boys of Lewes and the South Coast, and much was made of the fact that once more there would be fireworks. One town alone was said to have a stock of four thousand for its celebrations. But to me it all seemed cheaply sensational and just a bit infantile. To an old stager like myself, convinced that there are no times like the old times, those promised cavortings and sophisticated fancy-dress parades of the South Coast were a poor substitute for the days when masks were in the windows of little shops and urchins paraded their home-made guys and pleaded earnestly for coppers in the streets.

But I have gone into all that only because I want to impress the actual date on your mind. I want you also to recall the weather of that early November of 1945. After the superbity of autumn's late summer there was a period of patchy fog, and once or twice—in London and the South at least—it was thick. Generally, too, the days were muggy and overcast. Guy Fawkes Day itself began with drizzle, then continued dull and with a threat of rain that did not come, and in the evening there was more patchy fog. I want you also to remember that all that period of weather was accurately forecast and broadcast. It was easy for a murderer, shall we say, to be sure that unexpected changes of weather would not interfere with his particular plans.

So perhaps you see why I have been harping on the weather that prevailed in that early November. Thanks to it, a murderer almost got away with his killing, which brings us back to Guy Fawkes Day and to this story.

But first let me do some very brief explaining. George Wharton had been counting on retiring from the Yard well before Christmas, and he and I were going to take over Bill Ellice's Broad Street Detective Agency as a lucrative occupation—or so we hoped—for our leisure. Bill's was an old-established and reliable business. If you care to consult back files of your papers you will notice that it was the only one that consistently advertised throughout the war.

Now George's retirement was looking as far off as ever. I myself had been a bit premature in relinquishing a wartime job at the Yard, and though I was still on their list of what they call unofficial experts, I had not been called upon, and maybe because George Wharton, with whom I had always worked, was occupying himself at the moment with other things than murders. So I was enjoying an ample leisure, and, with the hope that George's retirement would eventuate much sooner than he pessimistically maintained, I was spending most of my time learning all the Detective Agency ropes from Bill Ellice.

Two of Bill's men had been demobilised, but the end of the war had brought more work than could be comfortably handled. That was why he had had to go North himself on the Sunday and had asked me to take over till his return on the Monday night. It was an interesting job, and it wasn't, if you know what I mean. Rather like fishing with a hook and float, when minutes and even hours pass with nothing to maintain interest but the expectation of a catch. All I had to do was sit in Bill's office at the end of a telephone and sign such papers as Miss Munney brought in. If reports arrived, she dealt with them or passed them to me. And all the time I would be hoping for a movement of the float, by which I mean the arrival of some new and interesting client. Arriving in person, I should have said, and not by telephone or post.

It was about eleven o'clock when the buzzer went.

"A Mr. Dorvan would like to speak to you," Miss Munney said, and with her up-to-the-minute efficiency proceeded to spell the name.

"What's he like?" I asked.

"Middle-aged. Quite well-spoken. A bit pompous perhaps."

"Right-ho," I said. "Put him through."

Were I ever to become Commandant of one of the new Police Colleges—I am far more likely to become Archbishop of Canterbury—I would insist to each student that the proper study of his fellow men is a paying hobby for a young detective. I have found it so, modestly though I say it. One can savour a new character as one can a new book. In a bus, a pub, a queue or even in casual walks abroad, there is the game of guessing the occupation, the character and the home county of this person and that, and if one has time and an inventive faculty, of proving one's self right or wrong. All that was why, as soon as I heard the voice of Mr. Dorvan, I tried to estimate just what kind of a person as well as a client he was likely to be.

"Is that the Broad Street Detective Agency?"

"It is," I said. "Mr. Travers speaking."

"My name's Dorvan, Mr. Travers. Herbert Dorvan. I'm at the Southern Hotel. Can you come and see me at four o'clock this afternoon?"

A voice, I thought, of an educated man, and with no trace whatever of local accent. Low-pitched and, though not exactly pompous as Miss Munney had described it, rather as if the speaker had a plum in his mouth, and a hot one at that. Before I could answer he was going on. Now the voice did have a certain pomposity.

"I'd like you to be on time. I'm a busy man and I've only a few minutes to spare."

"You can rely on me for four o'clock, Mr. Dorvan," I told him. "But pardon my mentioning something. Hadn't you better give me some idea of what it is that you want us to do for you? If it should be something we can't handle, we should only be wasting your valuable time and our own."

I waited while he cleared his throat. That would be an excuse of his for a bit of quick thinking.

"There are two things, as a matter of fact. I want you to find a nephew of mine."

"Yes," I said slowly. "Carry on, Mr. Dorvan, and I'll take down preliminary details."

"That doesn't matter," he told me rather testily. "I can discuss that when I see you. He's just a returned prisoner of war in Japanese hands. He should have been home days ago but he's never got in touch with me."

"The name?"

"Of course, of course. Robert Dorvan."

"Robert Dorvan," I repeated. "By the way, have you applied to the War Office?"

"I haven't." He seemed to snap that at me. "That's nobody's business but my own. In any case I'll explain when I see you. I saw your advertisement and I hoped you'd look after my interests."

"We certainly *shall* do so if you see fit to employ us. And you can treat a firm of our standing with the same confidence as you would your lawyer or doctor."

"Glad to hear it. Glad to hear it."

He cleared his throat again and I cut hastily in.

"You said there was one other matter."

"Yes, yes." Another little nervous clearing of his throat. The voice lowered, and at what he said my eyes fairly bulged.

"I think—in fact I know—that my life's in danger."

"You mean, someone's threatening you?"

"Not in words," he said, "but I know what I'm talking about. There's been one attempt to kill me already. You think I'm talking rubbish, perhaps. You think I'm mad."

"Certainly not, sir," I assured him. "We hear far stranger things than that from people just as sane as you are."

"We'll discuss it later," he said, and with a very definite finality. "But one thing's linked up with the other. That's why I want you to find Robert, my nephew. I want him to live with me and look after me. But you come and see me, young man. You *are* a young man?"

"Not a bit of it," I said. "I'm far too near middle age for my liking. But before I forget it, would you give me the number of your room?"

"Quite unnecessary." The throaty pompousness was there again. "Ask for me at the desk. How shall I recognise *you*? I've got to be sure you're the man I'm talking to."

"I'm well over six foot," I said, "and lean. I shall be wearing horn-rimmed glasses. I shall have on a grey soft felt hat and a light-grey overcoat."

"Right," he said. "I'll see you at four o'clock this afternoon. Four o'clock sharp."

With that he rang off. I sat thinking for a moment or two and then pressed the buzzer for Bertha Munney. She'd been with Bill Ellice for fifteen years, and, though no pin-up girl, was worth every penny of her eight quid a week.

"You heard all that?" I asked her. "If so, what did you make of it, and him?"

"I don't quite know," she told me in that dry, rather humorous voice of hers. "But I do think that nephew, if we find him, is in for a thin time."

"Old Dorvan's hard to live with, you mean. But what about that life-in-danger business?"

"I think there's possibly something in it." She didn't sound too sure. "Mind you, I do think he may have a bat or two in his belfry."

"Well, we shall know more in a few hours' time," I said sententiously. "But you might get hold of Cable and Wireless and find out if the Robert Dorvan sent home any message. And try the War Office lists. It'd be rather nice to have something to confront the old boy with as soon as he's signed on the dotted line."

"O.K.," she told me, and then within ten seconds the buzzer went again.

"Like to check up on Dorvan at the hotel, Mr. Travers?"

"Why?"

"Just a hunch," she said. "It paid in that Clarke case, didn't it? Hallows is back if you'd like him to slip along."

"Right-ho," I said. "You give Hallows the low-down but for the love of heaven tell him to be tactful. Dorvan struck me as a man who'd turn us down flat if he had a suspicion of anything fishy."

At half-past twelve, just when I was thinking of lunch, the buzzer went.

"You're through," Bertha Munney said, and I found myself listening to Hallows.

"That you, Mr. Travers? Oh, about that Mr. Dorvan. He's O.K. Arrived at the hotel last night. I pretended to be wanting a man named Donovan and that let me get a squint at the book. H. Dorvan is here all right. Gave his address as Porthaven."

"You took no chances?"

"Nothing to worry about, sir. I was interested in a man named Donovan. Ginger-haired young chap with a Belfast accent. I told the clerk I wasn't interested when he mentioned Dorvan."

"Good work," I said, and that was that. But it was interesting to know that Dorvan came from Porthaven. I'd been closely identified with George Wharton in a Case down there, and from what I'd been thinking about Dorvan's few and brief revelations, I guessed I might have to ask for the co-operation of the Porthaven police. If so, I'd be among friends.

In the incipient fog the taxi deposited me outside Charing Cross Station. My kind of punctuality is that a definite hour means one minute to that hour, and it's Army life that has taught me that. Dorvan had insisted on four o'clock sharp and it was not quite a minute to when I approached the hotel bureau. There was a youngish male clerk who raised courteous eyebrows.

"I have an appointment with a Mr. Herbert Dorvan," I said. "Will you tell me the number of his room?"

"You're Mr. Travers?"

"I am."

"Then there's a message for you, Mr. Travers."

I must have looked rather blank as he handed me a letter. "You mean that Mr. Dorvan is no longer here?"

"He's this second left, sir." The polite smile became somewhat rueful. "He'd made a mistake about the time of his train, sir. Thought it was half-past four instead of ten minutes past."

"Pity he didn't ring me up," I said as I began opening the letter.

"We did, sir, only a few moments ago, but you'd already left."

I glanced quickly through the letter. It was on hotel paper with the headings crossed out. The writing was old-fashioned copper-plate.

MOST CONFIDENTIAL.

> Midgley,
> Nr. Porthaven.
> Nov. 5th, 1945.

DEAR MR. TRAVERS,

The desk clerk will explain why I am unable to see you as arranged. Please accept my apologies for my stupidity. Will you come and see me next Wednesday at the above address. I would say tomorrow, but I have urgent business with my lawyer about my will.

I am prepared to pay any charges whatever. No need to fix a time or confirm as I shall be in all Wednesday.

Yours truly,

> Herbert Dorvan.

P.S.—Please make my business a priority. Your firm will not regret it. And I would ask you to burn this letter.—H.D.

The clerk suddenly spoke, and briskly.

"If you'd like to see Mr. Dorvan after all, sir, I think we might catch him."

Before I could do more than look interested, he was springing into action.

"This way, sir."

I bustled along at his heels and in a matter of seconds we were out at the platform. Everything was murky there and I could hardly distinguish the people swirling round the bookstall. But that clerk could see all right.

"There he is, sir! Just going towards the barrier now. The white-haired gentleman with the muffler round his neck."

I couldn't see but I took his word for it, and as I moved towards the barrier I gave my glasses a quick polish. Just as I got there Dorvan had gone through. But there was still a small queue. A slot machine was within reach and I got myself a platform ticket. Then I watched Dorvan slowly making his way along the train.

A back view from twenty yards showed a man of about five foot eight or nine, stooping slightly with rounded shoulders and with white hair showing above the muffler round his neck, or rather between it and the dark felt hat. Then suddenly he turned and looked into a compartment and I had a sideways view of him. The face was a curious one, with a curving beak of a nose and a prominent chin. And then he shifted position again, fingers feeling quickly in various pockets. There was something that apparently he'd lost, and he began walking back towards the barrier.

Now I could see that his face was sallow and his moustache untidy, and then he suddenly halted and turned. A feel in a waistcoat pocket had evidently produced the missing object, and, rather more quickly than before, he made his way along the train again. A porter was standing outside a compartment. He flicked his peak to Dorvan and again when he received a tip. Evidently he'd taken Dorvan's bag and retained his seat. Meanwhile I was almost at the head of the barrier queue.

You may be wondering why I should wish to thrust myself, as it were, upon a client whose new instructions were perfectly explicit. Perhaps the main reason was that I suddenly thought I ought to confirm the Wednesday's visit and give him some idea of the time. I thought too that it might be as well if he had a look at the man who would pay that visit, and especially since he had been so meticulously careful to ensure that the Travers of the telephone should be the Travels of the hotel. In any case I did not propose to speak more than a very few words. I am only too well aware of the limitations of my elongated appearance, but I do at least claim to look intelligent and reliable, and I trusted that the little Dorvan saw of me would exhibit me as tactful, understanding and courteous.

I had marked down the compartment but I was not to see Dorvan after all. There was his seat with a folded newspaper to retain it, and on the rack above was a bag.

"Is this seat taken?" I asked the nearest occupant. He looked like a lawyer or a confidential clerk, with a portfolio on his knees and a legal-looking document he was examining.

"I'm afraid it is," he told me, and went on with his reading. I closed the door and moved back a bit, polishing my glasses and blinking away as I stood there—a nervous trick of mine when at a sudden mental loss or on the edge of decision or discovery. Then all at once there was a final bustle of those in authority and within a few seconds the whistle shrilled and the train began to move. I shrugged my shoulders as I turned back to the barrier. Dorvan had evidently been disregarding the injunction not to use the lavatory while the train was standing at a station, and with my usual fluent theorising I told myself that men of his age often suffered with weak bladders. Then I felt my breast pocket and assured myself that his letter was still there.

Courtesy is always a valuable investment and I made up my mind to thank that young clerk. For some reason or other he didn't seem overjoyed to see me.

"Thank you for your kindness," I said, "but I just missed Mr. Dorvan after all."

"That's all right, sir," he told me, just a bit off-handedly.

"A regular client here, is he?"

He smiled regretfully.

"I'm sorry, sir, but we're not allowed to talk about our clients." Then, perhaps at the rueful look on my face, he gave a quick look round. "Between ourselves I don't remember him coming here before, but I've only been back a couple of months. I do know he had his meals sent up to his room."

"He had his lunch there?"

"Yes," he said, and was obviously regretting that he'd said what he had.

"Why I mentioned that, was this," I said. "A client is supposed to quit his room by midday. I was wondering how he could do that and still have lunch here."

"You can always book for a second night, if accommodation's available."

"I suppose you can," I said, and still didn't knew if he'd answered my question or avoided it. In any case it didn't matter much, except to leave unsatisfied my usual and often flagrant curiosity. So I gave him a smile of thanks and moved off, and then before I was out of the Station yard, I knew there was one question I ought to have asked him. Then I shrugged my shoulders. Wednesday wasn't so far away and then I'd know all the answers.

I didn't see Bill Ellice till the following morning, and then I went over everything I'd done with regard to Dorvan. He didn't seem too happy about the new client.

"Probably got a bee in his bonnet. Suffering from delusions. May be thinking his relatives need his money."

"Has he money?"

"Well, he put up at that hotel and it's a far from cheap one," Bill told me in his mild way. "And if he had all his meals in his room, that cost him a packet for extras."

"Doesn't that meals-in-his-room business rather prove someone is after his blood?" I said. "Surely it means he was keeping himself very much to himself? And there was that business about making sure it was myself who saw him at the hotel."

"Did anyone else see him at the hotel?" Bill asked pertinently. "Any callers?"

"I knew you'd come to that," I told him ruefully. "That's the one question I ought to have asked that clerk."

But there was one good thing about that Wednesday visit to Dorvan—that a goodish bit had been discovered already about the missing nephew. He had not sent a cable home, but home he was, having landed at Southampton from the *Caronia* about a fortnight previously. What we now had to know was if his discharge into civil life had been definitely completed, and if he had given any address for himself or of any relative. We didn't anticipate much difficulty there. Robert Dorvan's was the sort of case which, as the fellow said, we hadn't much else of but.

"Funny about Dorvan not applying to the War Office himself?" Bill said. "What was his idea?"

"Fallen foul of them at some time or other," was all I could suggest.

"That shows he's sane at any rate," Bill said dryly. "How are you going down there tomorrow, by the way?"

Trains weren't any too good, and as the petrol would run to it, I decided to take the car. What I was proposing was to start off as soon as it was light and that should bring me back to town well before it was dark. When I got to St. Martin's Chambers that afternoon I asked my wife if she'd like to make the trip, but she'd half promised a friend to do a matinée. So I made the trip alone, which was just as well, and in a very few minutes you'll know why.

Chapter II

THE MAN WHO COULDN'T HEAR

My old Bentley was running remarkably well, and it was exactly nine o'clock when I reached Sevenoaks. At Tonbridge I knew I had time in hand, so I pulled up at a roadhouse a few miles beyond the town and had some coffee. I also did a bit of thinking. I realised, for instance, that before I actually saw Dorvan I ought to know something of what the village of Midgley thought of him. Suppose, as Bill Ellice and Bertha Munney had both suggested, he had some bats in his belfry, then the village ought to have become aware of the fact, and I should know from the very outset how to guide and manipulate the conversation.

It was about ten o'clock when from a high ridge road I had a momentary glimpse of the sea through a gap in the hills above Porthaven. It was a grand morning of late autumn, with visibility uncannily good and the sun just breaking through the clouds, but for once I wasn't interested in scenery. I was thinking about our client—a man who had claimed that his life was in danger; that there'd been an attempt to kill him and that he needed a protector. I was interested in knowing just how much those statements were worth, and I was anxious to have a little more preliminary information about the man who had made them. And then about a mile along a side road I saw a roadman, so I slowed the car down. He was cutting back the encroaching grass verges and he gave a start as the car drew quietly alongside him.

"I'm right for Midgley, am I?"

"That's right," he said. "About half a mile on. You'll see it soon as you get round that bend."

I got out to stretch my legs. Then I offered him a cigarette and lighted one for myself.

"You're a stranger about here?" he asked me, and his eyes were busy probing who and what I was.

"Yes," I said. "I happen to have business with a Mr. Dorvan of Midgley. I've never seen him and I don't know where he actually lives."

The last part was easy, he said. Just short of the four cross-roads was a chestnut wood. Mr. Dorvan's bungalow—Woodlands by name—was in it. I couldn't miss it.

"An elderly man, is he?"

"About sixty or so," he said. "Perhaps a bit older. He ain't so spry as he was when he first came here."

"When was that?"

He thought for a moment and then said it would be about two years ago.

"What's he like personally? You'd call him a gentleman, for instance?"

"Well," he said, and frowned, "I don't know as you'd call him real gentry, but he's not a bad sort of gentleman. Keeps himself to himself a good deal."

"Just between ourselves," I said. "Suppose I wanted to do a business deal with him. Would you say he's a tough nut to crack? I mean, has he got all his wits about him?"

"Oh yes, sir," he told me with a sideways nod of the head. "He ain't no fool. I often see him out walking and we always have a word or two. Very well educated, I should say."

"But he doesn't take any part in village life?"

"No," he said reflectively. "I can't say as he do. I've never seen him at no meetings or things."

"He lives alone in the bungalow?"

"Oh yes. He live by himself. Don't have no woman to come in neither. And they reckon the house is as clean as a new pin."

"Ah well," I said resignedly. "Let's hope he doesn't drive too hard a bargain."

"You're not after his bungalow?"

"Oh no," I said as I got back in the car. "Something quite different from that."

As I pushed the car on I wondered just how much that little chat had been worth. But there was no time to assess its value for just round that bend was the village and there was the bungalow roof. It was in a chestnut wood of about a couple of acres, set almost in the angle made by the two roads—the one on which I was and another that came from Porthaven and went on to Cleavesham. It was that other road that seemed the main street of Midgley, for houses were dotted along its sides. Beyond the roof of Dorvan's bungalow I could see the church tower.

There was a gate with a track, roughly concreted, that led through the wood to the bungalow. The trees were young, for it looked as if that wood had been cut, except for its few slim oaks, about three years before. From their stubs the chestnuts stood about twelve feet high again, with stray beech a bit lower and ash saplings slightly above. Then as the car bumped on round a curve I saw the bungalow and it was plain that I had come in at the back way. It looked a well-built brick building of four or five small rooms at the most, and a wooden garage stood just clear of it. A small kitchen-garden, wire-netted against rabbits, had quite a good show of winter greens. To the front of the bungalow I could now see that the chestnut stubs had been grubbed out and the ground roughly turfed, and that gave something of a clear view towards the village and admitted more air and sun from the south.

I left the car by the garage, and as I neared the back door of the bungalow I noticed something white. On the green wood-work of that door was a sheet of paper, held in position by two drawing-pins.

> Away till Wednesday. Leave paper but no milk till Thursday.
>
> H. DORVAN.

A curious uneasiness came over me as I read that brief notice. The writing was definitely Dorvan's as I remembered it from the letter he had left for me at the hotel, but the thought that at once went through my mind was that, since he had been back since the Monday night, he ought to have removed the notice. It followed that, since he had not removed the notice, he had not come back, and my journey had been a wasted one.

I was half expecting to find another notice on the front door, but there was none, but I did see that the window curtains were closely drawn and that the house had electricity laid on. The door had both bell and knocker, so I pushed the bell. I could hear it ringing inside, but when I listened for a step there was never a sound. I rang again, and again without result, and then I wondered if the curtained windows meant that Dorvan was not yet up. Maybe he was a heavy sleeper, so I gave the door a bang or two with the knocker and then listened again. Within the house there was never the faintest sound. Then I squinted through the letter-box, but all I could see was a thin slit of what must have been the living-room wall.

I went round to the back again. The lean-to shed was un-locked so I peeped in. It was chock-a-block with gardening tools, firewood and about five hundredweight of coal. I don't know what I'd expected to see in it, but I closed the door again and did some more thinking. Dorvan had definitely assured me that he would be in the house all Wednesday. He had left London on the Monday night bound for Midgley. No changing was necessary. He simply got out at Porthaven and took a car or bus, and in a quarter of an hour or less he was home. He had not telephoned or telegraphed the Agency to cancel the visit, and therefore either something had happened suddenly to make him change all his plans or else he was in the house and I was unable to wake him. What if he had been taken ill. What if he were dead?

Round to the front I went again and listened at the door. The house was still as death itself, and then as I turned away I caught sight of something. There were three somethings, and within an area of three or four square yards—burnt-out crackers or squibs with a faint tang of powder still hanging about them. But they were not the kind I had known as a boy. These had a diameter of quite half an inch and originally must have been six or eight inches long. And they must have gone off with the very devil of a bang.

But I had been so engrossed in my examination of that bungalow that I had forgotten that my investigations were being carried out in almost the full view of some of the back windows of the village. I only realised that fact when I looked up to see a policeman in uniform almost on top of me.

"Having any trouble?" he asked, and it seemed to me somewhat ironically.

"Yes," I said. "I had a definite appointment with Mr. Dorvan for this morning. I've come all the way from London by road, and now I can't make him hear."

The policeman—he was quite a young fellow—gave a superior sort of grin.

"Probably because he's out."

"And therefore I ought to go away before I succumb to the temptation to do a bit of house-breaking?"

He grinned again.

"You can put it that way if you like, sir."

I asked him to step round to the back of the bungalow, and there I took him to a certain extent into my confidence. I learned that Inspector Galley was still at Porthaven, and I said he'd vouch for me, and that brought a certain respect.

"All sorts of things keep occurring to me," I said. "Look at that notice of his again. He arrived at the London hotel on Sunday so he probably put up that notice sometime earlier on Sunday and left here then. But if he announced there on that notice that he wouldn't be back till Wednesday, why did he leave London for here on the *Monday* night? And there's something else. He told me he had an appointment with his solicitors at Porthaven that would occupy him most of yesterday."

"But mayn't all this be what they call a mare's nest, sir? Why shouldn't Mr. Dorvan be out for a walk, for instance?"

"Then why the undrawn curtains? Why isn't this notice removed?"

"You're getting me out of my depth, sir," was all he could say to that. "The question is—to get down to brass tacks, as they say—what do you want me to do about it?"

"I'll answer you just as bluntly," I told him. "What I think is that I've given you good and sufficient reasons for making an entry. Any damage suffered in the process I'll pay for."

He shook his head.

"Daren't do it, sir. Not without higher authority."

We went by the front path. I showed him the squib things I'd picked up. Then he began telling me about Guy Fawkes Night in Midgley.

It had been a great night, he said. The local Bonfire Society had organised a torchlight procession that had started from our end of the village and ended at the other, and it had been headed by a band. Midgley, you should know, is shaped like a dumb-bell. Where we were was the church, the school, an inn and a cluster of houses with a shop or two. Then came a mile of road with a few houses along it, and lastly was another cluster of houses with another inn and another shop or two.

But to get back to Guy Fawkes Night. There had been a good stock of fireworks, though chiefly of the squib or banger variety. Prizes had been given for the best fancy costumes and the decorated carts, trailers and cars. There had been collectors with boxes who held up onlookers and called at every house for contributions for the hospital fund. The whole show had ended with a bonfire in a meadow near the centre of the village.

"Why the three squibs I picked up?" I asked him. Sprat, by the way, was his name.

He explained that each of the collectors was given a supply of them. The idea was to let them off near any house that stood well back from the road. Then the occupants would know the collecting-box was coming.

"But surely they must already have heard the very devil of a din?"

"I suppose they must, sir, but that's the custom. Very keen they are on these old customs."

We were at the main road. Twenty yards left was a house with a notice that it was Constabulary Headquarters. We went in and through to a back room. Sprat grinned as he pointed to the window.

"I happened to be working in here, sir, when I first caught sight of you. We've had a few burglaries in the district lately, so I wondered just what it was you were up to. And now if you'll take a chair, sir, I'll see if I can get the Inspector."

Galley was there and the explanations began. Then Sprat was beckoning to me to take the receiver.

"Hallo, Galley!" I said. "This is Ludovic Travers. You remember that little matter to do with your late Chief?"

He remembered only too well. It didn't take long to give him an idea of what I wanted, and why.

"I'll be over myself inside ten minutes," he told me. "The car's ready now."

"Hold on a minute," I said, and cupped the receiver. "Do you happen to know, Sprat, who Mr. Dorvan's solicitors are?"

I hardly expected an answer but I got one.

"I've seen him coming out of Cavendish and Clare's. That's just opposite the station, sir."

"Hallo there, Galley," I said. "Dorvan assured me that he would have business yesterday with his solicitors. Sprat here tells me it's likely that Cavendish and Clare are the solicitors. Could you find out, and if Dorvan *was* with them yesterday?"

*　*　*　*　*

"Tell you what we might do, sir," Sprat said when we came out to the road again. "The secretary of the Bonfire Society lives a yard or two along here. We might try to find out who went to Mr. Dorvan's place with the collecting-box on Monday night."

The secretary was one of the two village grocers. He told Sprat he'd come to the right place, and then began hollering at the back door for Fred.

"His son," Sprat whispered.

Fred, a young fellow of about eighteen, had been the collector we wanted.

"What happened at Mr. Dorvan's?" Sprat asked him.

"Nothing at all," Fred said. "The place was all dark and there wasn't anybody there."

"Pardon me," I said, "but what time was that?"

"Practically as soon as we started off," Fred said. "We should have started at seven but it was more like a quarter to eight."

Sprat and I exchanged glances. Even to him it was plain that if Dorvan had reached Porthaven that night at about six o'clock, he should have been at the bungalow long before the start of the procession.

"How many squibs did you let off there?"

"Only one," Fred said. "I was sort of rationing them out."

"Where'd you let that one off?"

"About twenty yards short of the house."

Sprat and I exchanged glances again. Sprat put another question.

"Did you see anybody else there collecting?"

"Why no!" Fred told him, rather surprised.

"But you do overlap sometimes, don't you?" He explained that to me. "There were two collectors for the houses each side of the road. They've been known to go both to the same house. Sort of rivalry to see who can collect the most."

"There wasn't anything of that," Fred said, and just a bit annoyedly, "and I'll tell you for why. Geoff Martin went to old Mrs. Mayne's while I did Dorvan's. We had it all worked out beforehand."

Sprat directed his summing-up at me.

"Why I've been asking all this, sir, is because I was given to understand there'd been trouble before the war. Unauthorised persons used to rig themselves up in costume and get on a bit ahead of the procession and do a little collecting for themselves."

"There *were* cases like that," Fred's father admitted a bit tartly, "though I don't remember the police ever catching any of 'em."

"They hadn't got real police then," Sprat told him with a grin. "But have you any reason to suspect there was anything of that sort this year?"

"You can take it from me there was nothing," he was told. "Perhaps the old gang hadn't time to get themselves organised."

"That's all then," said Sprat. "Thank you both very much. I might have to see you again, Fred, but I can't say for sure at the moment."

On that ominous note we went out. Sprat said we ought to have a look for the squib that Fred had let off. We found it roughly where he had described, and so easily that it was a wonder we had missed it when we came that way before.

"Not the same sort as these, is it?" I said.

It wasn't, though the difference was only one of colour. Fred's was white: those I had picked up were red.

"Better put yours back where you found them, sir," Sprat suggested, and when we'd done that he did some hammering on the front door for himself, and without result. After that there seemed nothing to do but wait for Inspector Galley.

"Something fishy about those three squibs, if you ask me, sir," Sprat said. "Either Fred was telling lies or else there was some unauthorised collecting."

"If the three squibs were let off before his one, would they have been heard?" I wanted to know.

"Now that's a real sensible question, sir," Sprat told me with a sideways nod of the head. "Let me see, now. I was on duty at the corner there from six o'clock and I didn't move off till the procession did."

He frowned in thought, then nodded.

"Depends on the time they were let off, sir. At any time after half-past six they wouldn't have been heard—or say a quarter to seven. The band began playing selections then, and there were boys letting off fireworks which I'd warned them not to. And there were all the people looking on at the fancy costumes, and young fellows larking about and all that, and traffic hooting to get through and me trying to keep the road clear." He shook his head. "No, sir, you can take it from me that if those squibs were let off at any time between a quarter to seven and the time Fred got there, they wouldn't have been heard."

His mouth gave a little gape.

"Wait a minute, sir, I can go further than that. I doubt if they'd have been noticed at any time that night. From as soon as it got dark, boys were letting off squibs all over the place. Who was to remember hearing any coming from the direction of Mr. Dorvan's?"

"By the way, what sort of a man *was* Dorvan?"

"Quite a nice gentleman I always found him," Sprat said. "Some used to reckon he was officious, as you might say, but that was only his way of speaking. Talked in a sort of blurting way. A bit like one of them Colonel Blimps."

"Someone told me he didn't take any part in village affairs. Used to keep himself to himself."

"In a way he did, I suppose, sir. He didn't seem to have any visitors. Used to go for regular walks, though. And he used to potter about in his garden. And I used to see him in Porthaven sometimes. That's why I guessed who his lawyers were. I saw him coming out of their office one afternoon. And I've seen him going into Barclay's Bank."

"How long's he been in Midgley?"

"Just a couple of years," he said. "I know because he came the same week as I did. Picked up this bungalow, furnished and everything, just at the right time. What do you think he gave for the whole lot, sir?"

"I don't know what the furniture's like," I said. "Twelve hundred?"

"Nine hundred and fifty, sir! And it'd make more than twice that tomorrow." Then he was hurriedly adjusting his tunic. "Here's the Inspector, sir."

Galley's eyes were wrinkling with pleasure as he held out his hand. Maybe he thought he owed me a good deal more than he did. In any case we had to do a bit of gossiping before we got down to the business in hand.

"About the solicitors," he said. "I rang Mr. Clare and he says his firm knew nothing about any interview for yesterday."

"Then Dorvan must have come to the decision some time on Monday to do something about his will," I said. "But it's curious all the same. Even more reason, don't you think, for having a look inside here?"

Sprat had been wandering about round the back of the bungalow while we were talking and now he had a good idea. He had found a door in the shed, cut through to the kitchen so that whoever needed fuel had no need to brave the weather. Galley hammered on that door and then listened before he got to work.

"Never a sound in there," he said, and looked round for a lever. There was a strong bill lying by the chopping-block and Sprat found a spade, and in a matter of seconds the door was burst open and with little more damage than a splintering of wood by the lock. Galley stepped into the kitchen.

"Nothing here that won't keep," he said. "Let's have a look at the other rooms."

He opened the only door and was going through. I was close at his heels and I ran full tilt into his back. For he had come to a sudden halt. With its closely-curtained windows that living-room was dim, and Galley's bulk hid the room from me. But I could see that it was the living-room, and I could just see the front door mat and count the four newspapers that lay on it. Then as Galley switched on the light, I saw the body of a man, feet towards that front door.

"Here he is then," Galley said grimly. "Must have had a heart attack or something. You recognise him, Sprat?"

"That's Mr. Dorvan all right," Sprat said.

"And you, Mr. Travers?"

"That's Dorvan," I said. "That's the man I saw at Charing Cross Station."

Galley stooped by the body. The hand that touched the face drew quickly back.

"Been dead since Monday night, so I'd say. . . . Hallo! What's this?"

I had been giving my glasses a quick polish and now I saw that his long lean fingers had gently raised the head from the floor. Now he raised it further and the underside was plainly visible. Near the right temple was a hole, brown and messy at its edges, and down the forehead and along the nose was dried blood.

"Shot, by God!" said Galley. "No wonder the poor old devil couldn't hear."

Chapter III

REVELATIONS

I DON'T quite know why, but that discovery of the murdered Dorvan came to me by no means as a shock. Maybe at the back of my mind, though I had not put it into words, there had been all along the premonition that he was dead. Besides, he was something almost impersonal. To me he had been three things, and none of them intimate or direct—a voice over a telephone, the writer of a letter and a stranger seen on a railway platform. Had I ever shaken him by the hand or talked with him face to face, then perhaps I should have felt something resembling a personal loss.

"There seems to have been some truth in that story of his after all," Galley said. "That bit about someone trying to do him in before."

"Yes," I said slowly, and was still frowning down at the body.

"Got an idea?"

"Idea?" I gathered what he meant and pulled myself together. "No ideas at all except those I've already told you. What I was looking at was his face."

Galley gave me a quick look.

"Oh, it's all right," I told him quickly. "He's Dorvan right enough. But things don't tally somehow."

"How do you mean?"

I addressed myself to Sprat.

"Your description of him was that he was quite a nice old gentleman."

"He always was—to me, sir. Polite, I mean, and all that."

"Maybe he had good reason for wanting to keep on the right side of the law," I said, and smiled disarmingly as I said it.

And there, strange as it must have appeared to Galley, I left it. But I couldn't say that for years I'd made the study of my fellow men something of a passion, and that the dead Dorvan hadn't to me the look of quite a nice old gentleman. Sprat had indeed ventured that the village had thought him officious because of his blustering way of speaking, but to me the dead Dorvan's face had a bitter and even a malignant look. It was a face, in fact, that I didn't like, and as I did that quick summing-up in my mind, I was trying to make allowances for the fact that he had been two days dead.

But Galley had ripped a page from his notebook and was scribbling a message for Sprat to send to Porthaven. When Sprat had gone he was asking my advice.

"Anything we might do, sir, outside routine?"

"You're the boss," I said, for he'd already told me that he was acting Chief Constable till his Chief recovered from an appendicitis operation. "But what I would do is get news of this murder to a Press Agency so that the London papers print it this afternoon. At the moment we know practically nothing about Dorvan. News of his murder should bring his relatives forward, if he has any, or someone who knew him. Then later in the day I suggest you see his solicitors."

You may have gathered that Galley was a good fellow in himself, and competent enough at his job. I admit that he had been in my debt in the past and yet few men in his position would have accepted the undoubted fact that I was more familiar with murder enquiries than himself. That was why I said I'd be delighted to stay on, even till late at night, provided I could get word through to Bill Ellice, and my wife. Galley said he'd see to all that for me, and when we'd drafted out a statement for the Press Agency, he went off to do the telephoning. A Sergeant Badcot would be arriving with the print and camera men, and of course there'd be the doctor. If Galley wasn't back when they arrived, I was to get them started.

I have no intention of boring you with the routine details of a preliminary enquiry into a murder case, for if you are a reader of detective novels you will know as much about procedure as myself. So you must take for granted the camera and fingerprint men, the chalked outline of the body when that body had gone, the measuring of this and that and the careful noting of the contents of the dead man's pockets. What I want to tell you are the unusual happenings or discoveries, though the real inwardness of some of them was not to be apparent at the immediate moment.

Take, for instance, the fact that Dorvan's pockets contained never a penny. If he had had a wallet, it was gone. I had a quick look in the writing-desk and there found a chequebook with a counterfoil that showed that on the previous Friday he had cashed a cheque on Self for twenty-five pounds. It was unthinkable that he should have cut things so fine as to have come back from London without a single cent. No wonder then that Sergeant Badcot was of the opinion that Dorvan had been murdered for his money. That kind of murder, as he said, was happening all over the country. Deserters, according to his ideas, were chiefly responsible. I agreed, and handsomely enough, I hope. Years of association with George Wharton have taught me the merits of dissimulation.

Then there was the mildly amusing episode with the old doctor. He and I were also old Porthaven acquaintances, and he couldn't help giving a roguish look at seeing me again, and in the company of yet another corpse. I told him it was a case of *non sequitur*. It wasn't that corpses sprang up at my approach but that cruel fate always had had to lead me to where corpses were. Just then Galley came bustling back. Everything had been fixed up, he whispered to me, and then the three of us chatted away as the doctor began making his preliminary examination.

"He wasn't shot at very close quarters," he said, as if to himself. "Five or six feet away at least."

"Looked to me as if he'd been lying there ever since he got back on Monday night," Galley told him. "I don't know if you agree."

"Why that particular time?" The old doctor had bridled up a bit. Maybe he thought Galley was trespassing.

"Oh, this and that," Galley told him enigmatically. "Tell you about it later. But it might help if you'd give a rough opinion; before you take him away, I mean."

The doctor grunted. Then maybe he realised he was taking himself a bit too seriously. "Isn't there something rather fishy about all this? Isn't this the first murder we've had since Mr. Travers was here last?"

"Don't you worry about Mr. Travers," Galley told him jocularly. "We've got him taped all right. You tell us if Monday night's all right and then we'll have the cuffs on him."

"Monday'll do to get along with," the doctor told him with a shrug of the shoulders. "Mind you, I may have to change my mind when I've had a good look at him." Then he had to labour the original joke, if joke it ever was. "Unless Mr. Travers saves both our times by owning up."

"I'm quite agreeable if it's going to be a help," I said. "I got on that train I was telling you about and followed him down here. It was seven o'clock on Monday night when I fired the fatal shot."

The old doctor raised humorous eyebrows.

"Is it permitted to ask why?"

"I'm afraid I'm the reason," I said. "It was he who took advantage of the virgin innocence of my Aunt Fanny. I was the result of their illicit passion. It wasn't till Monday that I found it out."

"Damned if that isn't good enough for *Punch*," guffawed Galley. And that was that, except that I would like you to keep the whole episode in mind. Many a true word, the saying has it, is spoken in jest. There's another side to that aphorism—that many a jest conceals a true word.

Then there was the argument about the newspapers. On the mat, as I have said, were four papers—the *Observer* for the Sunday and *The Times* for Monday, Tuesday and Wednesday. We had agreed that the choice of papers showed Dorvan as a man of taste, and I had said—perversely perhaps—that the *Telegraph* and the *Sunday Times* or any combination of the four papers would have still shown taste, but a slightly different kind of taste. Then it had struck me as peculiar that Dorvan hadn't picked up those papers as soon as he arrived on the Monday night. It was a natural thing to do. It was a thing that I myself would have *had* to do.

"Wouldn't you?" I asked Galley.

"Depends which door he came in by," he said. "Both the back and the front doors have Yale locks and there're the keys on his ring."

"The back door, then," I said. "And if so, why didn't he tear off that notice he'd put up?"

"Was it absolutely necessary that he should?" he countered. "It said milk was to be left on Thursday. Suppose they hadn't left it tomorrow morning, as it were. Then he could have shown them the notice and asked why."

I let it go at that. He carried the argument a step further.

"Say he came in the back way. He came in here and then to the bedroom. We know he put his bag on the bed and opened it. All he took out were his slippers, because the rest of the things he'd needed in London were still in the bag. He put his hat and muffler and overcoat in the wardrobe. I'd say it was then about a quarter to seven. No sooner did he step back in here than there was the knock at the door. He'd just changed into his slippers and he pushed the papers aside with his foot as he opened the door. Then he was shot."

I said, quite mildly, that the papers couldn't really be said to have been *aside*. I admitted that—as the photograph would show—they had left ample room for Dorvan to step round them when opening the door. And I added that the murderer must have been a remarkably fine shot.

"But what about that murderer?" I said. "Why didn't he kick against the newspapers with his dirty boots? Both the paths are pretty sticky, you know. He might even have trodden on them, though he didn't."

"*Did* the murderer come in?"

"If not, who emptied Dorvan's pockets of money?" I said.

There, for the moment, we left it, and chiefly because Galley had a brainwave.

"No use keeping Badcot hanging around," he said. "It mightn't be a bad idea if he enquired at the post-office about letters and telegrams. I don't know what you think, sir, but I've got it into my head that Dorvan went to town for some special reason."

He went off to brief Badcot and I wandered into the one room we hadn't examined—the spare bedroom. At once something struck me as odd about it, and it was quite a few moments before I knew what. Sprat had assured me that Dorvan had never had any visitors, and yet the bed was made up. I turned back the counterpane from the pillows and had a good look. I even felt the mattress. The bed was cold, as one would have expected, but it certainly wasn't damp. Galley came in and couldn't help staring.

"Looking for something, sir?"

He pursed his lips in thought when I told him that things didn't seem to tally. Then he had an idea.

"Perhaps he made up the bed for you, sir."

"For me!"

"That's right, sir. Only a theory, of course. Perhaps he knew he'd have a long story to tell you, sir, or there might have been something he wanted you to do locally. So he made up the bed in case you'd have to stay the night."

"But, my dear fellow," I told him, and tried to be jocular, "when he left here he didn't know that I or anyone similar was coming. When he got back on Monday night he wouldn't get to work on making up a bed for me on the Wednesday. If it *was* for me, then he wouldn't have made it up till yesterday." I added that he was a family man and ought to know that.

"Yes," he said. "I think you're right. But why *was* the bed made up?"

"Don't know," I said. "Unless it was that Dorvan often had visitors of whom the village was quite unaware. People couldn't be seen entering by that back way, you know. Maybe, then, the bed was always kept made up and aired ready for eventualities."

"I wouldn't be surprised," he said. "Not that the bed makes all that difference."

I told him I quite agreed. What I didn't like were things I couldn't satisfactorily explain.

We had another look at the kitchen. Dorvan had made himself no meal when he reached home that Monday night, or if he had, he had washed up after it. Everything in that kitchen was spotless and in place. In the table drawer was his ration book and in the pantry his rations, delivered, apparently, the previous Saturday. There was also a tiny joint of beef, roasted and uncut on its dish.

"Doesn't that rather tend to prove that he left here before lunch on Sunday?" I put to Galley. "Probably he cooked the joint when it came on the Saturday and left it for when he got back home."

"All I wish is he'd been a bit more untidy," Galley said feelingly. "Even the dustbin's clean as a new pin. If he'd left things lying about we might have found some sort of a clue." He didn't say to what, but went on muttering about the sin of being house-proud, and how a sister-in-law of his had to clean or wash up everything the very minute it was dirty.

We went back to the living-room to find everything finished there. Dorvan's prints were naturally everywhere, but no others except on a couple of gardening catalogues and the newspapers. So as we had room to operate, we got to work on an examination of the writing-desk. The first thing of interest we found was a drawer almost full of clippings from various periodicals and newspapers, and all relating to music-hall artists. Most dated from the ten years preceding the war. Then there were a few until 1940, and then no more than half a dozen cuttings from *The Times* or *Observer* for 1944 and 1945.

"Looks as if he was once in the theatrical business," I said. "If nothing comes from the Press I think I'd go through them carefully. They ought to tell you why he was interested."

There were one or two loose sheets of scribbling-paper, and when he unfolded one of them Galley really found something.

> Trains 11.0 arr. 1.55. 3.30 arr. 6.31.
> Ring Peters re car.

Above the first train there was a tick, as if upon examination, or after ringing Peters, that train had been decided upon and the other rejected.

"They're both Sunday trains too," Galley said, and frowned. "He cashed a cheque on Friday and therefore he went into Porthaven. That was when he made the notes about the trains. The paper's been folded because he had it in his pocket."

"And he might have rung Peters from there—whoever Peters is."

"He might, sir. Or from the local call-box against the post-office. And that explains how he got to London. This Peters called for him in a car. If we don't get any information at Porthaven, then we'll know Peters took him all the way there. Or to Tonbridge or Ashford."

Then just as we'd decided that there was nothing else of interest in the desk and were about to have an argument on the reasons why we'd found not one single private letter, Badcot came in.

"Get anything?" Galley asked him.

Badcot said yes and no. It was a rare thing for Dorvan to have a letter, but on Friday morning he had had a telegram.

"Did you get a copy?" asked Galley, getting to his feet.

Badcot shook his head.

"Shingler said he daren't let me have it. There'd have to be official application to his Head Office."

"That's Porthaven, isn't it?" Galley asked aggressively.

Badcot motioned as if for silence and then listened at the bedroom door beyond which the fingerprint men were at work. His voice lowered dramatically.

"I made application to Porthaven and they said they'd see what could be done. Then I had a quiet word with Shingler. I swore blind no one'd ever know. He reckoned he'd get hung, drawn and quartered if it ever got out."

Galley fairly snatched the paper from him, and the three of us went into the kitchen.

"This is just what we want, sir," he told me. "Listen to this. Handed in at the Strand Post-office at nine-fifteen on Friday morning. Received Midgley eleven-ten. Delivered at once, was it?"

"Straightaway, sir," Badcot told him. "Fred brought it over."

Then tantalisingly Galley went into a huddle with himself.

"That's it. He got the telegram in the morning and went into Porthaven as a result in the afternoon. Everything fits in snug."

"But what's the message say?"

We had a look at it together.

SEEING YOU SUNDAY CONFIDENTIALLY. SUGGEST YOU HAVE READY KNOWLEDGE EXPECTED YIELD. MEANWHILE AM BUYING OUT BUSINESS.

PETERS.

Galley had another look at it, and even then was still frowning.

"Some sort of a business transaction. Is that what you make of it, sir?"

"That's all it can be," I said. "Peters confirmed an appointment with Dorvan for the Sunday. Perhaps he came round the back way with the car. I merely mention that in case you can get no information about a car being seen at the front. Peters probably took him to London—he *was* already in London—and there we have a reason for the visit. As for what it means, I'd say that Peters was a seller of something or acting as Dorvan's agent. Dorvan was asked to find out more about the yield of something—perhaps the likely dividend of some particular firm or company—and in the meanwhile Peters was buying up a certain business concern—and probably as agreed." Then I had to shrug my shoulders. "Pure conjecture, but that's what it reads like."

Galley was about to put that copy of the telegram in his pocket when I asked for a copy for myself. Badcot looked agitated, even when I assured him that Shingler was still safe. Then Galley happened to glance at his watch. The time had passed so quickly that I was staggered to learn it was nearer two o'clock than one.

Galley had taken the precaution of ordering a cold meal of sorts at the local pub and there we had quite a cosy little room to ourselves. At three o'clock we were due to see Mr. Desmond Clare, head of the firm who had handled Dorvan's affairs. Almost before we had got our teeth into the corned beef, Galley was wanting to know if I had any ideas. I told him I'd been just about to ask him the same thing. We compromised by pooling all the ideas we had, and we agreed to accept no theory that wasn't supported by a considerable basis of fact.

First of all, then, we agreed that everything depended on one hypothesis: if there was any truth in Dorvan's statement that there had been a previous attempt on his life. We accepted the statement as true, and for two reasons. Firstly the real murder seemed to prove the truth of a previous attempt, and secondly there was the reason why Dorvan had approached the Broad Street Detective Agency, which was to put him in touch with his nephew, Robert, and with a view to inviting that nephew to live at Midgley as a kind of protection against any future murder attempt.

Next we agreed that the reason for the murder lay in Dorvan himself, by which we meant that it was no sporadic, unplanned affair for the sake of robbery. In other words, the murder had been committed by someone who knew Dorvan well; by someone who would profit financially by his death, or whom he had been blackmailing, or about whom Dorvan knew far too much. We were in agreement, therefore, that the cleaning out of the dead Dorvan's pockets and the possible removal of his wallet had been only a blind.

"The whole business is tied up with the fact that it was Guy Fawkes Night," I said. "Dorvan was shot, and that was the only night when nobody would have paid any attention to a shot."

"Because they wouldn't have thought it a shot."

"Exactly. They'd have known it was boys letting off a squib. And if anybody was really suspicious, there were the three squibs lying near the house for anyone to see. But just one point in connection with that. The murderer—probably wearing some kind of fancy-dress—"

"Why the fancy-dress exactly?"

"For two reasons," I said. "That would disguise him effectively so that Dorvan wouldn't recognise him when he opened the door. It would also have allowed him to move about in Midgley without being actually noticed. But the question I was going to put was this. The murderer knocked at the front door. He may have let off a couple of squibs just before he did so, but in any case Dorvan opened the door. That made a sudden flash of light. Surely someone in the crowd milling about round the cross-roads must have seen that light? That would determine the actual time of the shooting."

Galley shook his head.

"As a matter of fact I thought of that, sir, so I did a bit of quick checking when I did that telephoning. If you look out of this window you'll see what I mean."

It didn't take me long to see. From the back room of the police station the bungalow was visible, simply because it *was* a back room looking across rising ground. But all round the four cross-roads were houses, and towards Dorvan's bungalow there was a terrace of quite a dozen cottages, and they effectively screened it from view. Besides, as Galley pointed out, the crowd hadn't any interest in anything but what was happening before their eyes, and there was plenty in all conscience of that.

There was one other thing on which we agreed—that the murderer must have had local knowledge. The murder had been planned to fit snugly into a South Coast Guy Fawkes Night, and he must have been aware of the programme which Midgley had arranged for that night.

"By the way," I said, "we know how Dorvan got to the train on Sunday, or to London direct, and that was in Peters's car. But how did he get from Porthaven to Midgley on Monday night?"

"By bus, almost certainly," Galley said. "The train got in on time—I got Badcot to enquire about that—and the bus leaves ten minutes later."

"Then you can check?"

He shook his head.

"What you mean, sir, is that we can *try* to check. What we'll be up against is Guy Fawkes Night again; that and the fact that the buses aren't local ones and the conductresses aren't local girls. These buses, you see, were the ones that brought the spectators from Porthaven and just beyond it to see the show at Midgley. You mayn't believe it, sir, but Midgley always puts on as good a show as Porthaven, if not better. What I'm getting at is that the bus would have been packed. It'd have got nearly to Midgley before the conductress had collected the fares. She wouldn't have had time to notice people's faces."

Galley hastily wiped his mouth with his handkerchief and got to his feet.

"Don't you be in any hurry, sir," he told me. "There's twenty minutes yet, only I must have another word with Badcot. One thing you might do for me while you're waiting. Jot down anything else you think we ought to do."

It was nearly twenty minutes later when we were nearing Porthaven that he remembered that request. I told him I'd thought of nothing that he almost certainly hadn't thought of for himself. Then, as he insisted, I put the three questions:

(1) Who is Peters? And can he be traced through the Telephone Directory?
(2) Why did Dorvan come home on Monday instead of Wednesday?
(3) Where is Robert Dorvan?

Galley admitted he'd noted all three in his book.

"But about that Robert Dorvan," he said. "Your firm was being employed to find him. Why can't you go on with the job and claim against the estate?"

We both had to laugh when I explained why. For one thing, there mightn't be any estate. Then a contract was null and void in the event of the death of one of the parties, except that there would be a claim against the estate for work up till then performed implicit in or arising out of the contract. But the chief reason was that there had never been any contract.

But the car was drawing up outside the solicitors' office.

"Mr. Clare's one of the nicest gentlemen you'd ever wish to meet," Galley told me in a tone undesignedly reminiscent of Robb Wilton.

He led the way through the main door and into an office where three or four girl clerks were at work. One rang through and then said that Mr. Clare would see us at once, so we passed through an outer baize-lined door and into the private office. Clare came forward to greet us. He was as unlike a solicitor as could be imagined; not dry-as-dust and thin and patrician, but shortish, plump, and with a pair of eyes that twinkled as at the perpetual remembering of some delicious joke.

"This is Mr. Travers, sir," Galley said. "Mr. Travers is closely associated with Scotland Yard."

That was far too handsomely spoken, but the twinkle in Clare's eyes became only mildly quizzical as we shook hands. Then as soon as we were seated Galley got a confirmation that Dorvan had been a client of the firm, and then he gave Clare the news. One would have expected Clare to be astonished, and he was. But he was also looking strangely perturbed He was frowning to himself and rubbing his chin. Then he got to his feet, and did some more frowning. Then he anchored himself back to the fire, hands under his coat tails, and looking rather like a perturbed Pickwick.

"I take it you gentlemen want me to give you all the information I can? Without prejudice, of course, to my late client."

We said that was so, and that any information, whatever bearing it might or might not have on the crime, would be treated with the utmost implicit confidence. Nor would there be any divulgence of the source of such information.

Clare said that was very gratifying, and then there was a moment or two of blankness as if he were still loth to begin. I thought I'd set the ball rolling with a question.

"When did he first come and see you, Mr. Clare?"

"When?" He frowned. "About two years ago. I can give you the exact date." He frowned again and his eyes rose reminiscently to the ceiling. "The chief thing I remember about that visit was that he told me he had just come out of jail."

Chapter IV

ENQUIRY END

My eyes nearly popped out of my head. What effect that revelation had on Galley I didn't know. I was watching Clare's face.

"I think I'd better consult my private diary," he said, and went across to a huge safe that stood on the floor in the far corner. He came back with a largish book that had an over-lapping cover and a small lock inset, and he had that book open at the place he wanted.

"This is for 1943," he said. "December the 7th is the date. At three o'clock that afternoon."

Dorvan had introduced himself and then had said at once that a client should have no secrets from his lawyer.

"I'm afraid I was not strictly accurate when I said he had been in jail," Clare said. "He had been interned under 18B, and had just been released."

But perhaps I'd better give a precis of what Clare had to tell us, and cut out interruptions and questions and references to the diary. I should add that Clare was at once of the opinion that what he was to tell us would have been discovered in any case by any competent authority, and that therefore he was doing his late client no bad turn. On the other hand, in helping to trace his murderer, he was in a way doing him a service.

Perhaps it might help, too, if I give at once a tiny Dorvan family tree, for the three of us compiled one before we left Clare's office.

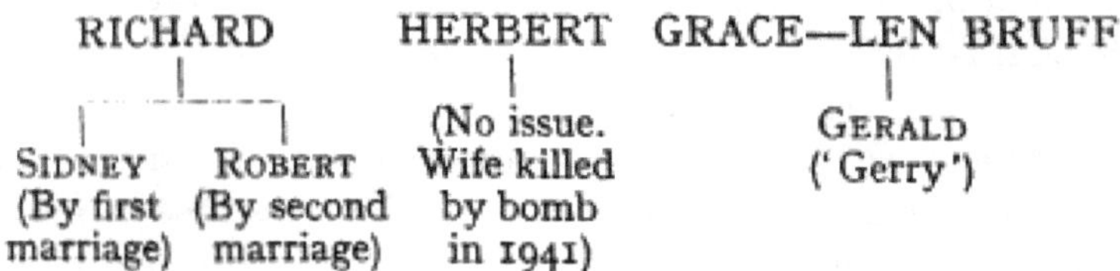

That was the Dorvan family, and their fortunes or misfortunes are easy enough to follow. Richard and Herbert had been left a flourishing East End furniture manufacturing business by their father. Herbert had retained only a small financial interest, for he had been the owner of a Variety and Stage Employment Agency. Grace, youngest of the three children, had married the famous Leonard Bruff, music-hall comedian and pantomime dame. The three were all dead. Grace had died just before the war; Herbert had been murdered, and Richard had committed suicide.

According to Herbert Dorvan, that last tragedy had come about like this. The furniture business had been ruined by Jewish undercutting, and to save anything out of the wreck, Richard had been forced to sell out at a ridiculous price to his Jewish competitors. From then on the story is simple. Herbert had declared war, as it were, on Jews in general. It was at the time of the rise of the British Fascist movement and Herbert contributed funds, spoke at meetings and was recognised as one of the big men by those in the know. When France fell the police swooped on him. His business was closed down, and his two nephews, who had been associated with him, were out of a job too.

Sidney, the elder, was now running a very well-conducted and successful night club, at least according to his dead uncle. Robert didn't matter so much, for as officer in a London Territorial Battalion, he had been called up in 1939, had been sent out East and had been taken prisoner by the Japs. But Herbert's bitterness against the Government had been partly concerned with Robert. If he had ever been brought to trial he would have claimed that a proof of his loyalty was the fact that his nephew—to whom he was in some ways a father—was a serving officer. Another source of even intenser bitterness was the death of his wife in a London bombing, for had Herbert been at liberty he would have removed her to the country as soon as bombing began. Then in the November of 1943 he was released. Since the person from whom he bought the bungalow was a very distant relation, he was allowed to take up residence there although it was still a prohibited area. As Clare ironically remarked, the ways of bureaucracy are unfathomable.

"Surely I've heard a chap called Gerry Bruff on the wireless," I said.

"You must have," Galley told me at once. "He's a comedian, and one of the few original ones, if you ask me. Does impersonations as well."

In any case there you have practically all that Clare had to tell us.

"I saw no reason why I shouldn't handle his affairs," he said. "Not that there was much to handle. There were certain securities which I hold and from time to time he would ask my advice about investments—not that he ever took it."

"He must have been rather a chatty person to have confided all that family history?" I suggested.

"I don't know that it was quite that," Clare said. "I think he wanted to unburden his mind. After all he'd been incarcerated—shall we call it?—for over three years." He smiled rather roguishly. "I'm a chatty person myself. I like the human side of my clients. I always have."

Then he remembered something else.

"I should have said that I had a special interest in Mr. Dorvan. The family originally came from Hastings. His father lived there. I think that's why Mr. Herbert Dorvan was pleased about coming to Midgley. He'd had a house in St. Leonards himself."

I didn't quite see the significance of that till a long while afterwards, and in any case Galley was putting a question in which I was interested.

"What sort of a man did you think him personally, Mr. Clare?"

"Well"—Clare pursed up his Puckish lips—"that's a hard thing to say. I wasn't attracted by him; I'll put it like that. In strict confidence I might go so far as to say that while I found no reason to distrust him, I saw no reason to trust him very far."

"He was mentally stable?" I asked.

"Oh yes. He was a man with a grievance, mind you, though he tried to give the impression that he wasn't." He shook his head. "A curious character. I felt all the time that he and I were talking through a kind of curtain. One thing he did mention more than once during his few visits here, was that he expected to come into possession of a considerable sum of money when the war was over. Then he would probably live abroad."

"He was well off?" asked Galley.

"I imagine so," Clare said frankly. "His expenses at Midgley couldn't have been great. We held about eight thousand pounds worth of first-class securities."

"He wouldn't starve on that," Galley said. "But about his will, sir. Could you divulge its contents?"

"Will?" He looked surprised. "We held no will."

"That's curious," I said. "I had it in writing from him that he was coming to see you yesterday about his will. That seemed to imply the existence of a will."

"You have that letter?"

"I haven't," I said. "His instructions were that it should be burnt. But we took the precaution of making a typewritten copy."

"This is quite interesting," Clare said. "I'd mentioned the matter of a will to him and he'd always put the matter off." He squinted up at the ceiling. "Now let me see. Yes. The last time I mentioned the matter we agreed that it would be highly advisable to make a will, but not till he came into that money which I've already mentioned."

"Just one last thing," I said. "He was in Porthaven on Friday last. Did he by any chance come and see you?"

Clare's eyes opened wide.

"As a matter of fact he did. He came to collect a sealed envelope. Quite a small envelope." He began to move towards the side table which was piled high with miscellaneous papers. "I have his receipt somewhere."

"Don't trouble," I said quickly. "We'll take your word for it, Mr. Clare."

"Well, I'll find it and have it ready for you if you wish to see it later. That envelope, by the way, was one of the reasons why I'd mentioned making a will. In the event of his death it would have to be handed over. But there we are. As far as I know, he died intestate."

It was only much later that I realised that he had left something unexplained: that he had hurried ahead, in fact, to avoid explanation. But Galley was getting to his feet, and in a couple of minutes we were in the outer office again.

"A message came for you, sir," one of the girls told Galley. "I didn't like to disturb you while you were with Mr. Clare, but you're to go to the police-station urgently."

"Here you are then, sir," the station-sergeant said. "The Yard rang up. A Mr. Sidney Dorvan rang them up about this Midgley business he'd just seen in the papers. The Yard got in touch with us and I said we'd ring him."

"You've got his number? . . . Right, then get him straight away."

"Now we're getting somewhere," Galley whispered to me. "But suppose I have to see him in town? What's the best way to go? Back with you?"

I said that seemed a good idea. The manager of the Southern Hotel could be interviewed at the same time.

"You get out a list of questions to ask that manager," Galley said. "I'll have them phoned through from here and then he'll be ready with the answers. There won't be a lot of time if I'm to get back tonight."

London was on the line and Galley took the receiver. I listened with only half an ear, for I was busy getting those questions ready, but I did hear the phrase 'Ginger Cat' and some questioning as to the whereabouts of a Palfrey Street. When Galley had finished I had hardly begun. All he wanted to know was if I'd be ready in a quarter of an hour. He was seeing the old doctor and meanwhile they'd find me a cup of tea.

This was my list of questions for the manager of the hotel:

(a) Exactly when was the room reservation made?
(b) At what time did Dorvan arrive?
(c) What reason did he give for having his meals in his room?
(d) Did he have any callers?
(e) Did he receive any telephone calls in his room through the hotel exchange?
(f) Did he leave his room during his stay?
(g) What reason did he give for suddenly relinquishing his room?
(h) Did he have tea before he left on the Monday?

I should add that that last question was added after Galley's return from seeing the doctor. The stomach content showed a meal taken about two to three hours before death. Sultanas were detected, which looked as if he had eaten tea-cake, taking into account the other contents. Galley also had the revolver bullet which would go to the Yard experts.

"What about the time of death?" I wanted to know.

"Near enough to what we thought," Galley told me, and then was bustling about and giving final orders. Badcot was to be warned that we would be at Midgley in ten minutes' time and then the hotel manager was to be given the list of questions. It mightn't be before nine o'clock that we would be ready to see him in town.

We must have done some hustling that afternoon, for it was only just after five o'clock when we left Midgley in my car. Galley was expecting to catch a London train back to Tonbridge at ten-thirty that night, and Badcot was to meet him there with the police car. As for our own journey, the night was fortunately clear and we made good time. Galley, by the way, had set my mind at rest about the inquest. It would be formal, and I should not be needed. He himself would give evidence about the finding of the body. Later, of course, I should be needed when the final inquest was deemed due.

It was striking seven as we went over Westminster Bridge. Twenty minutes later we were in Palfrey Street, and that, as I had known as soon as Galley had mentioned it, was within a quarter of a mile of my flat. The rather narrow street seemed singularly deserted except for a parked car or two. One rakish looking American car was drawn up outside the night-club itself. Over the door was an illuminated sign.

THE GINGER CAT
First Floor

"Not a very pretentious place," I said to Galley. But the stairs were wider than I expected and they led up to a very wide landing from which doors opened out. There was a general cloakroom, but no attendant, and only the usual basin and a decoy shilling to indicate his existence. There were Ladies' and Men's Rooms, and what looked like a main door. We went through.

The room was dim, for only a couple of lights were on, but rarely have I been taken so aback. It was a superb room with a magnificent dancing floor. On a deep-piled carpet surround were modernistic chromium-plated chairs and tables. To the far left was a platform with only the seats and a few instrument cases to hint at the band. Across the room was an immense bar with the usual rail and high chairs, and the only sign of life in all that huge room was the bar attendant, and he had his back to us and seemed to be busy rearranging innumerable bottles.

Our feet had made no sound on that luscious carpet and he gave a start when I coughed just behind him.

"Mr. Dorvan in?" I asked. "We have an appointment with him."

I didn't mention any time, for we were almost half an hour early. But we needn't have worried.

"Through there, sir," he said, and jerked a thumb at the only door.

We went through to a short passage at the end of which was a door, and the light came through to reveal the word OFFICE. I gave a tap at the door and a man's voice called a 'Come in'.

The man was sitting in his shirt sleeves at a desk. In front of that desk was a mahogany table on which stood a bottle, a siphon and glasses. On a corner of that table a woman was sitting, and she was definitely at her ease. She was a blonde and what they call a good-looker, though I own frankly that what I chiefly recall were the handsome legs and the sheer silk stockings. I remember the turquoise ring and the earrings to match, but, above all, I remember the elegant way in which she blew the smoke from her cigarette and then, as our eyes met, the supercilious look and the lifted eyebrows. If ever a look said, "What the hell's all this?" it was the one that drifted across that bored —or was it ironically amused—face.

Galley was speaking.

"You're Mr. Sidney Dorvan?"

"Yes?" the man said, and made no move. He was about forty by the look of him: black-haired, fleshy and what they call tough. The thin streak of black moustache gave him a foreign look. The mouth was sensual and the eyes hard and cold.

"I'm Inspector Galley. We have an appointment."

Dorvan scrambled—that was all I could call it—to his feet. When he smiled his teeth were like small white pearls, and the whole character of the man had changed. He held out his hand.

"Glad to see you, Inspector. You're a bit early."

There was a movement behind me, but all I caught was the swish of a skirt as the door closed behind the blonde. We sat down. Galley introduced me. Dorvan passed a box of expensive-looking cigarettes, then put on his tails.

"I'm afraid you caught me on the hop, gentlemen." He gave a little cough. "I was just going over the evening's business. We don't get cracking for another hour or so yet." He pretended to notice the absence of the lady. "I ought to have introduced Miss Malone. She's one of our cabaret artists."

"You run a cabaret here?" I asked politely.

He gave a little laugh and those pearly teeth fairly fascinated me again.

"I'm glad to hear you didn't know that, Mr. Travers. It shows the police haven't had reason to be interested in the Ginger Cat." He gave himself a nod of approval. "We've got a pretty good record here—as things go."

Then his face straightened. His fingers rapped the evening paper that was lying on the desk.

"A bad business about my uncle. This didn't tell us much either."

Galley and I had decided what and what not to divulge, and I might tell you that for nine parts of the latter there was about one of the former. Dorvan sat nodding and giving an occasional grunt, but he asked never a question.

"There we are then," Galley told him resignedly. "The point now is if you can give us any help."

Dorvan shrugged his shoulders.

"The whole thing's a mystery to me. You could have knocked me down with a feather when someone—when I saw it in the papers. 'There can't be any other Herbert Dorvan, not at Midgley,' I told myself, and even then I couldn't believe it. So I rang up Scotland Yard."

"You knew he was at Midgley then?"

Dorvan's lips clamped together for a quick moment and his eyes narrowed.

"Yes," he said. "I did. Of course I did." He was talking more rapidly. "I'd never actually been down there, but I'd written to him once or twice."

Then into his eyes came a look that was definitely calculating.

"If you went through his house you probably found one or two of the letters."

I didn't want Galley to answer that.

"You knew Midgley?" I cut in.

"Knew it quite well," he told me heartily. "We originally came from Hastings—our family, I mean. My Uncle Len—Len Bruff, you know—made his home there when he retired. Poor Aunt

Ethel—perhaps you know about her—she was Uncle Herbert's wife—is buried in the cemetery there. I got special permission."

There was a tap at the door. The bar attendant looked in.

"Sorry, Mr. Dorvan. . . ."

"I'll see you later, Peter," Dorvan told him. "Come in as soon as these gentlemen have gone."

It seemed to me that the tone held a certain threat. That bartender was going to get hell for letting us through unannounced. Dorvan was leaning back in his chair.

"One of the best men at his job in London," he told us. "Peter, you called him?" The question was crudely put and no wonder he looked momentarily surprised. I added that I'd known a Peter Perelli, a cocktail-shaker at the old—and fictitious—Golden Goose.

"This chap's Peter Camber," he told me. "Only been demobilised about a couple of months."

Galley got to his feet.

"Well, we won't take up any more of your valuable time at the moment, Mr. Dorvan. Just one last question and then we'll go. I hope you'll take it the right way. It's just a routine question that everyone concerned will have to be asked. Where were you yourself last Monday night?"

"I?" His eyebrows lifted. "I was here. It's my business to be here. Where else should I be?"

"That's all we want to know," Galley told him. But he had forgotten something and I cut in again.

"Would it surprise you to know that your uncle was staying at the Southern Hotel on Sunday night last?"

He stared in amazement.

"You didn't know it?"

"I hadn't the foggiest notion." The wary look came again. "What on earth was he doing there?"

"That's what we've got to find out," I said. "You can't help us?"

He shook his head.

"Then one really last question," I went on. "Someone murdered your uncle. What did you think when you read the news? Did you have anybody in your mind?"

His eyes met mine, then turned away.

"You mean, did I have any idea who'd done it?"

The question played for time.

"That's what I said," I told him bluntly. He shook his head again.

"I don't know anyone who should want to do him in." He moved back towards the desk and the question came almost casually. "It's none of my business perhaps, but didn't you find any correspondence from anybody? Any stranger, I mean?"

"Nothing of any importance," I said, "but we haven't gone into everything yet."

I hoped, if he had anything to conceal, that that wouldn't ease his mind, and he certainly didn't look too happy. Then Galley was telling him he'd be informed about the funeral and inquest, and was holding out his hand.

"You'll have a drink, gentlemen, before you go? Just a spot of whisky?"

We thanked him but said we were in a desperate hurry. Then he let us out by a back door which he unlocked and he actually went down the stone stairs with us.

"One thing I meant to ask you," he said. "What about his will?"

"The solicitors will be communicating with you about that," I told him. And there we left him. Forty yards on and to the right and we were back in Palfrey Street.

"We've got tons of time in hand," I said. "What about slipping along to my place?"

My wife had left a note to say she had gone to see a friend but would be home at ten. I found beer and then rang the Yard.

We had said little in that short cut round to St. Martin's Chambers and now I asked him what he thought of Sidney Dorvan.

"He said a lot about being knocked down with a feather." Galley said, "but you could have knocked me down with a feather when that chap poked his head round the door and he called him Peter. I know *Peter* isn't *Peters*, but it made me think."

"Yes," I said. "Another alibi you'll have to enquire into."

"And I didn't like the way Dorvan was so anxious to know if we'd found any letters. He'd tried to be too damn clever about it."

I was glad Galley had spotted that, not that it hadn't stood out a mile.

"What I noticed even more," I said, "was the way he reacted to the question of knowing who did it. What did you think?"

"He knows something."

"You're dead right he does," I said. "I wouldn't like to go as far as saying he knows who did it, but I'll bet you a fiver he has a shrewd idea of who was mixed up in it."

"That alibi of his will have to be a pretty sound one," Galley said belligerently, and then he went off on another tack. He'd see his Chief in the morning, but it looked as if the Case was going to be too involved for Porthaven to handle, what with a London and a Sussex end. Not that he had any intention of throwing in his hand for a day or two. Something lucky might turn up. If not—and he left it like that.

Then the messenger came round from the Yard to collect the parcel, and after that we emptied the last bottle of beer and walked the few yards to the Southern Hotel.

The manager was waiting for us. He had taken a great deal of pains to get the information we needed, so he said, and to see that it was complete. The answers, categorically, were these, and he signed the paper on which they and the questions were written.

(a) Dorvan made the hotel reservation by telephone on the Saturday afternoon. Where the call was from he couldn't say. The room was taken for three days, and he asked then about meals in his room.

(b) He arrived at nine-thirty on the Sunday night, and had no meal then.

(c) The reason he gave at breakfast the next morning for having meals in his room was that he hated lifts and stairs were bad for his heart. He said he was prepared to pay.

(d) As far as was known he had no callers. But that was something difficult to check. Anyone might have gone up to his room direct.

(e) There was a telephone in his room but he didn't use it in any way.

(f) It was impossible to check whether or not he left his room and the hotel.

(g) He gave no explicit reason for leaving the hotel on the Monday, except that 'something urgent had cropped up'. He was perfectly willing to pay for the three days but was actually charged only for two.

(h) He did have tea in his room. He ordered it when he'd made the discovery about the time of his train—i.e., about three-thirty. A tea-cake containing sultanas was part of the meal. The rest was one pastry and, of course, tea.

Well, that was that. There was nothing else to do at the hotel except thank the manager for his trouble. When Galley found he could get a meal of sorts while waiting for his train, I thought I might as well get back home. So we said goodbye then and there and he promised to keep me in touch with things.

It was not till the Friday night that he rang me. Nothing particular had happened at the formal inquest, he said, and there had been no discoveries at the Midgley end. Dorvan was being buried at Hastings on the Saturday and Sidney Dorvan was coming down. The postscript was the most interesting part of the conversation, for it came as a kind of afterthought, and when I'd been commiserating with him on his bad luck.

"I wouldn't be surprised, sir, if the Yard takes over in a very few days."

He wasn't a long way out. On the Monday afternoon, and it was only by chance that I happened to be in, the telephone went.

"That you, Mr. Travers?"

"Yes," I said. "It isn't you, George, is it?" George has two methods of address. In his ceremonial moments I'm Travers, and on very rare occasions when he considers it desirable to be frolicsome or placatory, then it's Ludo.

"George Wharton speaking," he told me.

"What's the matter, George?" I cut in. The tone had been more lugubrious than official. "Holding a prayer-meeting or something?"

He gave a Whartonian snort.

"Never mind about me. Bill Ellice told me I'd probably find you at home. I'd like to see you if you can manage it."

"When?"

"Soon as you can make it," he told me, and then rang off.

PART II

Chapter V
THE G.O.C.

Perhaps you are not acquainted with George Wharton. If so, and because he now enters the Case, you might like an introduction, even if that introduction is made, as it were, behind his back.

George is known at the Yard as the Old General, a nickname arising not only from a wholesome respect, but also from a very definite pride and even affection. But about his outward appearance there is nothing but contradictions, since no one could possibly look less like one of what is popularly known as the Big Four. He is tall and massive, for instance, but disguises his height with a stoop. His huge walrus moustache and those antiquated spectacles which he occasionally dons, give him the look of a shopkeeper harassed by too many Government forms, or of a hawker of vacuum cleaners with whom business could not conceivably be worse.

All that is part of his technique, for his back can suddenly be ramrod straight when wrath or indignation or excitement makes him forget the pose, and since he can read the smallest print with the best of us, the spectacles are donned for his own obscure and deceptive purposes. For George is a showman who is the master of his art—or should I say craft? His sleeves are crammed with innumerable tricks and his personality alert with innumerable disguises to be assumed on each apt occasion. I, who have been associated with him for years as a supposed-to-be consultative expert of the Yard, have still not seen the whole of his repertoire, though I have long since learned to place something like their true value on his grunts, snortings, bluffs and blusterings, his meeknesses and sly wheedlings, his hypocritical deprecations, spurious indignations and crafty concealments, and those guileful blandishments which, had they been known to Bret Harte, might have substituted the name of George Wharton for that of Ah Sin.

But make no mistake. George is no mountebank. No man can show more dignity when he so pleases, and on few men could that dignity better sit. For his tenacity, prodigious memory and shrewd judgment of character I have a very deep respect, and at our twin jobs he has forgotten more than I have ever known. For the man himself I have an enormous liking, and though at times tricks and subterfuges can exasperate, it is only they that make him the unique and lovable character that he is. A rich and fruity personality is George, and his portrait by Belcher would be the sensation of any Academy. But perhaps the best final comment I can make on him is my wife's—that if George ever died she would love to have him stuffed.

But to be fair to George, I should be equally frank about myself, and, thank God, the years have left me with very few illusions. Perhaps my only virtue is that I never take myself too seriously, which maybe is why I have been told that I am easy to get along with. There was a time when I was described as an intellectual—though never, thank heaven, as a pink one—but long association with George has, I think, removed most of that reproach. I have a brain which might be called alert, though flibbertigibbet is the epithet I myself prefer: the crossword kind of brain, shall we say, that loves problems and is quick to find solutions. That they are not always the right ones is a matter for endless sarcasms on the part of George, though nevertheless he makes no bones about assimilating as his own such theories of mine as prove to have been well on the mark. For the rest, I am lucky enough, even in these times, to be independent of work, but since work—with George at least—is the very salt of life, work I do, though with an independence and a what-the-hell approach that must sometimes drive George to profanity.

But together—make no mistake about that—we work very well. We may cuss each other and blaspheme, which after all is only an elaborate pulling of legs, but when on a Case we do know where we're going, nor have we often failed to arrive. And when attacked by any third party, we can form a mightily solid front. But it is high time we got back to the story.

I tapped at George's door and then walked in.

"You're quite a stranger," I told him disarmingly. "Bernice and I were saying only a few minutes ago that we'd have to ring you up."

He grunted a something as I helped myself to a chair. Then he adjusted those old-fashioned spectacles and peered belligerently over their tops. His knuckles rapped a pile of papers he had evidently been studying.

"You didn't tell me you'd been down in Porthaven with Galley?"

"Why should I?" I asked blandly.

"Why should you!" Amazement and grief were suddenly on his face.

"Exactly. Why should I? If it comes to that, there are plenty of things I don't tell you."

I was trying to think of a list.

"There's nothing funny about it," George told me reprovingly. "This is a murder case you were mixed up in."

"Mixed up?" I said. "That's rather a vulgar phrase for you to use, George, isn't it?"

Flippancy is the only weapon when George simulates a tantrum.

"Murder I said and murder I mean." He glared, then shook a sad head. "Dammit all, anyone'd have thought you'd have mentioned it, if only as a matter of courtesy."

"You've got something there," I told him. "Maybe if I'd seen you or heard from you I would have mentioned the matter. But you didn't send for me to do this schoolmaster act? Or did you?"

He gave a grunt or two, and I knew the wind was almost out of his sails.

"The Porthaven police have called us in," he told me, and rapped those papers again. "I thought perhaps you'd like to help."

I was going to say, "That's very good of you, George," but he had to spoil it by cutting in with, "After all, you have been mixed up in it, far as I can make out."

I drew my chair in closer.

"Do I gather that I'm being called in again?"

"Well, yes," George said grudgingly, and began turning those papers over. Then he was asking if I'd had tea. When I said I hadn't, he rang down for some. That was meant as an outward and visible sign that I was restored to grace.

"I was in Porthaven most of yesterday," he told me. "As soon as Galley mentioned your name I couldn't believe my ears. That was why I decided to take over the business myself."

"You needn't put it as if you're graciously getting me out of some scrape," I said. "But those are all the notes on the Case, are they?"

"I spent most of this morning going into them," he said. "Galley was a fool. He ought to have known inside twenty-four hours that he couldn't handle things."

Buttered—or margarined—toast came in and a pot of sergeant-major's tea. Over it I told George everything I knew. He was good enough to say it didn't differ much from the notes. Then he was wanting to know if I'd any ideas. I told him I'd naturally done nothing after I left Galley on the Wednesday night, and then I wanted to know if that bartender at the Ginger Cat had been interviewed.

"He's got a cast-iron alibi," George said, and then added shrewdly that there were quite a few people called Peter in the world, and that *Peter* wasn't *Peters*.

"And Gerry Bruff, the other nephew. What about him?"

"He hasn't been interviewed yet," George said.

"He wasn't at the funeral?"

"No," George said slowly, and I thought guardedly. "Galley says that Sidney Dorvan rather gave him the impression that Gerry Bruff and his uncle didn't hit it off very well together."

He set the ruined tea-tray on a side table and from there put his apparently artless question. The tone of voice should have warned me that something dramatic was coming.

"That nephew, Robert Dorvan. Is Bill Ellice doing anything about finding him?"

"How can he be?" I said. "Old Dorvan never was signed on as a client. Any expenses Bill incurred is just money down the drain."

"That's business all over," George pronounced piously. "Ups and downs, downs and ups."

The spectacles had served whatever turn he had had in mind and he began putting them away.

"You can start in at once on this Case?" He was glancing at his watch, and I wondered why.

"At any moment you like, George," I told him, "provided it goes down on the pay-sheet."

"You will have your little joke," he told me with an ersatz chuckle. "A good many months since you and I were showing 'em how to do it. Just like old times again."

"Just like old times," I echoed, and hoped my heartiness didn't sound too ersatz either.

"Afraid you'll have to pull more than your weight," George went on. "I'm getting a bit rusty in my joints."

"Rubbish!" I told him, which was what he'd been angling to hear. "You're still the old dog who knows all the tricks."

He hardly knew how to take that, and then he was hastily getting into his coat.

"I've got a call to pay. Thought you'd like to come along."

The car was ready and the driver evidently knew the destination. Our route lay along Piccadilly and towards South Kensington. George kept noticeably away from the Case and confined his few remarks to enquiries about Bill Ellice, and, when that petered out, Bernice and myself. Then the car turned left near Queen's Gate and in a couple of minutes was pulling up outside what looked like a private house. Then above the fanlight of the front door I saw the words—TEMPLEMORE HOTEL.

We went in and found ourselves in a large vestibule. That hotel looked a comfortable place, and the faint odour of cooking had nothing cheap and cabbagey about it but was somehow redolent of vast sirloins of beef. George motioned for me to stay put, so I took a seat while he interviewed the very presentable young lady at the desk. In a matter of seconds he was back.

"All right," he told me. "We can go right up. No need to use the lift."

On the first-floor landing he consulted the room numbers, then turned left. A few yards along was Room 15. George tapped at the door and a man's voice called a "Come in!"

In we went and found ourselves in a remarkably comfortable bed-sitting-room. A youngish-looking man got to his feet and came forward with a welcoming smile.

"Mr. Robert Dorvan?" asked Wharton.

A smile and a nod gave the answer.

"You were expecting me," Wharton told him. "I'm Superintendent Wharton of New Scotland Yard. Allow me to introduce my colleague, Mr. Ludovic Travers."

Robert Dorvan was a slim young fellow of about five-foot-nine. His face was a bit peaked and rather pale. I liked the look of him, and he spoke well too.

"You must have had a very thin time," Wharton told him.

"No worse than most," he said. "I did have a bit of luck towards the end. I got taken on as a kind of orderly by one of our doctors whom the Japs were allowing to look after some of the internees. We didn't have too good a time, but it wasn't quite hell like it had been before."

"And what's England seem like to you now?" I asked.

"A damn queer place," he said frankly. "That's one of the reasons why I slipped away quietly to have a few days by myself and think things over. Get acclimatised, you might call it. I just felt I couldn't face anybody I knew—in the old life I mean."

"And you didn't know about your uncle's death till this morning?" Wharton asked.

"That's right. And I rang you at once. It was Miss Sanbridge—the receptionist here—who put me up to it. She asked if the Mr. Dorvan was any relation."

"Just tell us your movements after you were—what shall I call it?—demobilised."

"Demobilised is good enough," Dorvan told him with a grin. "What I did first was to come to London and fix myself some sort of headquarters. I knew this place before the war so I managed to get in. Afraid I had to work the Japanese prisoner sob-stuff pretty heavily. I stayed here a bit, then went down to the country. Went to a show or two and had a look at the bomb damage and so on while I was here. Got back here from the country last Monday."

"You didn't look at the newspapers?"

"I suppose I did," he said. "If you mean why didn't I notice the mention of my uncle's murder, all I can say is that I didn't see a paper on the Tuesday morning, which was when I went away again." He smiled rather ruefully. "Also I'm not particularly interested in newspapers."

"I can well imagine it," Wharton told him sympathetically. "But you said you were in the country. May I ask where? Just for the records?"

Dorvan shifted a bit uneasily in his seat.

"Well. It's rather personal. I mean, it's . . . well, it's . . ."

"Everything's in strict confidence," Wharton told him heartily. "Nothing said in this room will ever go out."

"That's very good of you," Dorvan said lamely. "To tell the truth there was a very nice girl I met on the boat. A Miss English. Her father's a General English. I thought I'd like to see a bit more of her."

"And you hoped she'd like to see a bit more of you?" Wharton suggested roguishly.

"Well, yes. And that was why I went down to Flampton and stayed at a pub there. That's a little village just beyond Woodford in Essex."

"Well, I hope you had a good time," Wharton said. "And you came back—when?"

"Last night, as a matter of fact. Then I rang you this morning."

I don't think Wharton was any too pleased about his letting that out. But I gave no sign that the brief bubble of George's omniscience had been pricked.

"You were surprised to hear your uncle had been murdered?"

"I was flabbergasted. I mean, it sounded ridiculous. Those things happen to other people's relatives, not to your own."

"And what were your relations with your uncle?"

He looked away for a moment.

"Not too good." Then he gave Wharton a straight look. "You knew about that Fascist business?"

"Oh yes."

"Then perhaps you'll understand," he said. "I was a kind of freelance at the time. As a family we always had theatrical interests, and I'd been doing some work for the B.B.C., and some talent-scouting. In my judgment, that anti-Semitic mania wasn't doing the Variety Agency any good. Do you know that my uncle had a huge sign outside his office—NO YIDS NEED APPLY? You may think I'm talking a bit snobbishly, but I knew his activities weren't doing either me or him any good. Particularly as I was a Territorial officer at the time."

"Quite understandable," Wharton said. "And where were you when he was roped in?"

"Luckily just going out to the Middle East."

Wharton grunted a something.

"But let's come to hypothesis," he went on. "What were your feelings towards your uncle when you got back home? If you had any."

"If I had any is right," he said. "I didn't know what had happened to him and I just didn't care. I was going to live my own life in any case. You may think that ingratitude," he went on. "Maybe it was. I owed him a few things, but . . . well, I guess one forgets a lot where I've been." He smiled disarmingly. "Sorry. Afraid I'm doing the sob-stuff again."

"Not a bit of it," Wharton said. "But what sort of job do you expect to do now?"

"Oh, a bit of writing perhaps. Revue or B.B.C. work if I can get it. I wouldn't turn anything down."

"That's the spirit," Wharton said approvingly. "An honest man's the noblest work of God," he quoted, and heaven knows why. Then he was off at a tangent.

"What about your other relatives? Your step-brother Sidney, for example."

"Sid's all right in his way," he said, and then gave that disarming smile again. "I'm not being superior." He hesitated. "I oughtn't to say it, but he was too hand in glove with my uncle in that Fascist business for my liking. I think he had a damn lucky escape." He gave a look almost of horror.

"Sorry. I shouldn't have said that."

"Why not?" asked Wharton blandly.

"Well, you might go making enquiries."

"Don't you believe it," Wharton told him, and turned to me with a smile of amusement. "The war's over. The policy is, let sleeping dogs lie."

Dorvan smiled relievedly. Then he was asking if we knew Sid's whereabouts. The last news he had of him was in a letter from Gerry Bruff that had reached him in the Middle East. When Wharton mentioned the night-club, he seemed rather amused.

"Trust Sid to drop on his feet. A pretty paying game, isn't it?"

"Depends how much you've got left over after paying the fines," George told him with a chuckle. Then he got to his feet. "You didn't ask me about your uncle's will?"

"Should I?"

"I thought you might be interested," George told him, rather taken aback by the directness. And then he sat down again.

"Between ourselves I think he died intestate," he said. "That ought to mean a nest-egg for you."

"I shall take it," Dorvan said. "I'm not all that altruistic. And I won't say I wish he were alive to enjoy it himself."

"A very sensible way to look at it," George told him. "But I was forgetting something. You tell Mr. Dorvan about his uncle and the Detective Agency."

His left eye had made some extraordinary motion that I gathered was a wink. So I made my news impersonal. It was just something we'd discovered.

"But this is preposterous!" Dorvan told us. "Sure you're not pulling my leg?"

"Not a bit of it," Wharton said. "Mr. Travers can guarantee it's absolute fact."

"I can't believe it." He shook his head. "He wanted this Detective Agency to find *me*, and I was to live at this Midgley place as a sort of bodyguard!" He shook his head again. "I know the old boy always had a bit of a liking for me, but, dammit all, this is ridiculous."

"Well, there are the facts," Wharton said and got once more to his feet.

Then came the old, old recitation, though I must add that no one could do the reciting like George. You know the recitation I mean, about honest men not fearing the law, and routine enquiry for the files, and Mr. Dorvan having far too much sense to think there was anything personal.

"Where was I on Monday night last?" Dorvan said. Then he fidgeted a bit nervously. "That's rather awkward—in a way."

"Yes?" asked Wharton expectantly. Another moment and there would have appeared on his face what I always call his Coliseum smile—the one that must have flashed across the face of a lion when espying a particularly plump Christian.

"You'll think I'm a bit of a swine. I mean, after telling you about Miss English."

"Nonsense. We're all men of the world."

"Well, the fact is I was at a bit of a loose end on the Monday, so I got Miss Sanbridge to do a dinner and a show with me. I'd rather that didn't get out."

"Bless my soul, I'd have done the same myself," George told him and clapped him on the shoulder. Then he gave one of his peering looks. "Got a pound note on you?"

"Why, yes."

"Let me have it," George said. Dorvan shot me a look and then gave George a note from his wallet.

"This Miss Sanbridge has no idea who I am? Or Mr. Travers?"

"Not the foggiest."

"Right," said George, and gave a belly-like rumbling that was meant to be a chuckle. "I'm your Uncle George. You leave everything else to the Old Gentleman."

That was one of George's deprecatory allusions to himself, though usually he'd make it the Old Gent.

"You just introduce me to the lady and I'll do the rest."

Down to the vestibule and the desk we went.

"Hallo, Miss Sanbridge?" Dorvan hailed her.

"Hallo, Captain Dorvan."

I couldn't help noticing the flush and the shy smile. If that girl wasn't in love with him, I told myself, then I'd eat my hat.

"This is my Uncle George."

"How do you do?" said George with just the right mixture of courtliness and pleasure. "I want you to settle a bet for me, young lady. Or I did, until I saw you. Now I know that I've lost."

"A bet?" she said, and smiled, but the smile was for Dorvan.

"Yes," said George sadly. "I had the nerve to bet my nephew here that he'd never have the pluck to take a girl out anywhere, and then he claimed he'd taken you out to dinner and a show on Guy Fawkes Night."

She laughed again, rather a shy laugh this time.

"Yes. We did go out."

"I want the particulars," Wharton said. "I'm not going to pay out a pound as easy as that."

"Well," she said, and she was still smiling shyly at Dorvan, "we had an early dinner at the Café Royal and then we saw *Happy and Glorious* at the Palladium. Then we had supper at a little place in Soho." Her brows wrinkled delightfully. "I forget the name."

"Good enough for me," Wharton said, and scowled ferociously as he produced the pound note. "There's your money, young man. You know what you ought to do with it?"

"Why no . . . uncle."

"Take Miss Sanbridge out again," Wharton told him with a final chuckle.

No sooner had we waved a goodbye to Dorvan and the car had moved off, than I had to tell George that his handling had been masterly.

"The old Gent still knows a trick or two," he told me. "Anywhere you'd like to be put down?"

"You mean there's nothing else doing tonight?"

"That's right," he said. "Tomorrow morning we'll get going. I want a good night's rest for a change."

"Anywhere near the flat will do," I said.

"You were going there in any case," he told me.

"For the love of heaven, George, don't be devious," I told him. "Why was I going home in any case?"

"Because you might want to change. And to tell Bernice you were taking her out for once."

"What *is* this?" I said. "Taking her out where?"

"Well," he said, "a night-club mightn't be a bad idea."

Chapter VI

A NIGHT OUT

I'D RATHER expected Bernice to turn down that night-club offer, but she didn't. When I told her what was in the wind, she said it would be perfectly thrilling. Maybe she would have adventures like those in American detective novels. Then, and I honestly believe she was serious, she was wondering if I'd be in any danger. I shrugged my shoulders nonchalantly. If Bernice liked to think that a London nightclub of the Ginger Cat class was peopled with molls and gunmen and black marketeers, who was I to disillusion her? In fact, being in one of my perverse and mischievous moods, I made a suggestion.

"I don't think you'd better be my wife," I said. "You're just a lady friend I've brought along."

She rather opened her eyes at that.

"It'll be a kind of excuse for my being there at all," I said. "You know the kind of thing. One of the quiet sort, kicking his heels up."

She liked the idea, I think, but when she began enquiring about the night's programme, I said we'd leave everything to chance. George Wharton's briefing had been that we should look round and keep our eyes open.

There's no particular point in my claiming that my wife is a mightily attractive woman, and looking ten years younger than her real age, which—I can only shrewdly surmise—is still the right side of forty. I repeat that there's no point in my making that claim, for when a man makes that kind of boast, it's less for the sake of his wife than to indicate a certain merit in himself. If that sounds obscure, just work it out. But I must say that when Bernice was ready to go, and I was asked to give an opinion of her get-up, I told her she'd be a sensation. Between ourselves that was a shade overdrawn, but I was pretty sure all the same that there'd be a head or two craned to look at her. But the main point is that because of that get-up I thought it better to take the car than walk.

It was half-past nine when we drew up outside the Ginger Cat. There was an attendant on the kerb and he told me that I'd have to park in Halford Street, round the corner to the left. There was plenty of space there, and I thought I recognised that rakish American car that had been parked in front of the club the night I went there with Galley.

I deposited my things in the cloak-room, and, while Bernice powdered her nose, had a word with the attendant. It was then a quarter to ten and he told me the first short cabaret was at ten o'clock and the second at eleven. I don't know, by the way, if you are familiar with the way that a club of that standing has its drinking controlled. Mind you, there are various modifications of licensing laws to suit special circumstances and according to the scrupulously legal way the club is run. In the case of the Ginger Cat, its own cocktail bar had to close at eleven o'clock promptly, but wholly independent of that there was an arrangement with an off-licence whereby runners brought drinks that had been ordered, and such drinking would go on till the small hours or when the club closed. Now you know what's meant nowadays by a Bottle Party.

People had been coming in and there had been plenty of movement around that vestibule, and through the main door had been coming the subdued sounds of the dance band and an occasional clapping of hands. When Bernice and I at last went through, that dance floor seemed crowded, and it was thanks to that that we got a table to ourselves. A white-coated attendant was there as by magic. I ordered a pint of iced lager for myself and Bernice said she'd have the special post-prandial cocktail that the attendant highly recommended. I was recalling that George had not told me if the Government would pay.

"What do you think of it?" I said.

"It's perfectly lovely," she said. "Quite nice people too. The band sounds good."

Perhaps you didn't know that my wife had been a professional dancer. A solo, concert dancer, I should have said, and, if the name conveys anything to you, as famous fifteen years ago as Maude Allen. That was why I made a face when she asked me if I'd like to dance. Modern clutching and slithering is quite out of my line, not that I hadn't always been a menace in any ballroom.

"You'd never be noticed in that crowd," she told me, and then we were too late. People were crowding back to the tables again. A naval officer and a charming girl gave us a disappointed look.

"Sorry. Have we taken your chairs?" I asked them.

"It's all right," the man said, and then grabbed two handy chairs like lightning. The girl laughed as they hastily sat.

"Mind if we share your table?"

"We'd love it," I said, and then our drinks appeared. They weren't too extortionate—five bob each for the lager and the cocktail. The naval man ordered drinks and then said we ought to have had ours on him. I said there was plenty of time.

I had a look round. There were quite a lot of uniforms and a good sprinkling of middle-aged men of the gay-old-dog type. The women looked a lively crowd and young for the most part, but with quite a few highly-decorated old stagers among them. There was the devil of a din, with chattering and laughing and even shrieking, and a good time was being had by all. I counted no less than four waiters dealing with drinks, and round the bar was a crowd that made that bar invisible except for its overhead lights.

"My name's Purley," the naval man suddenly said. "This is Doris Carter." I think he said Carter, but the din was terrific.

I pressed Bernice's foot and bellowed that my name was Wharton and this was Bernice Haire. I knew the name would convey nothing but I didn't dare look at Bernice's face. Then the band began what I was told was a rumba. Purley looked smilingly at Bernice and off they went.

"You dancing?" Doris asked me, and I had to make my shameful confession.

"Sorry I'm cramping your style," I said.

"Not a bit of it," she told me laughingly. "I like an occasional squat."

"Another drink?" I suggested.

"Not now," she said, and she had a charming smile. "I hate getting woozy, don't you?"

"I certainly do," I said. "No half measures, what? Do you come here often, by the way?"

"Fairly," she said. "But only when Ted happens to get leave."

"What's the cabaret like?"

"Quite good."

Then she peered.

"See that girl in black just coming in by the bar? That's Netta Malone."

"Ought to be Let 'em Alone, by the look of her," I said facetiously.

"Frightfully attractive, isn't she. Sings rather well, too."

It flashed through my mind that Netta must have come from Sidney Dorvan's office.

"Your friend Miss Haire dances awfully well," Doris was telling me. I gave my glasses a polish for they were a bit misty.

"So I believe," I said. "Rather tough on an old-stager like me."

"Oh, but you're not old!" Then, before I could bask in any more assurances, she was nodding again towards the bar door.

"That's Sidney Dorvan who owns this place. The cabaret's going to begin."

Sidney was wearing his tails, and I must say they sat on him well. I lost sight of him as he went round by the bar. Then the dance ended, the waiters scurried round with drinks and the lights were lowered except for a spotlight over the platform-stage. Netta Malone stepped forward to the microphone and the band began some catchy number that I'd heard a score of times on the wireless.

"Rather effective that," Bernice whispered, and maybe she meant the spotlight. Or was it the black frock Netta was wearing, that seemed to stand by itself from the waist up and yet left shoulders bare.

Her voice was no different from that of a dozen croonerettes I'd been forced to hear; just a husky, sob-ridden contralto lagging well behind the beat. But the company lapped it up. Then when the applause had died down she announced that she'd sing 'Solitude', at which there was more applause. But I had to admit that she had a way with her, though quite what the way was I couldn't fathom. In that black frock and the misery-ridden face that ought, I suppose, to accompany the Duke Ellington song, she looked quite a different person from the hard-bitten baby who had sat cross-legged on the office table, and who'd given Galley and me that supercilious stare.

"What'd you think of her?" Doris asked me when the applause had died down again. Ted cut in and spared me an answer.

"Something about that girl always gets me. Damned if I know why."

I said nothing. To him she might have been a lump in the throat; to me she'd been a pain in the neck.

"Don't let it get you too far, darling," Doris told him. "They say she's a very close pal of Dorvan's."

The lights went off again and this time we had a juggling, patter merchant. He was pretty good, for he made me laugh. When he wanted a member of the audience to come forward, a special light began moving round the room, and where should it stop but on our table. I felt as if I was suddenly naked.

"You, madame, in the red frock. Will you kindly step up to the stage? . . . Thank you, madame. You'll get her back again, sir. Don't worry."

Doris went forward and the light followed her. She had to hold a handkerchief or something—you know the kind of thing— and then find the same handkerchief somewhere up her sleeve. It would have been quite funny if I hadn't been feeling annoyed about that light. Doris came back amid cheers, up went the lights and up struck the band. Ted hailed a pal and introduced him to Bernice, and off they moved. Ted swung off with Doris and no one gave a damn about me. I was just keeping the table.

Then I saw Netta coming round from the right on the edge of the carpet. She was looking at nothing in particular even when she slowly passed my table, and yet I knew somehow she'd had a good and special look at me. Perhaps, I thought, when she'd passed, I'd been spotted before and that light had been turned on our table so that someone might get a good look at me. And yet somehow I didn't think she'd recognised me. My legs were tucked well under and hid a lot of my height, and I was in glad rags and wearing different glasses. When she had seen me in that office I had had on a heavy overcoat with a felt hat well down over my eyes. Not that I gave a damn whether she'd recognised me or not. The interesting thing was why she should be interested enough to make the attempt.

I don't want to bore you with the long succession of dances or describe the one attempt I made to waltz-chasse a two-step with Bernice. What matters is that when we were having yet another drink between dances, Dorvan began making the round of the tables. As he neared ours, I slipped my glasses into my pocket, and lowered myself a bit in my seat.

"Good evening," came Dorvan's smooth voice. "You have everything you wish?"

"What a hope!" Ted told him facetiously.

He laughed. I heard Dorvan laugh, though his face was a blur.

"I hope you're enjoying yourselves, nevertheless."

"Having a great time," Doris told him.

"A delightful place," added Bernice, and Dorvan bowed from the waist and moved on. At the next table I heard the same questions, and as Dorvan's progress was towards the bar, I slipped on my glasses again.

There seemed to be even more people in the room than ever. Soon the second cabaret was over, and it had been pretty good too. Quite a good bass had sung a couple of popular ballads and then there'd been a frozen-faced comedian with a new line in patter. Perhaps I thought him so good because I'd had a drink or two or three, but when dancing began again, I was getting a bit bored. Bernice seemed to be having the time of her life. Once or twice she didn't come back at all to the home table but seemed to have got attached to another party. All I could do was take an occasional drink and look round. Netta danced once with what looked like a fat stockbroker, and Dorvan had at least one dance with an elderly dame whose jewellery was too sparkling for paste and whose make-up had been laid on with a palette knife. Then Ted sat down beside me. He had lost his girl too.

"You're having an exciting evening, old-timer?" he told me commiseratingly.

"I'm all right," I said. "My time's coming. The wife's away in the country for a fortnight."

His grin expressed a lot of things.

"Tell me," I said. "Does this chap Dorvan always make the round of the tables? You know—that shop-walker act."

"I don't remember him," he said, and frowned.

"Funny thing," I said, "but the bloke who recommended this place must have got mixed up with some other place. He was here on Guy Fawkes Night."

"So was I," Ted said.

"Was Dorvan here?"

"Good lord, yes. He's always here."

"What about that bartender? What's his name—Pete or something."

"Peter was here all right," he told me, and then gave me a wink. "You're feeling all right? Haven't taken too much aboard?"

"Me?" I said owlishly. "My dear young man, I haven't begun to drink yet. I was taking my liquor when your backside was corrugated with cradle marks."

"Good for you, old-timer," he told me cheerfully, and then off he went. And in that same moment I saw something that interested me. Netta and Dorvan were at that door by the bar. She was putting her hand to her head and making gestures that seemed to me to indicate a headache. Dorvan seemed a bit annoyed about something, then he shrugged his shoulders and went through the door towards his office. Netta went by the band—I had to stand up to see that—and through a door labelled ARTISTES ONLY.

Something told me that Netta was going home, and on a sudden impulse I made for the outer door. Then luckily I saw Bernice, and I pointed frantically to the door and made the motions of steering a car. All she did was wave to me. Maybe she thought I was tight.

I collected my hat and coat and nipped round to my car. Just when I was telling myself that I'd been a fool, Netta appeared round the corner about twenty yards away, and Dorvan was holding her arm and steering her. They got in the car and almost at once it moved off. Just as their tail-light was disappearing round the bend, I moved my car off too, and for the next fifteen minutes I was well on their heels.

The route lay along Regent's Park, or so I thought at first, but then we dipped a bit south towards Lords and then slightly north to St. John's Wood. There were two or three turns, with me at a discreet distance, and then when I was entering a quiet little road with rows of maisonette-flats, the car ahead of me pulled up. I drew quickly in at the kerb some fifty yards behind. The door of their car opened and Netta emerged. She gave a wave of the hand and Dorvan's car shot off again. Maybe there was no need for him to reverse his car if he knew a way round, and as I thought that I glanced at my watch. It was just short of midnight.

I walked slowly along the pavement trying to make sure which house Netta had entered, and then another queer thing happened. A taxi was suddenly drawing past me and it stopped at the kerb. From across the road, and it looked as if he had been waiting in the shadow of the trees, came a man, and we almost collided at the taxi door.

"All right," he told the driver, "I shan't wait."

The taxi slewed round and was off. I moved on and thought I'd identified the house I wanted. Then I walked on again for a bit before I turned back. And then what should appear but yet another taxi, and it too stopped quite near the house.

"This is it, sir," I heard the driver say.

A man got out. He paid the driver, and as I passed them my hat was well down over my eyes. Then I knew who the man was, and as I moved on I realised I was instinctively polishing my glasses. When I put them on again and took a quick look back, I was too late. The taxi was moving off and Robert Dorvan had disappeared. But that he had gone into that one particular house seemed certain. And at that moment, in the silence of that little road, it was something bewildering and amazing.

I waited in my car for the best part of an hour, and when I was thinking of driving off, Robert Dorvan appeared again. He was walking away from me like a man certain of his direction and I watched him till he was out of sight. Then I waited another quarter of an hour, thinking perhaps that Netta might go back to the club. Then, when I began working things out I knew she had pretended a headache, and there'd be no more going out for her that night. All the same I sat on for a bit, and it was almost half-past one when I moved the car on again. It was two o'clock when I'd parked it and got back to my flat.

I'd expected Bernice to be in, but she wasn't. So I made some coffee and told myself I'd give her another quarter of an hour, after which I'd walk back to the Ginger Cat. And over my coffee I naturally did a bit of quick thinking, and it was then that I remembered something, and about that man who, I'd casually told myself, had been waiting for a taxi in the shadow of the trees on the opposite side of the road from Netta's flat. What I remembered was that just as I'd got out of my own car, I'd seen a sudden flash of light and from where I knew later that that man had stood. Maybe then that quick flash of a lighter or a match had been a signal, and the taxi had at once come up. Maybe then the unknown man had been watching Netta's flat—for it looked to me as if those houses were each of two flats—and if so there were more unlikely things than that he was an employee of some Enquiry Agency. What if Netta were married, I thought, and her husband was after grounds for divorce. Then I remembered what Doris had said about Netta and Dorvan, and I couldn't help recalling the free and easy scene that had met the eyes of Galley and myself when we had stepped into Sidney Dorvan's office, and the pains Dorvan had afterwards taken to explain Netta away. "One of our cabaret artistes, Netta Malone," was what he had too casually said.

Then just when I was beginning to puzzle my wits over that extraordinary affair of Robert Dorvan, and had got to the point of being sure that the midnight appointment must have been fixed beforehand, I heard a key in the outer door, and there was Bernice.

"Here you are then, darling," she said happily.

I began to apologise, but she said everything had been all right. That nice naval officer had given her a lift home, not that she wouldn't have minded walking.

I heated the coffee again and brought her a cup.

"How're you feeling?" I asked meaningly.

"Simply splendid," she said. "I hadn't even got to my gracious stage."

When Bernice—on the rarest occasions—knows that she's really had a drink, she always becomes very gracious, and that is her own description. It means that she holds herself well in hand, does as little talking as possible, and beams on everybody.

"But you had a good time?"

"A marvellous time," she said. "I met some perfectly charming people."

"Well, I saw a man just going out in whom Wharton was interested," I said, "so I took a chance and followed him in the car and when I got back it was rather late. As a matter of fact, I was just going back to the club to fetch you."

"Something curious happened to me too," she said. "That proprietor, Mr. Dorvan, came up to our table. Our old table, I mean. There were about six of us there, and he got talking, and then Ted, the naval officer, introduced me."

"He got your name right?"

"Oh yes," she said. "Bernice Haire. Then that man Dorvan attached himself to me in the most obvious way. He asked if I'd been there before, and of course I had to say no. Then I thought I'd better tell him the truth about having been nursing during the war and only just being released. Then he said he thought he'd seen my friend before." She gave a little titter. "Darling, I had the most astounding brainwave. I told him he mustn't say a word. I said, 'If ever his wife finds out, heaven knows what will happen!' Then I said you'd been a patient of mine and we were just friends, so to speak. Then, darling, he simply leered at me. Well, a polite sort of leer. You know—a meaning look. So I leered back."

"My God!" I said. "Anything else?"

"He said wasn't your name Walford, and then I had to be horrified again. Then he assured me he was the soul of discretion and asked me to dance. So we danced."

"And that was that?"

"Yes, except that he said I danced amazingly well, or superbly, or something like that. I didn't want him to begin talking about us again, so I said I'd once thought of taking it up as a profession. I can't think what made me so reckless."

"I can," I said. "The sooner you're in bed the better, and me too."

A quarter of an hour later Bernice switched off her bedside light.

"Good night, darling. I had a perfectly wonderful evening."

I said good night and knew I'd be asleep in a couple of seconds. Five minutes passed and her voice suddenly came.

"You still awake, darling?"

I grunted a something.

"I think it was a wonderful idea of us going incognito." I grunted something else and settled to sleep once more. Another minute and her voice came again.

"Darling?"

"Yes," I said, and I fear a bit irritably.

"When are we going to the Ginger Cat again?"

Chapter VII
THE GERRY BRUFF SHOW

GEORGE HAD asked me to drop in at his office at about ten o'clock. For once in a while he seemed in a genial mood, and perhaps out of cussedness at the sight of my none-too-genial face. When he asked if I wasn't feeling fit, I told him a few things.

"Damn all night-clubs," I said. "My head's still muzzy—not that that matters. What I object to is having my private life disorganised and demoralised."

I told him about the time Bernice and I had had, particularly Bernice. All he wanted to know was if it had been a paying place.

"By my computation," I said, "I reckon each person there spent an average of at least thirty bob. I didn't get off so cheap myself, but there we are. If there was one person there last night, there must have been a couple of hundred from first to last. I counted seventy couples on the floor at one time. Now work it out for yourself."

"It's well run?"

"Very well, indeed. One big family party. They don't even have dance hostesses or whatever you call the girls."

He grunted. Then he was asking if anything had happened.

I didn't see why George should hog all the dramatic moments so I led him up the garden for a bit. I told him about Netta Malone and recalled the first time Galley and I had seen her. I said I was sure Dorvan had sent her to try to recognise me, and when she hadn't been sure, then he'd had a shot himself. Then he'd had a go at Bernice.

"What was it? Pure curiosity?"

"You're asking me," I said. "But if the place is well run—and it is—and even if he thought I was the police bloke who came with Galley, what had he got to be nervous about?"

"That amounts to saying he *was* nervous."

"Well, wasn't he? And if it wasn't the club, then what was it?"

"Maybe that business that Robert hinted at," George said. "You know, that old Mosley business."

I went on to tell him about my following Netta home, and about the man who'd been watching the house. George gave a snort of contempt.

"That's all divorce-court stuff. What's it got to do with the Case?"

I shrugged my shoulders indifferently. Then I told him about the arrival of the second taxi and the man who'd kept a midnight appointment. That made George sit up a bit.

"Faked the headache, did she? And I'll bet you didn't get a good look at the man."

"I saw him as well as I'm seeing you," I said.

"You didn't happen to recognise him?"

"Oh yes," I said airily. "It was Robert Dorvan."

"What!" His eyes bulged, then he shook his head. Then his eyes bulged again. "Why, dammit, that's the third woman we know he's been mixed up with! What's the idea? Where's it connect?"

"I've tried to think it out," I said, "and all I can arrive at is this. He wanted news of Sid and wasn't prepared to see Sid personally. Someone mentioned Netta Malone, so he asked her to give him a confidential interview. She said she never was free till three or four in the morning, and after that she slept all day. He asked her to make it as early as she could. Probably he made it worth her while, and she managed midnight."

"Not a bad theory," George said. "Except that it doesn't exactly tally. Robert told us nothing to indicate that he'd refuse to meet Sid. He even apologised for letting slip that Fascist business. So why shouldn't he have seen Sid for himself?"

"Don't know," I said. "But here's a suggestion. Maybe he suspected Sid of murdering old Dorvan. Maybe he hoped Netta might let something slip."

"That's an idea," George said. "We might do worse than put a man on both their tails."

"Tail Robert by all means," I said. "About Sid, I've got another suggestion. Here's a rough plan of the Ginger Cat. Somewhere above Sid's private office there must be some sort of a room. In fact there's at least a whole floor or two above the club. I suggest we put a man up there with listening apparatus, and from seven o'clock when Sid arrives till the time the club closes down. Sid and this Malone woman are bound to do some talking. They might even talk about me—if they did recognise me. Somebody might drop in. Some unexpected character like that man Peters we're looking for. Just a lead of some sort; that's all we want."

When George makes up his mind he doesn't hesitate. Inside two minutes a Sergeant Jewle was coming in. George introduced him and said he'd be lending a hand generally.

"Postpone that Midgley business for a couple of hours," George told him, and to me: "Jewle's got a couple of men down there trying to pick up something."

As for the new orders, nothing was said about tailing Robert Dorvan. It was that Ginger-Cat job that Wharton was keen on.

"Find out what's on the floor above," he said. "Then ring me here as soon as you can; inside an hour if you can work it. Make it snappy, but don't panic. I'll be here till best part of midday."

"We're going to interview somebody in a rather peculiar way," George told me when Jewle had gone. "Another ten minutes yet."

I had raised enquiring eyebrows but George was filling his pipe and grumbling about the price of tobacco.

"Something I remembered as I was coming along here," I said. "What about the bullet that killed Herbert Dorvan?"

"A German bullet."

"German?"

"Nothing unusual about that, is there?" he told me with a glare. "Thousands of our men and Americans coming back from there on leave or demobilised, and they come back lousy with souvenirs and black-market stuff. I ought to know. I've been working on it."

"What you mean is that anybody might now own a German gun."

"Why not? Especially in London." He gave a grunt or two. "That's what makes this Case a bit complicated. It isn't all in one piece. There's a London end and a Midgley end. Old Dorvan came to London, did some business here—or we presume so—and then went back . . ."

"Two days sooner than he expected."

"Exactly, and the reason for that must be at the London end. All the beneficiaries under his will—if he'd made one—live in London. But he was killed in Midgley and that's two hours from London, unless you take a plane."

"I think the London end's the more important of the two," I said.

He shrugged his shoulders.

"Maybe. But there's something connecting up those two ends. Have you thought of that?"

I shook my head. He gave a snort that might have indicated scorn or pity.

"Hastings. That's the connecting link. Dorvan was killed on a special night, wasn't he? Guy Fawkes Night, when all that mumbo-jumbo business was due to go on in Midgley. It was a murder that was planned to fit in."

"I see what you're getting at," I told him. "The murder couldn't have been committed by anyone not familiar with the

Guy-Fawkes-Night procedure in that particular village. But all the Dorvan family, so to speak, were born and bred down there."

"And the three nephews will get his money," George pointed out. "The solicitor will be temporary administrator and I'm given to understand that the total will be about twelve thousand. That's four thousand quid apiece. Not a lot, but it's not to be sneezed at. And one other little matter. It must have been what I'll call an old inhabitant who did the murder, and I'll tell you why. There haven't been any Guy Fawkes antics down there for six years. Work that out."

I saw the point well enough. The murderer knew that when the celebrations were resumed, there'd be a sort of continuity of tradition. He knew too much, in other words, to have gathered his vital advance information solely from the newspapers.

"Assuming Dorvan was murdered for his money," I said, "four thousand isn't much and it'll be a long time before the beneficiaries handle it. Meanwhile, is there one of the three who's badly in need of money?"

George shrugged his shoulders.

"Sid Dorvan doesn't seem to be. That's one reason why I wanted you to run an eye over that club of his. But money needn't be the only motive. The net's got to be thrown pretty wide. For instance, Herbert Dorvan might have been done in by some chap or other whom he did the dirty on in his Fascist days."

He glanced at the clock, then hurriedly pushed the buzzer. A portable wireless set came in, and he began twiddling the knobs. Then he altered its position and in a few seconds there was the sound of a brass band. He tuned it down.

"There's one of those three nephews nobody seems to have paid much attention to," he told me. "The one known as Gerry Bruff."

"He's on the wireless now?"

"That's the idea," George said. "A re-broadcast or whatever they call it. The Gerry Bruff Show."

I'm afraid I winced. Those shows in which the B.B.C. works various comedians to tatters are about the last word in inanity, futility and the more emetical kinds of ballyhoo. And sure enough, when George turned the knob again, there was the same old fanfare and the same hysterical announcer shrieking—"The GERRY *BRUFF* SHOW!!"

We'll skip the hammy—or should it be corny?—preliminaries. The Where-oh-where-can-Gerry-Bruff-be? stuff, and the star's ultimate arrival amid colossal applause from the usual audience of morons. Then I heard Gerry Bruff's voice.

It was different, there was no doubt about that. Handled aright and with a script writer like Ted Kavanagh, he could have been the pivot of another ITMA. His was dry humour, chatty, confidential and informal after the style of Gillie Potter or Michael Howard at his best, and even at that hour of the morning he was definitely funny, if only in some queer, incongruous way of his own.

"This chap's good," I whispered to George, but I needn't have bothered, for frantic applause announced that the opening phase was over. A dance band began to swing it hilariously, then quietened as the announcer did some more hysterics. In came the usual croonerette. When she came to

> Maybe, maybe
> I'm no lady,
> But my baby
> Doesn't seem to mind . . .

I had a bad moment or two. But it was over pretty soon, and then, after a minute or two of dreary back-chat between the croonerette, the band-leader and Bruff himself, came the announcer.

"Ladies and gentlemen, for the first of our guest artists to-night we have none other than the Prime Minister of Mirth himself—George ROBEY!!"

I heaved a sigh. George Robey is part of my lost youth and the days when I frequented the Oxford and the Tivoli. I hoped he'd have material that would transport me back there—and he had. As soon as the band struck up, I knew we were in for that ballad I'd heard scores of times; one of the many that had kept him on the map—"I stopped, I looked and I listened."

"Takes you back a bit?" I told Wharton, and he gave a sideways nod.

"Everything there," he said when the applause had died down. "Except those eyebrows of his and the dirty look."

There was more dance band and a crooner for what is known as the vocal. Then came another announcement, this time by the crooner, who seemed to have recovered miraculously from his three minutes of lachrymose despair.

"For our second guest star tonight, ladies and gentlemen, we have none other than our old friend, Nellie WALLACE!!"

"This show's costing a packet?" I remarked to George. He made a gesture for silence.

There was Nellie, kittenish and tremulous as ever, and I'd never heard her come through so well. One joke, over which the blue pencil must have hovered, made me laugh, but then I am of a Rabelaisian turn of mind. Nellie was playing Anne Boleyn and describing her wedding night, and how, when she'd undressed, she'd passed the time playing patience. Then came a tap at the door and Henry came in. "What do you want?" demanded Anne, and then Nellie—"Wasn't I a silly girl? As if I didn't know!"

The short remainder of the programme was very much anti-climax, and when the band struck up for the last time, I expected George to switch off. But he didn't and we had to hear the final announcement.

"You have been listening to the Gerry Bruff show, with So-and-So and So-and-So and So-and-So and Gerry Bruff both as himself and as George Robey and Nellie Wallace. Look out for the same show, same time, same day next week . . ."

Wharton switched off.

"What did you think of him?"

"Damn clever," I said. "He took me completely in. Didn't he you?"

"I heard the original show," he told me, and then glanced at the clock. The buzzer was pressed and he lifted the receiver. Someone was told to bring someone in. Then he dumped that portable set under the table.

Steps were heard and George himself went to the door.

"Ah, very glad to see you," I heard him say. "I'm Superintendent Wharton, as you probably know."

He was ushering into the room a neatly-dressed young fellow of well under thirty. No sooner did I take a look at him than my fingers went instinctively up to my glasses.

"This is my colleague, Mr. Travers," George was saying. "Travers, this is Mr. Gerry Bruff."

I didn't grudge George his look of—what shall I call it?—triumph or self-appreciation, for it had certainly been a masterpiece of timing.

"Mr. Bruff has been good enough to come round and see if he can help us," he went on, "and we're very grateful. Take your coat off, Mr. Bruff. Make yourself comfortable. This is Liberty Hall. Cigarette?"

I held the lighter. George gave a chuckle.

"I shouldn't be surprised if we found ourselves on the air next week," he told me.

"You wouldn't make at all a bad first guest artist," I said feelingly.

"You gentlemen been listening to my show?" Bruff asked us.

You couldn't call his a cultured voice, but it was a pleasant one, and the slightly Cockney accent made it friendly. And, curiously enough. I'd never have spotted it was the voice I'd just heard over the air.

"Oh yes, we've heard you," Wharton assured him.

Bruff shook his head.

"Not too good, between ourselves." He gave a dry look. "Still, comedians must live. Or mustn't they?"

If I'd have said that, nobody would have moved a muscle. Bruff had something I'll never have: just a lift of the eyebrows, perhaps, and a shifting of his mouth, that made even that old joke seem spontaneous and new.

Wharton ended his chuckle and hooked on his antiquated spectacles.

"Your uncle's death was a shock?"

And here I must interpose a brief word about the handling of evidence. Wharton has claimed that he can smell a liar a mile off, and so can I on the rare occasions when the smell reaches that far. But interviews with the law can be disturbing to the most honest of citizens, and it is only too easy to misinterpret an uneasiness here or a hesitation there. That's why Wharton and I always like to be together when a witness or suspect is questioned, and he is generally the questioner. He can look where he likes: reminiscently at the ceiling, for instance, or at his papers, or even at the one to whom he is talking. But I keep my eyes on that person's face and rarely let them waver. He isn't looking at me but at George. I'm in the background, only noticed at chance times, and I'm the one who watches reactions.

"It was a bit of a shock," Bruff said. "Not so much his dying as the way he was killed."

"I know, I know," said Wharton piously. "You were pretty friendly with him, I take it?"

Bruff shifted uneasily in his chair.

"Well, I can't say I was."

"A pity when relations fall out," Wharton observed piously, and then waited.

"You know all about him?" The *all* had been slightly accentuated.

"That Fascist business—yes. It's part of our job here, or was."

"That's what got my goat," Bruff said annoyedly. "All that Jew-baiting and hot air. Live and let live, that's my motto. Besides, I've got some good friends among the Yids. And he was making himself too conspicuous. Asking for trouble. I was just making a start then, and it wasn't doing me any good, either."

"I bet it wasn't," George told him sympathetically. "And when he ran up against 18B, that didn't make it any better."

"True enough, it didn't. Only there was a war on then and people had other things to read about in the papers. I don't mind telling you I let him drop out. That business of his had gone phut, but I could stand on my own feet by then."

"You weren't called up?"

"No," he said. "You mayn't think it, but my heart isn't all that good. I did a lot of work for Ensa though. Had one trip out to the Middle East and another to Italy. I should have been going to Burma this month, only it fell through."

"You fellows certainly see the world," George told him. "Been to Germany?"

"Only just got back, as a matter of fact. About a fortnight ago."

I don't know why, unless it was at some loathing for the Hun, but he had made a sort of pout as he said that, thrusting out his lower lip, and all at once it struck me how like he was to Sidney Dorvan. Not so fleshy, certainly, but the same cast of face. Give him a streak of a moustache and he'd pass for Sidney in a bad light, so I was telling myself.

Maybe George was trying to connect up that trip to Germany with the gun that had killed old Dorvan, I thought too, and I knew it when he gently slid away.

"There's something I've often wondered," he said. "Strictly between ourselves, how does Ensa pay?"

"Can't grumble," Bruff said. "I'm doing all right." The dry smile came again. "Doing my bit for the income-tax down-and-outs."

"Aren't we all?" Wharton said heavily. "But to get back to what I might call business. Your uncle was murdered, and that's a nasty word. You've no idea who might have done it?"

"Me?" He shook his head. "He must have made plenty of enemies; that's all I know."

"I suppose we all have if it comes to that." George heaved a sigh then gave another peer over the spectacle tops. "One thing I didn't make clear. You can be as frank in this room as you like. What's said here never goes outside. That's why I'd like the opinion of a man of the world like yourself about one or two of your relations. Sidney, your cousin, for one."

That unpleasant look definitely came again. It gave a vulgarity to the face and cheapened it.

"Sid?" he grunted. "Not a bad chap in his way. Always was a bit of a Yid himself. You know, after the shekels."

"Yes," said Wharton as if to himself. "We had our eyes on him over that Fascist business."

"I'm not surprised," Bruff told him eagerly. "He was in it up to the neck, only he covered up his tracks better than the old man."

"Well, luckily for him that's all over and gone," Wharton said, and made play with looking through some papers. "Oh yes. And there's his half-brother, Robert. What's he like?"

There was no doubt about the uneasiness and the hesitation.

"Well," he said, "Bob's quite a good sort. I had an idea once, mind you, that he was mixed up in that Fascist business too, but I was wrong."

He paused for a moment, mouth slightly agape, as if he were thinking out something.

"You won't think I'm crazy if I mention something, Superintendent?"

"Go ahead," Wharton told him genially. "We're all crazy here in any case. What's one more among so many?"

Bruff nodded to himself and with never a trace of a smile at Wharton's joke.

"Well, I thought there was more in it than that anti-Jew, black-shirt sort of stuff, and I'll tell you why. My uncle had a place at St. Leonards. Used to spend all his weekends down there, and you know what a hotbed of Fascism all that South Coast was. Brighton and Worthing, for instance. All the way down in the train you'd see the slogans chalked on the walls. But that's not what I was going to tell you about. What I wanted to tell you was that I had to go down to my uncle's place—in July it was, just before the war—and I walked in unexpected like, right into the dining-room, and he had three or four men there with him, all sitting round the table like a committee meeting. I didn't know any of them, but what I wanted to tell you was that he was damned angry. The maid brought me a message to another room that he couldn't see me and I'd better see him in town. But the point's this, Superintendent. I saw a photograph a day or two later in a picture paper. Ribbentrop at some function or other, and just behind Ribbentrop was one of the men

I'd seen down at St. Leonards! Only then he'd been in civilian clothes and in the picture he was all dolled up in uniform."

"That's mighty interesting," Wharton told him, and turned to me for confirmation. "Unfortunately we can't do anything about it now. Very good of you, though, to tell us."

He made a show again of looking through the papers on his desk.

"Oh, yes. Robert Dorvan. I understand he's just back from a Japanese Camp. You haven't seen him yet?"

Bruff shook his head and then said no. Something about the answer told me it was a lie. When he went on it was as if he'd recovered from the suddenness of an awkward question.

"I expect he'll be looking me up any old time now."

"I expect he will," Wharton said politely, and then turned to me again.

"Mr. Bruff's been so helpful that we might give him that bit of information about his uncle, don't you think?"

"Yes, I think so," I said, and hadn't a notion what piece of information he meant.

"Would you be surprised to hear, Mr. Bruff, that your uncle was here in town last Sunday week and stayed at an hotel till the following Monday afternoon?"

Bruff was very much of a character actor as I knew, but if he was acting when he showed that particular surprise, then my name's Sarah Bernhardt.

"You hadn't any idea, then?"

"Not the faintest," Bruff told him.

"I thought it would surprise you," Wharton said, and his smile was the second of his Coliseum ones—that of the lion who takes a snap at the plump Christian and misses by yards.

Then at last came the old, old recitation again, if with variations. Bruff was sure to be a beneficiary under his uncle's will, for instance, and as long as Scotland Yard existed, Wharton supposed there'd be red tape and sealing wax.

"Where was I on Guy Fawkes Night?" Bruff asked himself aloud, and again I knew the question had been an awkward one and he was sparring for time. "That's a fairish way back, Superintendent."

"Guy Fawkes Night," he said to himself again, then shook his head. "Afraid you've got me beaten. Wait a minute, though. The Saturday I was making records, and I did that show at the New Empire. All the Sunday I was working at scripts. The next week—last week that would be—I was free. Giving myself a holiday and doing just a spot of work for Ensa."

"I get you," Wharton said. "And say from six o'clock on the Monday till you went to bed. Remember what you were doing then?"

"Now you come to speak of it, I do," he said. "I had a busman's holiday. Went to that show at the Palladium."

"Meet anybody you knew?"

He frowned. "Can't say I did. I just slipped in, if you know what I mean. It wasn't so full as it might have been. The Command Performance was on at the Stoll."

"I remember," Wharton said, and got to his feet. Bruff didn't notice it, but he pressed the buzzer two or three times.

"Well, we're very grateful to you," he said and held out his hand. Then came the old joke. "Any time you want bail, just send for me."

"That's a good one," Bruff told him as one pro to another. "I hope to God I'll never have to call on you."

Wharton went through the door with him. The door closed behind them and then the buzzer went.

"Sergeant Jewle on the line," a voice said.

I told them to hang on, and then Wharton came back in time to take the call. From what he was saying, I gathered that things had gone pretty well with Jewle.

"Everything's working out fine," George told me when he'd rung off. Jewle was coming back at once and I was to take over. A Sergeant Francis, whom I'd worked with before, would be my assistant. George said he'd get in touch with the Department who were using that floor and have everything fixed by the time we got there. Then he was mentioning our late visitor.

"A bit thin, that alibi of his, wasn't it?"

"It was," I said. "And I'm glad you left it where you did. It's going to pay to give him a bit of rope."

"How do you mean?"

"This," I said. "I don't know where he was on Guy Fawkes Night, but I do know where he was some of the time last night. He was the man who was in that road where Netta Malone hangs out, watching her flat."

Chapter VIII
LISTENING IN

"You're dead sure?" George said.

"Dead sure," I told him. "I was nearer to him than I am to you now. I spotted him the moment he stepped into this room."

"What's the idea?" George said. "One of those eternal triangle affairs?" He shook his head. "Maybe you're right. We'll leave him alone for a bit. Perhaps we'll be able to get at him through another angle. Notice anything queer about what he told us?"

"There's one bit of confirmatory evidence," I said. "If Netta was his girl, then Sid's taken her. Perhaps that's why he did all he unobtrusively could to put Sid in bad with us."

"Right, for a fiver," George said.

"On the other hand, unless he's playing a very deep game, he did a bit towards clearing himself of suspicion of being concerned in his uncle's murder, alibi or no alibi."

"How do you mean?"

"Well, look at what he told us about the old man. And he said just as frankly that he had no use for him. I know that doesn't amount to saying he wished him out of the way, but you'll admit he was frank enough. And another point—a minor one. I'd say Bruff is making plenty of money. He wouldn't have risked his neck for four thousand pounds. Besides, he didn't know his uncle was going to die intestate, therefore he must have imagined—if he thought of it at all—that there was a will. And by his own admissions, he knew damn well he'd never benefit under that will. Therefore there was no money motive."

"Good logic," said George. "A bit too good, in fact."

"What's wrong with it?"

"Nothing—ostensibly. But I've got an idea that there's more in this Case than what anyone might think. What else did you notice about him?"

"I think he was definitely lying when he said he hadn't yet got in touch with Robert."

"I had a hunch like that too," he said. "Now you've told me where he was last night, it seems to me to bear it out. Just after he saw that Netta woman come home, he left in a taxi he'd had waiting. He told the driver he wouldn't wait. Therefore he had originally intended to wait. What for?"

He fairly threw the question at me.

"Don't know," I said. "But if he had waited, he'd have seen his cousin Robert arrive."

"Just what I was saying. Wheels within wheels." He gave an exasperated click of the tongue, then began rummaging among the papers on his desk.

"Take another look at that," he said, and what he handed me was the telegram that Herbert Dorvan had received on the Friday before his death. "That's the telegram that's supposed to have brought him to London. It's about some financial coup or other he was expecting to bring off in partnership with a man of the name of Peters. That's so, isn't it?"

I knew that telegram by heart, and naturally I agreed.

SUGGEST YOU HAVE READY KNOWLEDGE EXPECT-
ED YIELD. MEANWHILE AM BUYING OUT BUSINESS.

That was how it went, but before I could make any comment, George was off again.

"We've been into Dorvan's account at the Porthaven Bank and with his solicitors. He's drawn out no money to finance the buying out of any business. His accounts are just as open and above-board as mine. He had his income from investments.

When he had a surplus after expenses, then he reinvested. It's as simple as that. Never a cheque drawn except on himself."

"The only solution is to get hold of this Peters," I said, and diffidently enough. "That looks like being a tough job, especially if the transaction they were engaged in was a bit shady."

"A tough job?" He snorted contemptuously. "Dorvan never talked to a soul in Midgley about his affairs. All he talked was hot air about himself to that solicitor fellow, and passed the time of day with his bank manager. There's nothing to get your teeth into. Everything's negative. Nobody remembers visitors. No one saw a car come or go on that Sunday." He raised an impatient hand as I made as if to cut in. "I know there was a back way. But Midgley isn't the middle of the Sahara. People use that back road, don't they? You used it yourself. Somebody might have seen the car."

He took that telegram copy back and threw it exasperatedly down.

"I think I'll go back to Midgley with Jewle myself," he said. "There's something there that we've missed. Perhaps if I hunted up traces of the Dorvan family at Hastings and St. Leonards, I might get hold of something. You can carry on?"

"Why not?"

He grunted dubiously.

"If I'm not back tomorrow morning, act as you think fit." The head shook lugubriously again. "I hope to God you hear something in Sidney Dorvan's place tonight."

I hoped so too. It wasn't much of a hope, but I didn't tell him that. Then the buzzer went.

"Put him through," Wharton said, and then: "Speaking."

"Good," he said, and then, "Good" again. "No need to follow him when he comes out? . . . I see. More than one exit. Then you'd better get back here."

"That's our friend Bruff," he told me, peering as if the spectacles were still on his nose. "I thought I'd have a man on his tail when he left here. Where do you think he went to?"

"Netta's flat?"

"The Templemore Hotel," George said, and waited for my reactions.

"Straight to Bob Dorvan," I said. "The man he hadn't seen."

Wharton was prowling about the room and pursing out his lips in thought. Then he came to a halt.

"If I'm not back in the morning, you go and see our friend Bruff. Start getting the screws on him."

He gave me the address of his flat.

"Get there early," he told me. "If he's in bed, haul him out."

At six o'clock that night Detective-Sergeant Francis and I were making ourselves comfortable above Sid Dorvan's office. It was Francis who had done the preliminary work; fixing a microphone of some sort under the floor-boards, and rigging up the earphones and lighting. He told me dubiously that he hadn't had enough time. What he ought to have done was to get that microphone down lower and in contact with the ceiling.

All that floor had been requisitioned by a Government Department as an overflow for old documents and correspondence, and we were in a kind of lane between two long stacks of them. We could whisper without being heard, Francis assured me, and sacks had been laid to deaden the sound of our feet. It was none too warm up there, but we'd had a square meal and we had another with us, and plenty of hot coffee. I had my back comfortably against a stack of papers that probably dated back to the South Sea Bubble, and was doing a crossword that I'd saved for the occasion.

Now I'm not proposing to bore you with the details of that long night and its happenings. What I will give is a rough time-table and a précis, and all you will be told is what seemed to us to have some bearing on the Case. On Francis's knees, by the way, was a pad, and behind his ear a pencil. I gathered he was pretty hot at shorthand.

6.45. First faint sounds in room. Francis guessed someone was giving it a clean. Confirmed by noise of vacuum cleaner. Sounds of humming, but Francis couldn't identify the tune.

7.5. Door closed. Five minutes later someone arrived. Turned out to be Sid. Everything very quiet. Francis said he caught the rustling of papers. Tap at door. Sid's, "Come in!" Then, "Set it down there. . . . Dammit, don't interfere with those papers!" Door closed. Quiet for a couple of minutes, then sound of siphon. Tray of drinks had apparently been brought in.

7.20. "Hallo, Netta. How're you feeling now?" Then to our exasperation we found Netta's voice practically inaudible. All that night we didn't get fifty words of hers and could fit none into any context.

Sid's voice, on the other hand, was generally clear. We gathered that the cabaret programme was being discussed. He was trying to induce her to go on at the beginning of the second cabaret for a change and she apparently consented. Then, "Say when", and after that the siphon squirted again. "Nonsense, it'll do you good!" Then only a faint movement and the two voices became a murmur. But they came from very close together.

"Damn quiet down there, isn't it?" I said.

"Probably a spot of canoodling," Francis told me imperturbably.

7.55. Tap at door. Pause and then, "Come in!" An unknown voice was mentioning spare electric-light bulbs and there was a bit of an argument. "I'd better go with you myself," came Sid's voice annoyedly. The door closed. Quiet for two minutes and then the sound of the siphon.

"Doing herself well, isn't she?" Francis remarked.

8.15. Sid's voice suddenly came again. "Damn fellows, you can't trust 'em an inch. What about another spot for you? . . . Perhaps you're right." Squirt of siphon for himself. Murmur from her. Sid's reply, and it made me prick my ears, or clamp the headphones tighter. "Haven't found out a thing. But I still think I'm right. . . . How the devil should I know. . . . I'm *not* shouting. I'm just explaining. . . . They've got nothing on me, have they? . . . What should you panic about? . . . Oh, him. He asked for it, didn't he?"

Then exasperatingly there was another tap at the door. This time it sounded like the bartender reporting a waiter as sick. He was told to rearrange tables and put Alf on. Again Sid said he'd better have a look himself. The door closed. For a minute or two there was never a sound. We guessed that Netta had gone too. I whispered to Francis to read me that last bit of argument with Netta. I'd explained the job in hand to him and we agreed that the argument might have been about me. Sid hadn't discovered a thing about me. Who the *him* was that had asked for it, I hadn't the foggiest notion—*unless* it was Herbert Dorvan.

8.45. The band-leader came in and there was a quarter of an hour's conference. From then on Sid was in and out, hut there were no more callers. Francis suggested a snack but I said it wasn't time yet. Round about midnight was when we'd feel like something, if only to pass the time.

9.30. Sound of the band from away on our right. Francis brightened up, then looked annoyed. Said it'd interfere with our hearing. Clamped my headphones on tightly, but could still faintly hear the band. Hoped he wouldn't be right. Various comings and goings, all apparently on the part of Sid. Undercurrent of voices from the main room, and Francis guessed rightly that things were livening up. And that sort of thing went on till almost eleven o'clock.

10.58. We had both got a bit browned off. We'd just had a second tot of coffee and were listening mechanically, so when the door closed once more, Francis didn't even bother to note the fact. Then in about five minutes—I didn't need to glance at my watch again for the band had begun and Netta was crooning—we heard voices. I guessed they were coming up those back stairs by which Sid had ushered out Galley and myself. Then as they reached the back door that led to the passage, they ceased. Then the door beneath us closed, and there was a sound like a turning of a key in a lock.

Now there were to be two voices—Sid's and a Voice I didn't at first definitely verify. What we heard had to be scrappily recorded, and the version you have is the final one made up after Francis and I had wrestled long and earnestly with the scraps we had. You must imagine how eerie it was, sitting up there in the utter silence and having disembodied voices coming up at you as if out of a fog. There were long periods of such fog when the voices were lowered or the band or applause made hearing even more blurred. All I can set down, then, are the reasonably coherent patches of conversation as Francis recorded them, and his hearing—and maybe his headphones—must have been better than my own.

PHASE ONE

S. How the hell can she affect us? Or him, if it comes to that.

V. I don't say she will, but you can't get away from the fact that trouble never did anyone any good. Gerry isn't a bad sort, in his way.

S. Here! What the hell *is* this. Whose side are you on?

F. Now, now, now. No need to get excited.

S. I'm not excited. . . .

PHASE TWO

S. Dammit, it makes *all* the difference! Did he have it or didn't he have it?

V. He had it. You bet he wouldn't part with it.

S. Then how the hell are *we* going to get it? Tell me that.

V. Why don't you go down there and have a look? You know the lay-out. Or don't you?

S. Just what are you getting at?

V. Sh! Want to broadcast all your business?

PHASE THREE

V. What sort of a bloody fool do you think I am! My cards are on the table. That's more than I can say for yours.

S. Just what are you hinting at?

V. I'm hinting at nothing. He's dead and somebody killed him.

S. Shut your bloody mouth! Who's broadcasting now.

V. You're the one who gets excited. . . .

(The voices had been so much nearer that it was plain that both men were on their feet.)

PHASE FOUR

V. All right. I'll tell you what we'll do. Grab your hat and we'll go round to Scotland Yard straightaway.

S. And benefit Bruff? You're balmy. And the fake names. How're you going to explain that away?

V. Take it easy. Just let me do the talking . . .

That was when there was a tap at the door, and then the sound of someone trying the handle. Sid's voice now came from the door.

"Who's that?"

"Me." That was Netta.

"Ready in five minutes, Netta. Got someone with me." There was silence as if he was listening. The door closed, and that showed he had unlocked it and looked out to see if she'd really gone.

"Wonder how the hell long she'd been there. That's what comes of all this bloody argument."

"Better talk this over somewhere else," Bob Dorvan told him, for I now hadn't any doubts whose voice it was.

"Wait a minute." Sid was probably seeing if the coast was clear.

"O.K.," he said, and we heard steps receding towards the back stairs.

"I thought one time there was going to be a bit of a scrap," Francis told me, but I was looking at my watch. The minutes went by and it was not till twenty minutes later that Sid returned. Almost at once Netta was back. She must have been in a bit of a temper, which was why for the first time she spoke loudly enough for Francis to catch most of the words.

"Who was that with you?" she was wanting to know.

"Just someone on business, my dear." The drawl was a hint to lay off.

"Not that police nark?"

"And what if it was? I'm in the clear, aren't I? He's got nothing on *me*."

"Oh, keep that for the customers," she told him contemptuously.

"And you shut your mouth. . . . Who's running this place, me or you? . . . What was it you wanted?"

"It's that Mrs. Friedman. She's a pretty good customer."

"Damn the old hag! . . . All right. I'll come."

"A Peep Behind the Scenes," Francis remarked casually, "or How They Run Night-Clubs. Wonder who that Mrs. Friedman is—if her name *was* Friedman. And what about that spot of supper now, sir?"

Everything that was likely to happen from then on seemed to me to be nothing but anti-climax.

"Don't think there's any need to stay any longer," I said. "We'll go round to my place and have our meal there."

It was after midnight when we got to St. Martin's Chambers. Bernice was in bed, so we made ourselves comfortable with the electric fire and a couple of bottles. When the meal was over, we got to an assembling of those scraps of conversation: compiling, in fact, the version that you've just read. And that took no less than an hour and a half. But we weren't grumbling. We'd anticipated being above the Ginger Cat till the best part of four o'clock, and, as Francis put it, we were quids in.

The next job was to try to connect up those four phases of conversation and to make something unified and consecutive of the twenty minutes the two men had spent in that office. Why not stop dead where you are reading, and turn back and make an attempt of your own? You know as much as Francis and I did, and you might like to set your wits against ours. But if you're not in the mood, then here's what we finally arrived at. How we arrived at it doesn't so much matter. If you turn back you can at least check that for yourself. You will notice that our version is in the present tense, which casts about it an air of the hypothetical. Had it been in the past tense it would have read too cocksure and ceased to some extent to be partly theory.

CONVERSATION BETWEEN SID AND BOB DORVAN
Place—S.D's office. *Time*—11.0 to 11.20.

Bob Dorvan must have rung Sid up and the appointment had been arranged for 11.0 p.m. sharp. That was why Netta had been transferred to the second cabaret. Allowing for the time between Sid's leaving the office and the time he and Bob entered it, there must have been some preliminary talk outside and on the way up. Doubtless there had also been talk over the telephone. That may account for no talk about Bob's experiences as a Jap prisoner. So to what happened in the office itself.

The talk begins with Netta. Bob apparently doesn't want any trouble to arise through Sid's taking Gerry's girl. Sid accuses him of being on Gerry's side. Probably the trouble that Bob envisages is a lack of harmonious settlement between the three beneficiaries of the estate of Herbert Dorvan.

The talk drifts naturally to Herbert's Dorvan's death and how it will affect the two men themselves. Herbert Dorvan was apparently in possession of a certain secret something when the police collared him in 1940, and he almost certainly had it at his death. But there is an idea that it is missing, and the two want it badly. Perhaps it is a document that will incriminate either or both in the Fascist business, and my guess is that it is that sealed envelope that Dorvan took back from his solicitor on the Friday before his death. And a point there arising is that Wharton has told me that *that* sealed envelope was not found among Dorvan's effects. The two men think it—whatever it is—so important that one of them should go to Midgley to look for it. When Bob suggests that Sid knows the bungalow, Sid flies off the handle. He takes it as an implication that he murdered his uncle for the sake of that something. Bob pacifies him but the same thing flares up again. Sid now hints that Bob might have done the murder. Bob keeps cool. He knows he didn't do the murder and he can afford to wait till Sid perhaps gives something away.

Then finally Bob calls for a showdown. Sid doesn't think he's bluffing. Bob proposes in fact that Scotland Yard be informed of the whole business. Bob's real idea is this. "I know Sid killed him, but the way we'll put it to the police is that whoever the murderer was, he murdered Herbert Dorvan for the sake of that document in the sealed envelope." But Sid, whatever else he realises, has objections. The document will mean, if found, the addition of money to the estate, which will mean Gerry Bruff having his share. If the two secured it, and the money dependent on it, then it would be a private matter shared only between two. And there's a difficulty about realising money on or through the document, for the names on it are faked ones. Maybe old Herbert Dorvan in his violent Fascist days worked under a pseudonym or pseudonyms. Then comes the interruption by Netta, and finally Bob suggests another talk.

Well, that's our idea of what happened, though maybe you've bettered it. Francis typed it all out ready for Wharton's perusal. Then he suggested keeping a tail on both Sid and Bob to find out their next meeting. I pointed out that it didn't matter. If they met we'd never be able to arrange on the spur of the moment to overhear their talk. Let them meet and let them talk. The sealed envelope had gone, and everything centred round it. If it were ever found, then ultimately the three beneficiaries would have to decide what was to be done with it. *But*, Sid and Bob might decide to take independent action after all. Ask to be present when the bungalow was thoroughly searched, for instance. If so, we should know about it.

"That's the lot then, sir?" Francis asked me.

"And plenty too," I told him. "In the morning—not too early—I'm seeing this chap Bruff. You'd better come with me. What about a quarter to ten, outside Randall's boot shop at this end of the Strand?"

But there was something which I didn't tell Sergeant Francis, and that was my private idea of what had been behind the whole evening, and, when I woke next morning, I saw no reason to change my mind. Bob Dorvan, I was pretty sure, was doing some detective work on his own. He was of a different type from Sid; more truly intelligent and more suave, and he was working from the impregnable position of his own innocence. Maybe Sid was his favourite for the murderer, but, whoever it was, Bob was doggedly going to find out.

Mind you, I had reservations. Everything told me that Bob was working warily. Maybe any disclosures might smirch his own name, and that would do him no good with that General's daughter he was smitten with. But that didn't so much matter, and as I set out for the rendezvous with Francis, I had the feeling we were really getting somewhere at last.

Chapter IX
COUNTRY RIDE

Francis had the car and we drew up outside a fine block of flats just off Knightsbridge. It looked, as Francis said, as if Bruff was making a packet.

In the big lounge entrance there was a kind of communal bureau, and they rang up from there to see if Bruff was in. To my surprise, he said we were to go up. To my greater surprise, he didn't look at all embarrassed at seeing us.

"A nice place you've got here," I said when I'd introduced Francis.

Bruff was proud of it, at least he took us on a quick tour round. There were two bedrooms, a fine bathroom, a lounge, a fair-sized dining-room and a tiny kitchen. That latter didn't matter, he said. They were service flats and one could have any meal provided reasonable notice was given. The furniture was his, he said. It looked expensive stuff, though a bit showy. The lounge where we sat was a really fine room with quite a good view.

"You're working this week?" I said.

"On and off," he told me. "Making some records tomorrow."

Perhaps he took a fancy to us. I try to be a friendly sort of inquisitor, and Francis looks uncommonly harmless. At any rate, he took us into his confidence.

"You pally with the Income Tax people, Mr. Travers?"

"God forbid," I said hastily.

"*God forbid* is good," he told me. He seemed the sort of chap who's always on the look-out for something that could be turned into a gag. "But I'll tell you two gentlemen how it is. I could make twice what I'm actually making now. But why should I? Working for the Income Tax, that's all it is. I get all the publicity I want and I'm keeping the wolf from the door, so why should I worry?" He got a hearty nod of agreement from Francis. "Still, you gentlemen don't want to hear my life story. Something about that business of my uncle, was it?"

Now I may have sat at the feet of General Wharton for a good few years, but an enquiry by me is very much *Hamlet* without the Prince of Denmark. My methods are less devious, and perhaps they don't pay the same dividends.

"It's about that alibi of yours for Guy Fawkes Night," I began. "No fault of mine, but I've got the Higher-ups to satisfy. What you told us isn't conclusive enough, so they say. They want it amplified. Surely you can remember someone who saw you at the Palladium? What about your ticket?"

"Me?" he said. "My face gets me in anywhere. I was in the last show but one they had there."

"You just walked in?"

"That's it, sir. Just waved a cheerful hand, like this, and Bob's your uncle."

"I take it you waved to the attendant at the door," I said. "Make a note of that, Sergeant Francis, will you?"

Then Bruff couldn't leave things like that. He had to go and deliver himself into my hands.

"It isn't too easy looking back and telling yourself where you were on a particular night."

"I don't know," I said. "Let me give you a little test. Let's take last Monday night. Twelve o' clock midnight. Where were you then?"

That caught him clean in the wind. It was a moment or two before he could pull himself together.

"Where was I? Tucked up in my little cot."

"Sure?"

"Of course I'm sure. It was me that did the tucking in."

"Well, I hate disagreeing with you," I said, "but I know for a fact that at that particular time you were in a certain road in St. John's Wood watching the flat of a cabaret artiste of the name of Netta Malone."

He was so flabbergasted that he couldn't even blurt a denial.

"The trouble with you people is that you won't believe *us*," I went on. "We assure you that we respect confidences. You agree and then you tell us a certain amount of truth mixed up with a stiffening of lies. When we prove they're lies, you give us another mixture. Before you know where you are, you're being held for giving false information and obstructing."

I looked round at Francis for confirmation.

"Mr. Bruff isn't going to land himself in that kind of mess," he told me. "No doubt he had good reason for watching the lady's flat."

"You're right I had good reason," Bruff told us. Then he licked his lips. "This isn't going to go any further?"

I let out an exasperated breath. Hadn't I already told him so? and I added that the confessional box was a broadcasting station compared with Scotland Yard.

"Well, I did have good reason for watching her," he said. "Any man's got the right to watch his own wife."

Then he told us his story. Once or twice I thought he was going to blubber, but he just staved it off. And he said he'd be prepared to put it in the form of a statement and sign it.

He'd married Netta Malone just over a year ago. That was her professional name; her real name was Daisy Carberry. He'd first met her when she was in the chorus of *Now You're Getting It*, a show in which he'd appeared and which had had a very short run. Previous to that she'd been on the road with a company touring in *How's Your Father?* and before that she'd been a hostess at a Palais de Danse. She was still only twenty-five—so she said. She had no people that he knew of and was supposed to have been brought up by an aunt.

Gerry Bruff was in search of domesticity. His idea of happiness was that handsome flat he took and a little wifie to greet his return, and already he was trying for a place near Hastings in the family tradition; a place where he and his wife could spend congenial weekends in the summer months. But that hadn't been Netta's idea. She'd stuck that flat for six months, though, as Bruff confessed, life had been none too easy. Then she'd packed up and gone. Bruff brought her back from a road-show in Coventry and a fresh start was made. Then she'd gone for good—so said the letter she left—and the next he heard of her, and that was about a month ago, was that she was a sort of hostess in chief for Sid Dorvan and doing a cabaret act. The next thing he discovered, and by following her and Sid, was that she was in that St. John's Wood flat. Since then he'd waylaid her twice and she'd refused even to open her mouth. He'd tried to get at Sid, but all he got was something in the course of a telephone call— that Netta had a right to earn her living, and, as far as Sid was concerned, she *was* earning a living at her job and nothing else.

"I tell you I've been nearly crazy," Bruff told us. "I know if she'd only listen I could make her see sense. And do you tell me that Sid Dorvan's on the level? Sid's no philanthropist and never was. And what about that driving her home? One night he took her home at half-past four and he didn't come out again for an hour."

"Why didn't you go for him as man to man?" demanded Francis, for whom the real-life drama had been somehow only too real.

"Yes," said Bruff. "And have my face slashed one dark night. Broken glass and razor blades make you think."

"He's in with a gang?" I suggested helpfully.

"You bet he is," he told me vaguely, then threw up his hands. "But what's the good? Driving me crazy it is."

I tried a longish shot.

"Hadn't you anyone to confide in?"

"Well, I . . ."

Then he pulled up short.

"It's all right," I said. "You stick to the truth and we'll wipe out what you told us about not having seen Robert Dorvan."

Then he said he'd heard from him quite suddenly on the telephone; just picked up the receiver, so to speak, and there was Bob. Bob had got his address through his agents, and that of the agents through the B.B.C. Bob said he wasn't keen on meeting any of the family for a time, though he might do so later.

"Then I went and saw him at his hotel," Bruff said. "Last Monday it was . . ."

"Mind telling me the time?"

"About five o'clock," he said, and I knew that would be soon after Wharton and I had left. "I told him I was in a jam and he said I was to come round. Absolutely at the end of my tether," he told us, "or I wouldn't have done it."

"I want to have this quite clear in my mind," I said. "You'd worked yourself up to breaking point over this trouble with your wife, so you went to see him about it."

"That's right," he said, "and he told me he'd try to straighten things out. He'd try to see Netta first, and I was to come back here and leave things to him. Then he rang me up to say he'd fixed with her for twelve o'clock. She was going to make an excuse to leave the club . . ."

"A curious time for an interview, wasn't it?"

"He couldn't fix it up any other way," he explained. "You see, he was leaving town yesterday, as it were, so he wanted to do the job quick. I was afraid Netta would do some double-crossing, so I went round to her flat myself to make sure that she'd come."

"You didn't wait to see if Bob would come?"

"You can trust old Bob," he told us quietly. "Bob wouldn't have let me down."

"And how did he get on with Netta?"

"She said she'd think it over. That's all he could get out of her. When he asked her if she'd mind if he saw Sid, she told him to go ahead. He told me that the next morning—yesterday morning— over the phone and how he'd fixed up with Sid to see him at the club that night. Then he rang me up about an hour ago and told me what happened. He reckoned he might get Netta to see sense if I left things to him and didn't go butting in. He'd try and fix everything up when he got back to town again."

"You mean he's now gone away?"

"Well, I sort of gathered so. He'd have gone yesterday if it hadn't been for me. He said he wouldn't be away long. Only a few days."

"Well, that's cleared up at last," I said. "And I don't think we shall ask you to make a statement—at the moment. But to get back to something. That Guy Fawkes Night alibi of yours? What about it?"

He hesitated only a moment or two.

"Well, you can guess for yourself," was how he put it. "To tell the truth, I didn't go where I said. I was watching that club all night."

"Yes," I said slowly. "The unfortunate part of the matter is that you still haven't an alibi. No one saw you there? You didn't speak to anyone? The door attendant, for instance?"

He shook his head dejectedly. He had brightened up when he had told us what Bob Dorvan was doing, and now he was full of his troubles again.

"Maybe something will come back to you," I said as I got to my feet. "Take things easy and don't do any worrying."

Then he said he'd like to get everything off his chest. That talk about Income Tax for example. There'd been a certain amount of truth in what he'd said, but the real truth was that he hadn't been able to work. He couldn't get his mind off Netta. Nearly crazy he'd been.

I did some more cheering up and then we left. We drove back to a tea-room and there had some coffee, and I told Francis something of what had been in my mind.

"I think he's now on the level," I said. "His story fits in with what we listened to last night—the early part, I mean. Sid Dorvan, as you and I know, takes careful handling."

"I can understand that Bob Dorvan going to all that trouble," Francis said. "That Gerry Bruff is absolutely crackers over that Netta. If you ask me, Mr. Travers, he'd have ended up by doing her in. I wouldn't be surprised if he told his cousin Bob as much."

"I think you're right," I said. "But what I'm wondering about is why Bob should have an idea that Sid did the uncle in. Something tells me I ought to see Bob Dorvan."

"You're not going to let on about last night?"

"I'm certainly not," I said. "If he gives me an opening I might nudge my way in, if you know what I mean. After all, there's a perfectly good reason for seeing him. We want confirmation of Bruff's story."

On the way to the Templemore Hotel we stopped at a telephone-box and I rang the Yard. They'd been trying to get in touch with me at the flat to say that Wharton would not be back till late that night. When we got to the hotel I went in for a word with Miss Sanbridge. She didn't recognise me for a minute.

"Is Captain Dorvan in?" I asked her.

"I'm afraid he's gone away for a few days," she told me. Then she recognised me. "Weren't you here with his uncle the other day?"

"That's right," I said. "I rather wanted to see him about something. Could I possibly have his address?"

She promptly gave it—The Blue Boar, Flampton, Woodford.

"I might run down and see him," I said. "It all depends if I can make time."

I smiled a thanks and goodbye, then turned back.

"Did you spend that pound note?"

"Oh rather!" she told me, and her cheeks flushed charmingly.

"Well, we're only young once," I told her sententiously, and left it at that.

Next we drove to my place. Francis took the listening-in papers to the Yard for Wharton's inspection as soon as he might arrive. I changed into something that looked a little more like the country, and then Francis was back with the car. It was a grand November morning, cold but sunny, though the forecast had predicted later fog. So it wasn't hard to induce Bernice to get out of town for an afternoon. What I didn't tell her was that she'd unknowingly be paying her passage.

We went by Epping, and when we got there I dropped in at the police-station and rang the pub at Flampton, for if Bob Dorvan was staying there, it seemed likely we might get lunch. The pub said reluctantly that they would find us lunch, but we'd have to wait till half-past one. I said that would suit us fine.

It was still short of midday, so we cruised along to Flampton. It was a larger village than I'd thought; the countryside well wooded and slightly undulating, and the village itself sufficiently off the beaten track to lack the pinkiness of suburbia's fringes. We went by the Blue Boar—quite a substantial-looking old place—and found the post-office. I went in ostensibly to telephone. The address of General English, C.B., D.S.O., was given as Flampton Grange.

"Could you direct me to Flampton Grange?—General English's place?" I asked the girl at the counter.

"It's over a mile from here," she told me, as if that might deter me. "Were you going to see the General? The reason I asked was that he's an invalid and isn't supposed to see anybody."

"That's all right," I said. "It isn't the General I'm seeing."

We went half a mile on, as directed, then took the left-hand fork. Well over half a mile from there we came to the large white gate and a private drive. Francis said if we went on up the hill we might see the house from there, and he was right.

It was an unpretentious, snug-looking Georgian house on two floors, something like a large country vicarage, and behind it among the elms were quite extensive outbuildings. It looked well-kept, and from our view-point just over a hundred yards away we could see a gardener, shirt-sleeves rolled up, sweeping a lawn clear of leaves. Late dahlias made a splash of colour in a bed.

"What do you think of it?" I asked Bernice.

"I like it," she said, and gave an enquiring look.

"I'm not thinking of buying," I told her. "Just interested in someone who's also interested. A General English lives there," I went on. "Tell me, just for curiosity's sake, what kind of a man you'd think he'd be—assuming I hadn't told you his rank."

"Well, obviously someone with taste. Quite a lot of money. County and all that."

"Just what I thought," I said.

Then Francis was craning and I was reaching for the field-glasses. A couple had appeared from nowhere, and were approaching the front of the house. The man, in grey flannel bags and tweed jacket, was Bob Dorvan. I was concentrating on the girl. Then as the two stood facing us as if looking at the view, I passed the glasses to Bernice.

"Take a look at that girl. Tell me what you make of her."

A spaniel came bounding up. The girl stooped and patted its flanks. A matter of half a minute and the three turned and went up the last few steps and into the house. Bernice handed the glasses back.

"Well?" I said.

"It's difficult," she said. "Everything I think of is so trite."

"The triter the better," I said encouragingly. "You just try placing her for us."

"Well, she's obviously what's called a lady. She's not handsome, but she has a nice, pleasant face. She was sensibly dressed for the country."

"Good," I said. "And her age?"

"Hard to say," she said, and frowned. "Under thirty, I think."

"Good," I said again. "And would it be too much to ask if you could gather if she was in love with the man?"

"Well, it was obvious they were pretty good friends." Then the informatory worm turned. "Is this something to do with the police?"

I caught Francis's eye and the face he made.

"In a way, yes," I said. "Though that isn't why I was keen on your coming out this afternoon. The fact is that . . . well, remember Sid Dorvan who owns the Ginger Cat? Well, the man you just had a look at is his half-brother."

We drove on to where I could reverse the car, then got back as far as the fork, and there I stopped.

"What have you been thinking about?" I asked Francis.

"You mean, about that?" and he nodded back. "Well, as Mrs. Travers was saying, sir, it's hard to say. But that Captain Dorvan looks as if he'd clicked."

"That's all I want to know," I told him, and moved the car on again.

We parked the car at the pub and then I made Francis do the enquiring. He came back to the lounge with the drinks on a tray. Dorvan was staying there all right, but wouldn't be in to lunch. They doubted if he'd be in much before dinner.

We had a repulsive lunch—minced and boiled corned beef with soggy potatoes and soggier cabbage, followed by a boiled pudding that stuck to the palate. I made up with cheese and what Bernice said was real butter. I said Dorvan must be very much in love if he endured such feeding. Bernice took the side of the enemy. After all, they'd had to get a meal at short notice.

I managed to get the current local paper and found that a Woodford cinema had quite a good picture. So we pushed on there, and when we came out we had tea in an arty sort of café, and after that we made our way to Flampton again. A slight breeze had sprung up and there wasn't any fog.

I did the enquiries this time, and was gratified to hear that Captain Dorvan had just come in. But he was going out again almost at once. I guessed he was dining at the Grange. They gave me his number and I went up the stairs and tapped at his door. At his call, I walked in. He was sitting at the dressing-table mirror, adjusting his tie, and it was in the glass that he saw me. The effect was extraordinary, and no wonder, for he must have been expecting to see the maid. His fingers stopped their movements as if he'd been stricken with paralysis, and all his body was suddenly rigid. Then he got to his feet.

"You gave me a regular shock," he said. "Mr. Travers, isn't it?"

I did a whole lot of explaining. My wife hadn't been any too fit and I'd thought an afternoon in the country might do her good. I'd called at the Templemore to see him, and so on and so on. When I'd finished he told me to take a seat and asked what I'd drink. I said I wasn't staying more than a second or two, since my wife and the driver were waiting in the car. I wished then that Francis had had a chauffeur's cap.

"I think you've got it right," he said, referring to Bruff's story. Then his eyes narrowed. "To be perfectly frank, you're not trying to catch me out in any way?"

"Heavens, no!" I said, and then realised what he meant. But he did the explaining.

"I admit I told you I hadn't got in touch with any of the family, but Gerry Bruff was different. Then when he told me about his wife I thought I'd better keep it under my hat. I wouldn't mind telling a lie or two for Gerry."

"He was pretty desperate?"

"Yes, the poor fool. Don't think I'm being cynical, but she isn't worth it. If I do get her back, I'll bet a fiver she leaves him again in a week. Not that that'll stop me trying."

"How'd you find your half-brother?" I asked him politely.

His lip dropped.

"The same old Sid. Well after the shekels. Not that we had much talk. Only family business."

I made play with opening the door and looking along the corridor.

"Absolutely between ourselves," I said in almost a whisper. "Is he so fond of the shekels as to be capable of committing a murder for the . . . well, you know what I mean."

His eyes narrowed and he moistened his lips.

"I'm not saying anything. I just have ideas. Do you mind if we leave it like that?"

"Perhaps we'd better," I said. "But if you do run across anything, I'd be grateful if you'd give me a quiet tip." Then I put as much earnestness into it as I could muster. "I'm only one of the understrappers at Scotland Yard. It might do me a bit of good."

"I certainly will," he assured me. Then he frowned for a moment or two in thought. "I've got an idea or two. How they're going to work out I can't say."

He gave his hair a quick brush and went with me downstairs.

"Look here," he said. "You really must have a drink. You can't go like this."

I hesitated and then said I would, if I could bring my wife in. Bring the chauffeur too, was what he told me.

I said he was an old family servant and a teetotaller, but I'd see.

I left Francis there and escorted Bernice in, and I'd warned her against surprise. And I'd told her to keep the collar of the fur coat well up round her ears. I didn't mind if any subsequent talk between Bob and Sid revealed the fact that I'd been at Flampton with a Bernice Haire, but I didn't want to make it too obvious.

Bernice was perfect. Dorvan had an Irish-hot mixed for her and we had a quarter of an hour's gossip, chiefly about the Japs. In fact, we could hardly tear ourselves away.

It was after seven when we set off back, and as Dorvan didn't go with us to the car, he didn't have a good look at Francis. When we were on the main Epping Road again, I asked Bernice what she thought of Bob Dorvan. Maybe that double Irish had made her a bit sleepy.

"I'm not going to answer any more of your questions," she told me. And then: "After all, darling, you were near enough to see him for yourself."

Then after a minute or so she relented, though all she said was that he could be very, very charming.

<h2 style="text-align:center">CHAPTER X</h2>

WHARTON HAS A THEORY

WE BROUGHT Francis in for a service meal at our flat, and while it was coming and as soon as I'd swallowed it, I did some work. There was a concise report of the day's doings to write for Wharton, and when I'd finished that I made a few notes on the things that had struck me while I was at Midgley with Galley. I hadn't expected to be drawn into the Case except possibly as a witness or I should have recorded my impressions long since. But I could remember that day only too well, and I don't think I left much out. Then I rang the Yard and found that George still wasn't back, so Francis took the whole bag of tricks for Wharton's perusal when he ultimately did arrive.

After breakfast the next morning I rang again. George was back and had left word that he'd be ringing me, so I had a peaceful morning which I spent in going over that day with Galley again. Then George rang to say he'd drop in on me about one o'clock. I said we'd rely on him for lunch, but when I wanted to know if he'd found anything out, he said that that could wait.

It was like old times having George in for a meal. He wasn't any too cheerful, I thought, though that might have been camouflage to mask some surprise he was keeping up his sleeve. I'll admit, however, that I've rarely seen him looking more tired. Bernice was going out that afternoon, and when I was drawing the easy chairs up to the fire, George said he'd prefer a hard seat at the table.

"A couple of minutes in that damn chair," he said, "and I'd be sound asleep."

"You've had a busy time?"

"Off and on," he said. "Didn't get back till past midnight and then I sat up reading those notes of yours. This morning I've been with the Special Branch, and I've had a look at Sid Dorvan."

"What you think of him?"

He snorted and spread his palms.

"I've handled his sort for years. Oily sort of customers. The wide-awake boys. Know just how far to go, or so they think. Butter wouldn't melt in their mouths."

Then he told me what he'd done in Midgley and Porthaven. He'd personally gone over the bungalow with a small-toothed comb and he'd had the whole neighbourhood searched for the gun. At Porthaven he'd seen the bank manager for himself, and the solicitor. He'd got every movement that Herbert Dorvan had made on that Friday—bank first, then a purchase of herrings on the way to the solicitor, then the purchase of a cake at a confectioner's, and so to the homeward bus.

"There were sultanas in the cake?" I asked him.

He said there were, and he saw the point of the question. Then he began telling me what he'd done at Hastings and St.

Leonards, and that might have been summed up as a devil of a lot of ado about absolutely nothing. Those towns have a hard core of old inhabitants, as he said, but the bulk of the population is transitory. It wasn't hard to find traces of Dorvans and Bruffs; the impossibility had been to find someone to gossip about them. The late Len Bruff had retired because he'd had a stroke, so he'd taken no part in the life of the town, while Herbert Dorvan had been little more than a week-ender.

"I don't mind owning up," George told me, "that I didn't know what I was looking for, in any case. Just hoping for a lead; that about sums it up."

It isn't George's way to do any back-patting—not that I deserved it—so he dismissed my day's efforts with the remark that I'd seemed to have had an interesting time. I had one correction to make.

"One thing in that listening-in report," I said. "You'll see a remark by Sid Dorvan to Netta Bruff. He asked for it, didn't he? I originally noted that as applying to Herbert Dorvan. I think he was talking about Gerry Bruff; that Bruff, in other words, had only himself to blame for his wife's leaving him."

George smiled dryly and showed me a note of his own he'd made to the same effect in the margin of the report.

"But about these items you say struck you when you were down there with Galley," he said. "This bit about the joint having been roasted and being intact. What's the point of it?"

"That purchase of herrings rather modifies it," I said. "We still can't say . . ." Then I thought of something. "How many herrings?"

"Two large ones."

"This is pure supposition, then," I said, "but he might have had one for his supper on the Friday night and the other for his main meal on the Saturday. With mashed potatoes there'd be a filling first course, and that would help out with his rations and leave the joint free. But he was expecting the elusive Peters to call for him with the car on the Sunday. I suggest he cooked the joint so as to give Peters lunch. *But*—and this is my point—that joint, though cooked, was not touched. Therefore Peters didn't have any of it. And Herbert Dorvan would be expecting Peters to arrive and so he'd wait. But Peters didn't arrive till the afternoon, and then he was in a hurry to get back to town. So the joint was put in the pantry."

"And they went all the way to town without a meal?"

"Peters had probably had one," I said. "Dorvan might have cut himself a snack of bread and cheese to eat in the car if he hadn't had the same kind of snatch-meal beforehand."

"Depends on too many hypotheses," George told me, but he didn't grunt or snort. "Even supposing you're right, what's it establish? Only that Dorvan left Midgley in the afternoon. Where's that get us?"

I had to admit that it got us nowhere, and I don't mind telling you now that was to be the devil of a way wrong. It was just, I explained, that my tidy mind didn't like loose ends.

"Then there's this business of Sid Dorvan being very anxious to find out if Galley and you had found any letters of his at the bungalow," George went on. "Where's that get us?"

"It proves that Sid and his uncle corresponded," I said. "It suggests that Sid wrote things he wasn't anxious for us to read. It might even suggest that the sealed envelope—if we'd found it—had in it something compromising. It seems to link up with that overheard conversation or argument or quarrel between Sid and Bob. The part that referred to some asset or other that they didn't want Bruff to share when the estate was finally settled."

"I think the whole thing has to do with that old Fascist business," George said. "You claim that Bob is doing some amateur detecting. Then why shouldn't he have been holding that sealed envelope over Sid's head. Showing he knew something, so as to get him to talk."

"Did you find any papers?" I went off at a partial tangent because George seemed in one of those moods when argument gets one nowhere.

"At Midgley? Never a one. Nothing but what you and Galley found. Whoever murdered Dorvan must have cleared the whole lot out, if Dorvan hadn't burnt everything himself beforehand. My idea is that the sealed envelope was in his wallet."

"If so, that puts Sid Dorvan in the clear," I said. "He hasn't got the sealed envelope."

George's snort was prodigious.

"What do you base that on? Sid Dorvan's as straight as a donkey's hind leg. He was bluffing Bob, that's what he was doing. How could he say he'd got the wallet? That'd have made him the murderer! That's what Bob was trying to get out of him. Trying to catch him out."

Already he was ruffling the papers and coming to something else.

"This last note about Dorvan's hinting to the solicitor that he'd be coming into money. What about that?"

"You tell me," I said, a bit tired of having ideas summarily dismissed.

"There may be something in it," George said reluctantly. "I told you I'd been having a confab with the Special Branch. They knew Dorvan was flirting with Germans up till the war and they gave him plenty of rope. But the old boy was too fly. When he was nabbed, there was nothing incriminating they could lay their hands on."

"They think Dorvan had been financed by the Germans?"

"Why not? They subsidised this and that. Spent thousands just to make trouble, and beyond what they spent over ordinary espionage. My guess is that he had a packet from the Germans just before the war and then daren't move when war broke out. He kept the money by him and then had to cache it when he knew we were after him."

"It's getting a bit too involved for me," I said. "I'd like time to think it out. But why didn't Dorvan get the cached money when he was released? His movements weren't restricted at the time of his death?"

"My guess is that he and Sid were in cahoots," he said. "Neither dare move without the other. Maybe they were quarrelling about dividing up the money."

The whole theory seemed to me to be as full of holes as a roll of wire-netting. Mind you, I could see a certain amount of solid surface, but the whole thing presented a problem in meticulous deduction. It was the kind of thing that had to be begun at the beginning—a vague beginning in 1939, when Bruff had blundered into that conference in the St. Leonards house—and it had to proceed slowly and logically, step by step. But George was looking at me quizzically. When he spoke, his voice was so mild that I knew something was in the wind.

"You don't think a lot of that theory?"

"Well, it has a lot to be said for it," I temporised.

"Only you don't feel like doing the saying," he retorted. Then the tone became positively unctuous. "I wouldn't have mentioned it at all if I hadn't had a hunch about that murder."

I didn't have long to wait to hear what the hunch was.

"What's Gerry Bruff's job?" he began.

I rather stared.

"His job? Why, you know that as well as I do."

I'd forgotten that that was the wrong answer. George likes putting leading questions and expects helpful answers. He likes an audience of stage hands so that finally he's only to wag a finger and up goes the curtain. But he didn't get ruffled as I'd expected, though he did look a bit chagrined.

"Well, he's a comedian and impersonator, isn't he? That convey anything to you?"

"Not at the moment," I said, and I admit I was being slow in the uptake.

"Good at impersonating, isn't he?"

"An absolute master," I said.

"Then why shouldn't he have impersonated Sid Dorvan?" I gaped. I began polishing my glasses. I even said I thought he'd got something there.

"There we are then," he went on. "All this Netta business is one big bluff. She's in it and Bruff is in it, and Sid's in it. They're all in it up to the neck."

I nodded. He left the hard chair for the easy one and he got his dead pipe going again.

"All worked out well beforehand, as I see it," he said. "It must have been pretty big stakes they were playing for. And it'd be cushy for Bruff. Did you notice how like Sid he is? Not that a bit of make-up wouldn't have put that right even if he hadn't been. And all he'd have to do was to keep in that office and occasionally show himself in the dance room. Imitating Sid's voice would be child's play. In other words, he held the fort on the Monday night while Sid slipped down in that big car of his and did the murder. And, mind you, Sid could have reached there at any time he liked. He might have been waiting for the old man. But that's not the point. The point is that Bruff wouldn't have to be holding the fort very long. Sid could have been out of the bungalow by—say—half-past seven. That car of his could have got him back in town in a couple of hours easily. And the night-club wouldn't even have got warmed up by then."

If he hadn't added a sort of "What about it?" look, I think I'd have left it there to think over.

"You've just said that Sid could have been back before the club was properly warmed up," I said. "Then why couldn't he have simply been late that night at the Club?" Then I knew I'd been slower-witted than ever. "Sorry. I see your point now. If he hadn't had Bruff at the club impersonating him, he wouldn't have had an alibi."

"That's it. That's the very point."

"There is just one other thing," I said. "I know from my listening-in experiences of the other night that all sorts of people had to keep coming to Sid's office. They'd have to see the pseudo-Sid at close quarters."

"Not necessarily," he said. "I've even got an idea how the whole thing could have been done without even bringing Netta in. Sid might say to her overnight, 'I've got a most important interview in the office tomorrow at eight o'clock—say. You carry on and here're the keys. I'll put a notice on the door that I'm not to be disturbed.' You see? All Bruff, as Sid, then had to do was to show himself once or twice, and, if he then expected Netta to think the interview or conference was over, to bolt back to the office and leave the notice on the door. A chap like Bruff could carry on a conversation with himself if he guessed someone was at the keyhole."

"It's damned ingenious," I said, and I might have added that if I'd thought of anything so melodramatic and even fantastic, George would have hooted the whole idea to hell. "But tell me just one more thing," I said. "Why should Bruff do this for Sid? What was the *quid pro quo*?"

"Dammit, you can see that for yourself," George told me pityingly. "'You do this,' he said to Bruff, 'and to show my good faith I'll give Netta the push. After that it's up to you!'"

"Bear with me, George," I said placatingly, "and take into account what I said about loose ends. Suppose Sid did as you say. Suppose everything worked as you say. Then why hasn't Netta been given the push?"

"Plenty of time yet," he told me. And, at that very moment, believe it or not, the telephone bell went.

"Yes?" I said. "Travers speaking."

It was the Yard on the line.

"A message just come for you, sir, from a Captain Dorvan. He said you'd understand what it meant. Ready to take it, sir?"

I took it. It said simply that he'd enquired about a certain lady from her employer and had been told that she'd packed up and gone.

"That O.K. for you, sir?"

I said it was. When I went back to George I was still shaking my head.

"The most incredible coincidence," I said. "I told you I'd asked Bob Dorvan to let me know if he picked up any ideas. Well, he just rang me at the Yard to say he'd wanted to get hold of Netta, apparently, so he'd applied to Sid and Sid told him she'd packed up and gone!"

"Why didn't he see Netta at her flat?" demanded George, and then, "Not that it matters."

Then he began frowning, and pursing his lips.

"A bit too good to be true. That's what worries me."

"You should worry," I told him. And then I remembered that other objection I'd meant to make to the scheme. "But going a bit back. George, you do realise, don't you, that Bruff wasn't a fool? He'd be bound to read about his uncle's death—*murder* is the real word. He couldn't help putting two and two together. He'd have Sid clean under his thumb—like this. You think Sid would have risked that?"

"I know," he said. "That's the one flaw in it. Not that I can't see one or two ways round."

We had lunched late and dusk was almost on us. I wanted him to stay on for a cup of tea, but he said he'd be getting back to the Yard. And there was something I might do there—check up all round on that news that Netta had left the Ginger Cat.

When we came out to the street it looked to me as if we were in for the father and mother of all fogs. Already there was a yellowish tint to the mist and visibility was no more than the length of a cricket pitch.

George went up to his room and I began my telephoning.

I tried Sid Dorvan first and couldn't get him at his private address. I tried the club, even if it was a hundred to one against its being open, so I wasn't disappointed when nothing came from there. Then I tried Gerry Bruff, and there I had better luck. I told him who I was and that I'd heard his wife had left the Ginger Cat for good, but I didn't say how I'd heard it. To my surprise he knew it already.

"Bob rang me up about half an hour ago," he said. "I don't know that I won't go round to see if she's in."

"Good luck to you," I told him, and before he could ring off: "Suppose you don't know why she quit?"

He hadn't a notion, unless it was the way Bob had argued with her.

"What was Bob doing back in town?" I said.

"He came up specially to see her," he said. "He hadn't got anything on down where he's staying, so he thought he'd see Netta again for me. Only when he called at her flat, she wasn't in. So he rang up Sid and Sid told him she'd quit."

That seemed clear enough. I asked him to ring me and let me know how he got on, and then I had another shot at Sid Dorvan. Again there was nothing doing, so I nipped round to a restaurant at the bottom of Whitehall and had tea. The fog was getting thicker, with visibility only a few yards.

As soon as I was back, I rang Sid again and this time he was in. I made no bones about telling him my name.

"That's right," he said, though his tone said plainly enough that he'd have liked to ask what the hell Netta had to do with me. "She rang me this afternoon early. Said she was quitting—just like that."

"Any idea why?"

"She's a bitch—that's why."

I waited a moment, and then he was mumbling that he shouldn't have said that.

"Go on," I said. "Get it off your chest. You knew she was letting you down."

"I couldn't get a word in with her," he said. "She said she'd quit and she'd taken her things away and it was no use coming round to see her because she'd made up her mind. 'You can't do this to me,' I told her. 'And what about our contract?' She'd rung off and there I was, talking to a dead line."

"Have you tried to see her?"

"I went round straightaway," he said. "Couldn't make anybody hear. Guess she was out."

I waited a few minutes and then rang the Blue Boar at Frampton.

"May I speak to Captain Dorvan, please?"

"Sorry, but he isn't in," a woman's voice said. "We're expecting him at any minute though. I expect it's the fog. It's pretty bad, they say."

I don't know why I gathered that he'd come up to town by car, but somehow I did.

"Oh yes," she said. "He was driving his own car. He said he'd be back for a late tea."

I couldn't very well ask her to ring Whitehall 1212. The wireless has made that number too familiar, so I said would she ask him not to go out again when he did come in, till I'd rung him, which would be in under an hour's time. No sooner had I hung up than a call was coming for me. It was Bruff.

"Nothing doing round at her place," he told me. "I reckon she must have gone out somewhere. Perhaps I shall go round again later."

There was nothing to do but thank him. Then to pass the time I went up to George's room to report progress. He wasn't there, so I strolled down again. At half-past seven I slipped out and bought myself an *Evening Standard*, and, a quarter of an hour before I'd intended, I rang the Blue Boar again.

"That you, Captain Dorvan?" I said, for it had sounded like his voice. "This is Travers speaking. Thanks very much for the tip you gave me."

"That's all right," he said and began to explain. "I was at a bit of a loose end for today, so I thought I'd run up to town and have a word with Netta. She wasn't in, so I rang Sid to ask if he knew where I could find her. Then he told me what I told you."

"What was travelling like?"

"Tonight? Absolutely hellish. A few yards clear and then patchy. I ought to have been back an hour and a half ago."

"I didn't know you had a car," I said. "What's she like?"

"Nothing on earth!" he said. "Well, she's not so bad as all that. An old Singer I picked up as soon as I got home. I was staggered when they asked me two hundred quid for her. Got her for a hundred and sixty, though."

"And how's the matrimonial business going?"

"Not too bad," he told me. "She happens to be away today. That's why I was at a loose end."

"I know," I said playfully, and, "Well, take care of yourself."

"Cheerio, sir," he told me, and on that merry note we hung up.

I went up to George's room and found him getting into his overcoat. I told him how I'd got on and asked if he wanted a written report. Then he made me go over everything again. Then he looked at his watch.

"Think we'll drift round to the Ginger Cat," he said, then changed his mind and pressed the buzzer. The number he asked for was that of the Ginger Cat all the same.

"This is Superintendent Wharton worrying you again, Mr. Dorvan," he said. "I suppose you don't happen to have a key to Miss Malone's flat. . . . You have! Then why didn't you use it when you went round to see her today? . . . I see. You'd expected her to be in and so you didn't have it in your pocket. . . . I see. But look here. I want you to meet us in the Piccadilly Underground Station by the booking office in a quarter of an hour's time, and have that key with you. . . . I know you're busy. . . . I know, I know. But I'm telling you it's a favour you'll be doing us. . . . Good. Thanks very much. Goodbye."

"What's the idea?" I said. "Think something's wrong?"

"Jumping to conclusions, aren't you?" he told me. "A good chance to look over that flat of hers, isn't it? Or she may have skipped altogether."

I might have asked him where that would get us, but he was already on the move. The visibility was better when we got outside, and we made fair time. We had in fact a good ten minutes to wait before Dorvan arrived. But we got the right train almost at once.

"Any inkling that this was going to happen?" Wharton asked as soon as we were on the move.

"Not the faintest," Dorvan told him, and I noticed that he was casting curious glances at myself. "Right as rain she was last night. Been a bit queer this last day or two though."

"How?" fired Wharton.

"Well, I don't know how to put it quite. She wasn't her usual self. A bit too short-tempered and then a bit too much the other way. Didn't know which way to take her."

"And which way was she last night?"

"A bit too gay," he said. "Perhaps she'd had a drink or two too much. We have to sometimes, at our game."

When we got out at St. John's Wood Station we were in a fog patch. Wharton said Dorvan probably knew the way, and off we set. The fog cleared slightly again, and inside five minutes we were at the end of the road. Another couple of minutes and we were mounting the steps that led up to the flat.

"An upper flat, is it?" whispered Wharton.

Dorvan said it wasn't. It was only that the ground sloped away at the back. His hand was going forward with the key, but Wharton held it back.

"Better ring first."

Dorvan rang and we waited. There was a knocker on the door and Wharton rapped smartly and we waited again.

"Right," he said. "Better try the key."

The door opened and Dorvan switched on the light. We were in a tiny hall. An old-fashioned hat-stand stood by the right-hand wall and an old beret was hanging there and a waterproof. Wharton motioned Dorvan on.

Now he opened the door immediately in front, and again reached for the light switch.

"Doesn't seem . . ."

Then he stopped. Wharton pushed him aside and moved forward.

I craned over Dorvan's shoulder.

Netta Malone was lying there on the carpeted floor as if she had slithered from the overturned chair. Wharton sniffed, then sniffed again. Then he stooped and his head hid her face. Then he got to his feet again.

"She's dead?"

"Dead as mutton," he told me, and gave an incipient glare. "Can't you smell the cyanide?"

PART III

Chapter XI

SO MANY OPINIONS

"You stay out in that hall, Mr. Dorvan," rapped out Wharton. "Unless you've anything you'd like to say."

Dorvan was moistening his lips and shaking his head. His cheeks looked suddenly sunken and more sallow.

"Why should she?" was all he could say.

"Why should she what?"

"Kill herself? I mean . . ." He shook his head bewilderedly again. Wharton grunted.

"Wait in that other room." Then he changed his mind. "Just a minute, though. Know where the nearest telephone is?"

Dorvan didn't, unless it was the one at the Underground.

Wharton began writing in his notebook. He ripped out the page.

"Find a telephone somewhere and get that through to Scotland Yard. They'll know what it means. Then get back here."

He motioned me to step inside, and I took up my stance just inside the door. On the table was a glass in which was about an inch of pinky liquid. Wharton sniffed at it, then looked round. There was a little arty kind of sideboard against the far wall, and one of its two doors was slightly open. On the sideboard itself stood a bottle. With his gloved hand he turned the bottle round and read the label:

VERSAC

THE COCKTAIL SUPREME

Of all Wine Merchants and Retail Agents

Sole Proprietors:

THE WEST END WINE COMPANY LTD.

33, Wendon Street, W.3.

"Screw stopper," he said. "One tot out of it."

He stooped and looked in the cupboard with the slightly open door.

"Regular little bar of her own. Whisky, vermouth, gin—and some stout bottles."

"What's that on the mantelpiece?" I said. "It looks like a note."

It was a note, propped against an ornament. It was written on a fancy biscuit-coloured paper. Had it been white paper, Wharton would have spotted it at once.

"Interesting," he said. "Just listen to this:

"DEAR GERRY,

This is goodbye for good. I'm sick of everything and the whole rotten lot of you. I'm going where none of you will ever be able to pester me again.

NETTA."

"Seems like suicide all right," I said. "Rather surprising, though, that she should speak so vindictively of Bruff. I had an idea she was fed up with domesticity and no more."

"It's early yet to talk," he said. "What I'm wondering is why she should get herself a special bottle when she'd already got a selection in this cupboard."

"To hide the taste of the cyanide," I suggested.

"Stout would have done that," he said. "And suicides aren't usually so fastidious. Down goes the stuff and that's that."

There didn't seem any chance of footmarks on the carpet, so I stepped round the table to where he was examining something at the other end of the sideboard. He pointed to the ink, the pen and the blotter. He opened the blotter and there was more of the biscuit-coloured paper and envelopes to match. The blotting paper sheet looked new, except for faint marks. Wharton held it against the mirror back of the sideboard. All we could see was a word that looked like that last *again* of the letter, and then the signature reasonably distinct.

"Why a new sheet?" I said. "There seem to be only a few envelopes left."

"Seven, to be exact," he said. "Therefore she'd done some writing. As you say, why a new sheet of blotting-paper for that last letter? And why wasn't it in an envelope?"

"Exactly," I said. "It's untidy. Either it assumed that Bruff would be coming here or that whoever discovered her would know who the Gerry of the letter was."

"No point in rushing to conclusions," he told me, and was turning to look down at the body again. I took one look at the distorted face, and no more. It wasn't so much the ghastliness of it all as the sudden obtrusion of a song—that song another croonerette had sung in the Gerry Bruff show.

Maybe, maybe
I'm no lady. . . .

Maybe Netta Malone *was* no lady, but then she'd been flesh and blood and vitality and an emanation of sex that could do things to people like that Ted we'd met at the Ginger Cat. There was the sound of steps. Dorvan looked in.

"I got that off, Superintendent."

"Much obliged to you," Wharton told him. "You can keep a still tongue in your head?"

Sid shot him a scared look.

"No one's to know about this," Wharton told him. "If it gets out, you're responsible. Understand?"

He said he did. And he ventured to ask if that meant he might go.

"We'll see you back here at midnight, sharp," Wharton told him. "And thank you again for what you've done." The steps receded, with Wharton cocking an ear.

"No use scaring him," he said. "Let him think he's on our side. Wonder what's in this handbag?"

The handbag—quite an expensive affair—was on the mantelpiece. Wharton brought it to the sideboard and emptied it with gloved fingers. There were the usual lipstick, rouge, face powder, nail polish; a pencil in a gold case, a Yale key, a used handkerchief and a clean one, a receipt dated a fortnight back for treatment at a beauty parlour, four pound-notes, three halves and, in a little purse, some silver and coppers.

"Nothing very informative there," George said, and then cocked an ear again. There was the sound of car brakes. The circus had arrived.

*　　*　　*　　*　　*

It wasn't only because it would have been crowded in that small flat that George sent me out on errands. What he was wanting was to save time and to get into action as soon as the body and the circus had gone. But in the flat above I had no luck, for there was nobody in.

When I enquired at the ground-floor flat on my right, I learnt that the flat above Netta's was in the occupation of a lady of leisure. The prim female who told me that didn't put it in those words; it was what she didn't say that said so much. Apparently the lady often had long weekends away, and this was one of them.

"What about Miss Malone in the flat underneath?" I said.

"She's most irregular too," she said. "She comes home at all hours and there's been a man with her." Then she added that Miss Malone hadn't had the flat very long, and as she'd been edging the door gradually to, I thanked her and departed.

Next I went round to the local police-station and from there rang the Blue Boar. It took quite a time.

"Travers bothering you again," I told Robert Dorvan. "But Miss Malone—Gerry Bruff's wife—has been found dead in her flat. . . ."

"My God, no!"

"Afraid it's only too true," I said, but he was cutting in again.

"What was it? I mean, did she do herself in or was she killed?"

"Why that last question?"

"Well," he said, and gave a nervous titter. "It's natural, isn't it?"

"Maybe you're right," I said. "But we want you here at midnight sharp. Everybody who called at the flat this afternoon is being questioned. . . . I know it's a hell of a night. I've just been out in it. . . . Right-ho, then. At midnight or before. At her flat."

So he'd expected Netta to be killed, I told myself, and made a note for Wharton's benefit. And if he'd expected her to be killed, then he certainly knew the one who might have done it. And that one was probably Bruff. When Bruff had unloaded his troubles he had doubtless uttered a few wild threats. Or hadn't they been wild?

Next I tried to get Gerry Bruff. But I had no luck. So I rang the bureau and was told that he'd gone out a few minutes before. I said that if they spotted him coming in, he was to ring the number I gave them, and would they consider the matter as most urgent. Then I wrote out a carefully-worded message for Bruff.

"Try him every half-hour," I told the station-sergeant. "If he happens to ring you, just read him this message. Don't have any backchat. Tell him he's to do as he's told."

When I got back to the flat I saw the ambulance drawn up at the kerb. A couple of electricians were doing something to the wires and I guessed George was having a temporary telephone. When I stepped gingerly inside the small lounge, the police-surgeon was just going.

"The time of death was round about four o'clock," Wharton told me. I wondered why he had spoken so low, and then he explained.

Gerry Bruff had come by the flat and the man on duty had thought he was acting suspiciously and had questioned him.

"He's in there," George said, nodding at the far door.

"How'd he take it?"

"Broke down," George said. "The doc. here gave him a dose to steady him."

The cocktail bottle and the glass had gone to the Yard. The body was moved out to the ambulance and George led me out with it, for the fingerprint sergeant and his men were still at work. George said there were plenty of Sid's fingerprints about, but no others up to the present.

"The writing on that suicide note was hers?" I asked him.

"No doubt about that," George said. "At least, Bruff identified it."

"Find any correspondence?"

"Not a thing," he said. "A few old souvenirs of the shows she'd been in and that was all."

"What about the kitchen?"

"Everything left after her breakfast," he said. "Toast, marmalade and tea was what she had. Nothing washed up. Nothing in the bathroom either."

"Why'd she have breakfast?" I said. "She was on duty last night, presumably till three or four this morning. Weren't we given to understand that she slept all day?"

"Breakfast's a relative term," George pointed out. "What she called breakfast mightn't be till the afternoon. All we know is that after she had it, she went out and telephoned Sid Dorvan."

He added that the stomach content would tell us all we wanted to know about that, and then we went indoors again. The fingerprint men were going over the best bedroom and George suggested that he and I should try to get a snack of sorts at the police-station. He'd had nothing since four o'clock, and it looked as if we'd be at that flat till the small hours. I rang my wife and then George did some telephoning.

"I fixed up for Bob Dorvan at his hotel," he told me over our sandwiches and cocoa.

I had thought that he had named midnight for Sid Dorvan to return so that it would coincide approximately with the arrival of Robert, and that he was going to have the three nephews together for the general enquiry. That would be rushing matters, he said. Sid had his club to see to, and it was just as well to go easy with a suspect of his temperament. As for Bruff, he'd be questioned when we got back, provided he'd recovered from that nervous breakdown.

"He wasn't putting on an act?"

"Don't know," George said. "The tears were real enough, but they don't mean a thing. Hess fooled all the experts, didn't he, and he wasn't a pro?"

When I told him about Robert Dorvan and the mention of murder, he didn't seem too interested. It was after eleven o'clock, in any case, and time we were getting back.

We found the telephone installed and George tried it out. Then he tapped at the door and went into the spare bedroom. In a couple of minutes the two came out. Bruff's eyes were red and swollen.

"Mr. Bruff is feeling better," George announced condolingly. "He might as well get along home and have a night's rest. Just a question or two if he feels equal to it." He gave Bruff a queer look. "I take it you want to do all you can to find out why she did this?"

"Yes," he said heavily, and all the time he was frowning away like a man too busy with thoughts of his own.

"Make yourself comfortable," Wharton told him. "Have a cigarette. It'll steady your nerves. A minute or two and you'll be away and gone. Now you just tell us what the time was when you came round here and found her out."

"It was round about half-past five," he said, and once he began talking, he stopped frowning.

"And when did Robert Dorvan give you the news about her leaving the Ginger Cat?"

"I think it was about three. You see," he explained, "I had to think it over. What it meant and so on. I really only made up my mind to see her after Mr. Travers had rung me up."

"That's clear enough," said Wharton. "I wish witnesses were always half as clear. Now will you run your eye over this jewellery. Anything missing?"

Bruff didn't think there was. There had been a valuable diamond ring he'd given her, but she'd hocked that or sold it when she'd cut loose the first time.

"You gave her everything she wanted?"

"Everything," he said. "She'd only got to speak. I gave her a fur coat. . . ."

"That squirrel one in the wardrobe?"

"That's the one." He smiled wryly. "Seventy-five quid was what it cost me. More money than she ever saw at one time in her life, and then it didn't satisfy her. That's what used to get my goat when she was having one of her goes. Reckoned I was a piker. When I started reminding her of things, then she . . ." He shook his head. "You know how they are."

"I know," said George feelingly. "Anything for a row. But what about her money? You allowed her plenty?"

"Ten quid a week," he said, "and I paid everything in connection with the flat. You might call it her spending money."

"Ten quid a week, eh?" Wharton looked round at me. "What did she spend it on? Or didn't she."

"It went all right," he said. "The pictures, night-clubs . . . you know."

"I know," George said. "Anything for a hectic life."

"Even then she was always fed up," he told us. "Wanted to get back to the show business. That was her all the time. You know how they are, Mr. Wharton. Give anything to get out of it, and when they do get out of it, everything's rosy and sentimental. It's a kind of home-sickness, I guess."

"That's it. It's in the blood." He got to his feet. "Well, I think that's about all. Unless you can think of any reason why she should want to commit suicide?"

His head shook bewilderedly.

"I still can't believe it. She was the last one to do a thing like that. She was having her own way, wasn't she? Doing what she wanted?"

"I know," George said. "That's why I couldn't understand her talking about being fed up with the whole rotten lot. Must have been temporarily out of her mind. That's why she wrote as if the rotten lot included you." A fatherly hand fell on Bruff's shoulder. "Forget it. You get along home now and mind you take two of those tablets the doctor gave you."

The two went out, and the last I heard was Wharton offering to take him home in the car. When George came back he said he'd preferred to walk round to the Underground.

"Before I forget it," I said, "did Bruff have any doubts when he identified his wife's writing?"

"No doubt at all," he said, and then shook his head. "A funny sort of ménage that flat of theirs must have been. A bit of a piker, Bruff, for all his protestations."

I didn't agree. I said I admired men like Bruff who looked after their money instead of scattering it about in handfuls like a good many of his profession. Besides, an allowance of ten pounds didn't sound like piking.

"Probably gave her that in the first flush of the honeymoon," George told me cynically. "Then he was terrified at what he'd done and kept the rest of the strings a bit tight."

I'd probably have asked where all that was getting us, but voices were heard outside. A plain-clothes man put his head in and said a Captain Dorvan was there. Wharton gave me a look.

Robert Dorvan set down his bag and wiped his forehead.

"Pretty warm walking," he told us. "I'd have been here a bit sooner if I hadn't got lost."

Wharton told him about the Templemore arrangements and Dorvan said he'd also thought of it, which was why he'd brought a bag. The roads had been a bit clearer, but he'd left his car at Palmer's Green as usual and taken the Piccadilly Tube.

"Is that how you came up today?" Wharton asked him. "But make yourself comfortable. Have a cigarette and take that overcoat off. You won't feel the benefit of it when you get out-side again."

He got his own pipe going, and there the three of us were seated in front of the electric fire, snug as bugs in a rug. No wonder Dorvan chatted away as if we'd been in the Blue Boar. At least when he'd recovered from the minor shock of being told what the chalk mark on the carpet was there for.

As to his movements of that day, we were able to work them out smoothly enough. He had had the idea of seeing a man named Merlin who, he'd discovered from something in the *Radio Times*, was still at Broadcasting House. Merlin had been a former colleague of his, and—he said so frankly—he was hoping something in the way of business might come out of the meeting. So he'd driven to town, by way of Epping as usual, and had parked his car at a garage at Palmer's Green, and from there had taken the tube to Piccadilly Circus. Then he'd walked to Broadcasting House and had taken his time because he thought he was a bit early. He'd had the luck to catch Merlin, and the two had had coffee and had yarned for half an hour or so.

It was then too early for lunch, so he dropped in at a Cinema—the Rialto in Coventry Street—to see Bob Hope in *The Princess and the Pirate*. There he ate a packet of sandwiches he'd brought with him from the Blue Boar, and when he came out it was just after two o'clock. That was really what he'd been waiting for, since Netta Bruff would be almost sure by then to be up and about. It was about two-thirty, then, when he called at her flat and could make nobody hear.

"Before we go any further," Wharton said, "would you mind telling us exactly why you were taking all this trouble about unravelling Bruff's domestic affairs?" He turned quickly to me. "Why, according to Bruff, Captain Dorvan came to town today specially to see his wife."

Dorvan smiled rather lamely.

"I'm afraid you gentlemen must think what you like, but what it amounts to is the same thing as I told you about my friend Merlin. Bruff knows everybody and he's got a lot of influence. We returned prisoners-of-war aren't going to find jobs so cushy as we thought. You can't afford to leave any stone unturned."

"And very laudable, too," Wharton told him. "We've all had to do it in our time. But what happened after you didn't get any answer here?"

Dorvan said he'd hung around for a bit and then had gone back to the station. There he had telephoned Sid, who'd given him the news about Netta's quitting the Ginger Cat. At once he'd passed on the news to Bruff. At Piccadilly Station again he passed on the news to me, and then he went in search of tea. Miss English had recommended French and Carter's, the Oxford Street store, but when he got there he found he had to queue up, not for tea but for the lifts that took you up to tea!

"That's right," I said. "My wife had the same experience only the other day."

Dorvan had stuck it out for a quarter of an hour, and as it still looked like being a good few minutes before he was taken up, he threw in his hand and took a chance on the Corner House. The queue there looked miles long, so he walked through to Leicester Square Station. A Winchmore Hill bus happened to draw up, so he took it. It ran into nasty fog patches and it was very near half-past five when he reached the garage where his car was. He'd intended finding somewhere for tea, but after so much wasted time and with the prospect of a slow journey on to Flampton, he pushed off at once.

"Now something personal," Wharton said, "and strictly between ourselves. What was in your mind when you let drop to Mr. Travers tonight that there was the possibility of murder?"

He thought for a minute. Then he said he'd rather not say.

"That's a pity," Wharton said. "It turned out to be suicide, but it's a pity. If you're asked the same question at the inquest, you'd have to answer it then. And you don't want to have to attend any inquest?"

Dorvan moistened his lips.

"Of course, the fact that it's suicide does make a difference. But this isn't going to get round to Bruff?"

"Not on your life."

"Well then, it was something he said to me when he first told me about Netta. He said if he couldn't have her, no one else should. I told him not to talk like a bloody fool. And that's about all there was to it."

"In fact, if she *had* been murdered, you'd have known he was probably the one who'd done her in."

"Well, yes. That's what it amounts to."

"That's cleared up then," Wharton said. "And now about *her*. Any suicidal tendencies, did you gather?"

"I don't think so," he said. "I only saw her once."

"What impressions did you get?"

"Well, I thought Gerry Bruff had been a good picker, as they say. Then I wasn't so sure. In fact she struck me as being common as dirt down at the bottom of her. She knew where she wanted to get, though, and that was into films. If Gerry had guaranteed her that, I think she'd have gone back to him—till it was time to double-cross him again." He shook his head. "I know you're supposed to speak well of the dead, but I take it you expected the truth."

"We did," Wharton told him, "and we're glad we got it. And that, I think, is about all." He looked at me for confirmation and I too got to my feet. Then off the two went, with Wharton profuse in his thanks. I looked at my watch and saw it was well after midnight.

Chapter XII
THE MINK COAT

I DON'T PROPOSE to drag you through that third enquiry. All I will say is that Sid Dorvan arrived twenty minutes late, and full of apologies. Everything had gone wrong at the club and the fog had been so thick in town that he'd taken fifteen minutes to reach Piccadilly Circus. He said it was about three o'clock that afternoon when he'd come to the flat and he admitted he'd no alibi for the rest of the afternoon.

But there are two things you ought to know. Wharton had asked whose flat it was, and Dorvan said it was rented by him. Wharton tried the man-of-the-world approach and Dorvan admitted that he'd had a girl friend installed there, but she'd left two months ago because her husband was coming back from the Far East.

"Let me put something to you straight," Wharton said. "Did this Netta commit suicide because you'd let her down? Promised marriage, for instance, if her husband divorced her, and then told her it couldn't be done?"

Dorvan swore there'd never been any talk of marriage. In any case, he knew Bruff wouldn't divorce her.

"How do you know that?" Wharton asked him.

"Because he told me so over the phone," he said. "If he couldn't have her, he'd take good care nobody else did, that's what he said."

"We all talk a bit wildly at times," Wharton told him mildly, and then shifted to another question. This was the vital one, though we didn't know it at the time.

"I'd like to be sure of her state of mind last night," he said. "You were the last one to see her alive, I take it. Did you bring her home?"

"I didn't," he said. "She left just before three and came home by herself."

"Well, just what was she like last night? Cheerful? Depressed?"

"I don't know how to put it," Dorvan said, and he was frowning away as if trying to find the right words. "Kittenish —that's what she was."

Wharton grunted.

"You mean in an amorous mood?"

"Not exactly." He frowned again, then obviously remembered something. "For instance, she . . ."

And then he stopped dead. For a moment or two his whole body was still. The eyes were across the room as at something barely seen. How can I describe his expression? Perhaps it was that of a father of a family approaching a ticket-barrier and suddenly saying to himself, "My God, I've left the tickets at home!"

"Yes?" said Wharton.

Dorvan looked at him unseeingly, then suddenly pulled himself together.

"You were asking something?"

"You were telling us something," Wharton reminded him. "Something she did last night."

"I was wrong," he said quickly. "That was some other night."

"Well, what was it she did some other night?" persisted Wharton.

"Oh, she was just kittenish. Pulling my ears and that sort of thing." He was smiling sheepishly, and yet there was no doubt about the ersatz quality of that smile. And all the remaining minutes he was in the room he was somehow a different man. I think Wharton knew it, and that was why he kept asking questions that had no bearing on the Case. Then as soon as he'd gone, Wharton was putting the question to me.

"What came over him so suddenly?"

"Something must have happened last night and he suddenly remembered it," I said. "Something damnably important because he couldn't think of anything else. When he was answering you, his thoughts were elsewhere. He had to keep pulling himself together. And whatever it was, it was to do with Netta Bruff."

Wharton shrugged his shoulders.

"No use guessing what it was. And no use being in too much of a hurry. I've got an idea everything's just beginning to make a sort of pattern."

"You think it wasn't suicide?"

He gave his first glare.

"Didn't I just say it was no use rushing at things? Anyone'd think we'd be hung if we didn't get the whole thing cleared up in five minutes." Then the tone was subtly altered. "What makes you think it wasn't suicide?"

"The line you took in all those three interrogations tonight," I said. "And a thing or two I pointed out already. But what about the poison bottle? Was there one?"

He said it had been on the floor beside her as if she'd knocked it off the table when falling. It had been the usual small bottle that one can buy at any chemist's for destroying wasps' nests.

"But that stuff isn't soluble in cold water?" I said. "I know, because I've used it. What I'm getting at is that the cocktail was cold. How'd she dissolve it?"

"Leave all that for the morning," he told me, and so placatingly that I knew he had something up his sleeve. "The bottle's gone to the Yard. Wait till we see what the prints are like. Let's get out that time-table while everything's clear in our minds."

At first we merely set down the times as they concerned the flat. Then George said we should make it more comprehensive and include every time even remotely concerned.

"I know Bob Dorvan probably hadn't anything to do with it," he said to my faint protests. "He hadn't a motive for one thing, but his movements dovetail with other people's movements, don't they? Suppose we can prove he was half an hour out somewhere? That'd upset other people's timings."

I didn't give a damn either way, so we compiled the timetable as George wanted it. In any case it wasn't very much of a job.

9.30 B.D. parks car at Palmer's Green.
10.30 Meets Merlin.
11.15 In cinema.
2.0 Leaves cinema.

2.15 Netta rings Sid.
2.30 B.D. at flat.
2.45 B.D. rings Sid and Bruff.
3.0 Sid at flat.
3.30 B.D. rings Travers. Travers rings Bruff.
5.30 Bruff at flat. B.D. leaves Palmer's Green.
(ASSUMED NETTA DEAD 3.45–4.15.)

Wharton said he had asked Bob Dorvan at what stage of the programme he had entered the cinema and when he had left it, and that would be one check. Then he said we might as well get away, and there'd be no point in my coming round to the flat in the morning much before ten. There might be some news from the Yard by then. And he'd have his own hands full, in any case. Each of the three men we'd seen would have to have their movements checked. People in the road would have to be questioned about what they might have seen. There'd have to be a round of the chemists to find out where the cyanide had been bought. The Press statement had to go out.

"It'll be put out as suicide," he said, "and normally that wouldn't make anything of a splash. But we want to know what her movements were all day, so we'll try and get a photograph. 'Wife of famous comedian commits suicide'—that'll be what makes the headlines."

"A bit tough for Bruff," I said.

"What's coming over you?" He gave a glare. "Getting tender-hearted in your old age?"

"No," I said. "But whatever else Bruff did, I'll bet you a new hat he didn't commit that particular murder."

"Who said it was a murder?"

"Like to bet another new hat that it wasn't?"

He didn't accept the challenge. As I went out of the front door I heard him talking over that temporary telephone.

It was just before ten o'clock when I reached the Netta Bruff flat the next morning. Sergeant Francis let me in and he was the only one there. Wharton had rung up to say he mightn't be round till midday, so I relieved Francis at the telephone when reports came in from the two men working the road. By midday there was nothing positive from that enquiry. The flats opposite or anywhere near seemed occupied largely by business women who were out all day, and those that were in said that the light had been so bad from the early afternoon onwards, that they had had to switch on the light, and that meant drawing curtains.

At half-past twelve Wharton rang. Would I meet him at the Yard at two o'clock and get myself lunch in the meantime. I asked if there was news.

"Prints are all right," he said. "Stomach content shows she had her lunch out."

He began the grisly details. I said the statement was good enough for me, but what about the time of death. That, he said, was as originally thought: 3.15 to 4.15. The fact that the electric fire had been on in the room made a nearer assessment difficult.

I didn't feel like lunch, so I hung on with Francis for a bit, and it was lucky that I did. I looked at my watch, remarked that I'd better be moving off, and then the telephone went.

I stayed on with my usual curiosity to see what it was, and found it was Wharton wanting me. Suspicious as ever, he wanted to know first of all why I was still at the flat.

"Never mind that," he told me impatiently, and before I could get out half a dozen words. "There's a job for you. May be something and may be not. A woman's seen that photograph in this afternoon's papers and says she's almost certain she saw Netta Bruff yesterday afternoon, She won't say any more over the telephone. Perhaps you'll slip along. A Mrs. Cross, of 33, Ensbury Road, Fulham."

Five minutes later I was boarding a bus outside the Underground Station and I'd bought one of the early editions. On the front page, left-hand side, was a photograph of Netta Bruff, and a first-class likeness too. She was wearing that low-cut black dress she'd had on that night at the Ginger Cat. The headings were roughly as George had foreshadowed, but of letter-press there was practically nothing but padding. Gerry Bruff, in fact, was mentioned more than his wife.

It didn't take so long to reach the house. The road was a kind of oasis in what had once been a good residential district. Mrs. Cross, who opened the door at my knock, was one of those highly-enamelled women who get about a bit. There was something about her of the stage, the saloon-bar and the ribbon-counter of a suburban store. Before I'd followed her three steps along the passage she told me she was a widow, and what her husband had died of.

We went into a frowsty drawing-room and I began pinning her down to Netta Bruff. It was hard work at first because I seemed to be fascinating her. What she had expected was a copper, and not my elongated civilian self. When I'd refused politely to 'have something', she began her story and she had her own newspaper—two in fact—to illustrate it.

"As soon as I clapped eyes on it I said to myself, 'That's the young lady who bought my coat!' Then I had another look at it—what did you say your name was? . . . Well, I had another look and then I was certain. 'That's her,' I said, 'as sure as my name's what it is.'"

"A coat?" I said.

She explained. She'd had a mink coat and, prices being what they were, she thought she'd sell, so she'd advertised in the *Telegraph*.

"No, I didn't have a box number," she said, "I just put 33, Ensbury Road."

"When did the advertisement appear?"

"Yesterday morning," she said, "and I had two enquiries on the telephone. Then this lady, she called direct. About half-past two or a quarter to three, it was. I saw she was a lady as soon as I opened the door."

"What clothes was she wearing?"

"A squirrel coat," she said. "That made me think at first she wasn't coming about my coat, then afterwards she told me she'd be selling the squirrel now she'd got mine. At any rate I brought her in here and we talked it over, same as you and me might be doing now. Then she tried the coat on and, do you know, it fitted her like a glove. Might have been made for her, as I told her. Suited her down to the ground. You never saw anything like it."

I raised polite eyebrows.

"So, of course, she bought it?"

"Bought it and paid for it straightaway," she said. "When she opened her bag it fairly took my breath away. Two packets of a hundred pound-notes each!"

"Really? And did she have any more?"

"Not that I could see," she said. "Not that I was trying to look."

"Of course," I said. "And that was the price of the coat—two hundred pounds?"

That was the price, she said, and worth every penny of it. The insurance man who'd called had advised insuring for more than that, and people like them ought to know.

"The lady didn't mention her name?" I asked.

"She didn't. What she told me was that she was in the films, and that the Studio she was working for didn't like their people giving names."

"And she seemed pleased with her bargain? Didn't argue or try to beat down the price?"

"Not a bit of it," she said. "That's what made me a bit suspicious when she'd gone—poor lady. I wondered if the notes were good ones, if you know what I mean, so first thing this morning I slipped round to my bank." She smiled. "Everything was all right, though."

"She took the coat with her?"

"Oh yes. We made a parcel of it. I said she ought to wear it and pack the squirrel, but she wouldn't. She didn't want to get the squirrel creased, she said, if she was going to sell it."

I got her to describe Netta's voice, her figure, the one ring she'd been wearing and everything else I could think of. At the end there didn't seem any doubt that it had been Netta Bruff who bought that coat.

"What was the time when she left here?" I wanted to know.

She thought it out and reckoned it might have been about three or quarter-past. It was getting foggy. In fact she hadn't been able to see the lady more than as far as Monkton Road. Then I asked if she'd be prepared to sign a short statement, and she didn't demur. In fact, when I said that her name might be in the papers, she was only too ready. She even expressed herself as willing to see the dead woman. A very helpful woman was Mrs. Cross. She even wanted to get me a cup of tea. I asked her if she'd got Mrs. Bruff a cup of tea.

"I offered," she said, "but she said she'd had such an enormous lunch."

"She didn't say where?"

She put her fingers to her lips. "Now did she?" Then she shook her head. "I don't think she did. But I know she mentioned the West End."

That was about all. We shook hands at the door, and as soon as I was round the bend by Monkton Road, I lengthened my stride. At the first kiosk I rang the Yard. Wharton was at the flat, so I asked them to get him there and say I was coming. Then I went back as far as Monkton Road and timed myself to the nearest Underground. Allowing for a change at Piccadilly, I found that a reasonable time it might take one to get from the Fulham house to the St. John's Wood flat was three-quarters of an hour. On the other hand it would be far more likely that Netta had splashed on a taxi, for the coat must have made a bulky parcel. That journey would have taken well under half an hour. Allowing a certain latitude for Mrs. Cross's 'three or a quarter-past', Netta should have been home before four o'clock. She might even have been home well before a quarter-to.

I'd expected to be something of a sensation, and I certainly was.

"That clinches it," Wharton said. "It must be murder! It can't be anything else." He had got to his feet and was looking down at me. "Where's the coat? Tell me that."

"There *is* just the possibility that she left it somewhere on her way home," I said. "At a furrier's, say, to be overhauled."

"But that Mrs. Cross said it was perfect. Just like new."

"I merely mentioned the possibility," I said. "If necessary, it could be checked."

"It doesn't matter what she did with the coat," Wharton said. "The vital fact is that she *bought* the coat. Are you going to tell me that a woman buys a mink coat—every woman's dream—and then commits suicide as soon as she's bought it!" He snorted. "It isn't human nature. Dammit, anybody wouldn't think you're a married man." Then he remembered something. "You seemed pretty certain last night that it was murder. What was that about betting me a new hat?"

"It was the suicide letter I didn't like," I said.

"Oh, that."

"Wait a moment," I said. "I don't mean what I mentioned about its being addressed to her husband. What I mean now is the actual content of the letter."

"The content?"

He began turning over his papers. I told him I knew the letter by heart.

"Listen to this," I said. "*This is goodbye for good. I'm sick of everything and the whole rotten lot of you. I'm going where none of you will ever be able to pester me again.*"

He nodded to himself as I duly emphasised each word.

"You see it now? How ambiguous it is? It needn't refer to death at all. It might be a letter to her husband telling him she was fed up with his pestering her to come back, and fed up with the rotten gang at the Ginger Cat. What she was doing was going away."

"Yes," said George slowly. "There's something in that or my name's Robinson. But wait a minute, though. Why *should* the letter be ambiguous? You can't achieve ambiguity unless it's consciously." He gave himself a little nod of approval. "At least, not in a whole letter."

"I'd say she was tricked into it."

"Tricked?"

"That's it—tricked. Someone—the murderer if you like—had kidded her that he was going to get her into pictures. She had that on her mind, by the way, when she was with that Mrs. Cross yesterday afternoon. He said, 'Write Gerry a letter.' She said she wasn't good at writing letters, so he told her what to write. She didn't like Gerry; that's why the murderer told her to tell him off good and proper. 'Tell the whole rotten lot what you think of them and him in particular.' The murderer knew the letter could have another meaning. He knew it because he'd composed it beforehand against just that situation."

Wharton's grunt was more like a purr.

"Just one other question," he said. "She thought she was going away. What was she going to live on?"

"Someone—the murderer again if you like—had already given her earnest money of two hundred pounds. He could have promised her a thousand more, or two thousand more. It didn't matter what he promised, because he'd take it off her again when he'd killed her. I'd say he was expecting to take the two hundred from her, and when he found she'd bought that mink coat with the money, he took the coat so as to conceal the fact that she'd been given the money. And just one other point. The fact that she'd been given two hundred pounds as earnest money would convince her that she was going to get the balance, however much that balance was."

"I think you're dead right," George said, and, between ourselves, it's a good theory in which he can find no flaws.

"Every bit of evidence is cumulative," he said. "Take the cyanide. The bottle was there, but how did she dissolve it in the cocktail? One would have thought in hot water, but there was no smell in the kitchen or the bathroom. There wasn't a spoon or cup with a trace of smell. If she washed up whatever it was she dissolved the cyanide in, then why didn't she wash the breakfast things? It wouldn't have taken a couple of minutes."

"My guess is that the murderer brought the cyanide ready dissolved," I said. "He poured the drinks—the cocktail for her and something else for himself. She wouldn't be sure of the flavour of a new kind of drink. But if all this is right, then we ought to know something about the murderer. It doesn't get us far beyond what we know already, but the murderer must have been someone who'd never used that wasp-killing cyanide.

He thought it would dissolve in the cocktail, and that's why he didn't fake evidence in the kitchen that she'd dissolved it there. He brought his own in a tiny little bottle that he could almost palm in his hand, but his was dissolved because he had to pour it straight into the cocktail."

"I see all that," George told me, "but what's the point?"

"That the murderer wasn't a countryman who'd taken wasps' nests, as they call it, with cyanide. Neither Bruff nor Sid Dorvan was a real countryman."

George halted an incipient glare. He had been going to say that we knew that already.

"Just a minute. The suicide letter was addressed to Bruff. How could he induce his wife to write a letter to himself?"

"It'd have been damned difficult," I said. "I doubt if he's got that amount of ingenuity."

"Then we're left with Sid Dorvan," Wharton said, and on his face was that first Coliseum smile. "Sid Dorvan's our man. What we've got to do is find his motive."

"That original theory of yours provides the motive," I said. "Netta was killed because she knew too much. Mind if I put it the way I see it?"

"Go ahead," he told me.

"Then every bit of evidence we've got points to this as the sequence of events," I said. "Sid and his uncle had money cached somewhere. The whereabouts of that money or the means of getting it was in the sealed envelope. Bob Dorvan was coming home and Sid felt the urgency of getting that money—or his own share of it—before that happened, because Bob knew something that might put a spoke in the wheel. He couldn't get his uncle to agree, but finally he got the old man to come to town and talk things over. Whatever he suggested, the old man didn't like it. He mistrusted Sid, and even thought his life might be in danger. That's why he rang the Broad Street Agency and asked to have Bob located. He intended perhaps to sell out Sid's share, in some way, to Bob, and it was Bob he trusted. You're with me so far?" Wharton nodded. He did say the money business was highly hypothetical, and I had to agree.

"Sid realised on the Monday that the old man would have to be killed. Perhaps the revelations in that sealed envelope might have given him a goodish term of imprisonment. But the only safe scheme he could think of was to get Bruff to impersonate him for the vital Monday night, if only for a certain time. He trusted to luck and his own glib tongue to get him out of things when Bruff knew that at that very time Herbert Dorvan had been murdered. Maybe when Bruff did realise that and when he told Sid his suspicions, Sid said that even if it was true—which he'd swear it wasn't—then Bruff himself had been an accessory before the fact. That might keep Bruff's mouth shut. In any case, if it came out at a trial, then Bruff's reputation would inevitably be badly smirched."

"That seems reasonable enough," Wharton admitted.

"As for the reward that Sid promised Bruff, I can't think of any unless it was giving up Netta. I don't want to upset your theory, George, but somehow I don't like that part of it. Still, we'll say tentatively that that's how things were. Sid had to take Netta into his confidence to a certain extent, and he had to make it well worth her while. Then he realised she'd have to be put out of the way."

"One thing occurs to me," he said. "If all this is true, then Sid should have given Netta the push immediately after the murder. Why all the delay?"

"That's one of the objections I was going to make," I said. "Mind you, I think that business of Netta ringing Sid and saying she'd quit was all a fake. But about the delay. Maybe Sid shilly-shallied because he had to find money and kept pleading he couldn't raise it. I don't know. It's a weak point in the argument."

"We'll by-pass it," George said. "What we'll work on is the main points—Bruff's impersonation and Sid as the one we want." Then he was giving me one of his leer-like squints. "Think we can make use of Bob Dorvan? Get him to tell us what he knew? Or suspected? That ought to be a job right up your alley."

With that we went into committee, and if I tell you what we decided, it will only be an anticipation of what happened. Maybe you'd like to follow those events for yourself.

CHAPTER XIII

LITTLE BY LITTLE

I HOPE you won't get impatient about the much we did and the little—or so we thought—we found. George was right when he said there was no hurry, at least in the sense that more haste is less speed. Nowadays the law can take its time. The world was suddenly smaller still. A murderer may bolt, but he cannot escape. When the remorseless enquiries of the law have established the final proof, then the murderer will be there. War-time restrictions alone would see to that.

At just before ten o'clock that night Sergeant Francis and I made our way to the Ginger Cat. We tried the back way first, only to find on the first landing a door locked against us. So we went in as clients through the main door and up the stairs. Neither of us looked too out of place.

Before a waiter could hail us for drinks we had made our way to the bar. Peter said the boss was in, and it struck me as curious that after his ticking-off on a previous occasion, he should tell us to go through. I tapped on the office door and an even more curious thing happened. The door opened about three inches, and a face appeared. It was a square, clean-shaven face, pasty-looking, and yet tough. It was a square kind of face with beetling eyebrows and a prominent jaw. Hair was smarmed down over the low forehead. Somehow it reminded me of an aged gorilla dressed up for a stunt at the Zoo.

"Yeah?"

The greeting took me aback. All I could manage to ask was if Mr. Dorvan was in.

"And what if he is?"

"Tell him I want to see him."

"Name of?"

"Travers."

The door was shut in our faces. Francis promptly stuck his ear against it. I heard a faint murmur, and in about a minute the door opened again, this time fairly wide. I had a look at that door-keeper. He was six foot, and with a back like the end of a barn. His nose was slightly askew and his ears were rather mangled. Altogether he might have had a head-on argument with a bulldozer. But he slipped out to the corridor behind us as we went in, and I was wondering who'd set him up with that dinner-jacket outfit.

Dorvan got to his feet, and as he did so he slid shut the table-drawer.

"Sorry to bother you, Mr. Dorvan," I said, and just a bit annoyedly. "We shan't keep you more than a very few minutes."

"That's all right," he said, eyes on Francis. "You'll have a drink?"

I said we were on duty. All we wanted was his written statement about his movements for the previous afternoon.

"That's O.K. by me," he said. "Mind if I pour myself a drink? Sure you gentlemen won't have one?"

While he was squirting the siphon I put the casual question.

"Why the bodyguard? Expecting a visit from some of the boys?"

He gave me a quick look. The siphon squirted over the side of the glass and he made play with mopping the table with his handkerchief.

"Something like that. You know how it is. Think they're entitled to a cut."

"Why don't you ask for police protection?"

"Because there won't be any trouble," he told me. "Not now."

In a quarter of an hour the statement was signed. I told Francis he could go. We'd thought that Dorvan might open up a bit in a friendly chat.

"How's the settlement of your uncle's estate getting along?" I asked him, and I'd told him I thought I'd change my mind about having that drink. "I only asked you because that's right up my alley and strictly outside business, I thought I might help."

The idea behind all that was to get him to talk, however indirectly, about that sealed envelope. I could almost see his cunning little brain working as he sipped his second drink.

"That's damn good of you," he said. "The way I get it is that Clare—the solicitor—is handling things. He's a sort of administrator."

"That's the way it goes," I said. "But if the likely beneficiaries—say you three nephews—squabble about anything, then the Court will decide who's to have letters of administration. That may be the solicitor again."

"You know, I have the idea the old boy left a will," he said. "I've mentioned the matter to Mr. Clare and he doesn't agree."

"Well, *he* hasn't a will," I said. "Do you mean that your uncle might have made a will and concealed it somewhere? In the bungalow, for instance?"

"Well, that was the general idea. Sounds a bit silly, perhaps."

"If I remember rightly," I said, "the bungalow's been thoroughly searched. Was your idea that you should have a look for yourself."

"Well, something of the sort. Clare seems to think that if that was done, then all three of us ought to be in it. I don't think the game's worth the candle. All damned red tape. Don't you think so?"

"My advice is to leave things as they are," I said. "If a will were found, you mightn't benefit." Then I gave him an arch look. "Strictly between ourselves, did you expect to benefit? To be better off than you will be by having a third share?"

"I wouldn't know," he said. "The way I look at it is that fair's fair and right's right. A matter of principle, if you get me. I don't want his money. I'm doing all right."

That was about all. The gorilla peeped round the back door as I left. Francis was waiting on the corner of Temple Street.

"Know who that bodyguard was?"

I said I didn't.

"Old Flatear Fred," he said. "I didn't bat an eyelid when I saw him."

"Who's Flatear Fred?"

"You must know Flatear Fred," he told me. "He fought Joe Beckett and Joe knocked him out in the first round. You remember all the row there was about it. Last I heard of him was about a year ago and then he was chucker-out at Alf Morgan's place."

I didn't give a damn about Fred's history. What I wanted to know was why he'd been suddenly installed at the Ginger Cat.

"Plain as the nose on your face," Francis said. "He's expecting trouble. And why did he close that drawer when we came in? Because he had a gun in it."

"There's a fairly sure way of finding out *where* he expects trouble," I said. "If it's only at the Ginger Cat, then Fred will go home when it closes. You put a man—better make it a couple—outside the Ginger Cat. Brief them yourself and take good care they don't slip up."

We had been walking towards the Yard. I took the statement up to Wharton and made my report. I said if we substituted for *will* the words *sealed envelope*, we'd know just what Sid's anxieties were.

"Unless he was bluffing, then he hasn't got the sealed envelope," George said.

"I don't think he's bluffing," I said. "But he can't adopt Clare's suggestion about a search because he can't get Bob to agree with him. Maybe Bruff as well. Neither could hope to benefit by a will."

"A hell of a position for him," George said. "If he did his uncle in as we think he did, he did it for nothing. No wonder he's worrying about what his next move will be."

Wharton knew Flatear Fred, but he couldn't work out why he'd been suddenly all dolled up for a bodyguard. But before I left he did give me some pieces of news. There had been no poison in the actual cocktail bottle. It hadn't been traced yet where the bottle had been bought, but a telephone enquiry from Sid had shown that there was no Versac at the Ginger Cat. Also it hadn't been established where the poison had been bought. The fingerprints on it were very questionable and a good case might be made out for impression after death. Analysis of the small amount of cocktail remaining in the overturned glass established that the dose had been just enough. Netta had died within seconds of taking that first gulp. As for the movements of the three men on the time-table, Bob Dorvan's had been proved reasonably correct —to within a few minutes, that is to say. Neither Sid nor Bruff had any alibi for the afternoon and early evening.

I was up early the following morning, and at half-past nine I was at the Templemore Hotel. Miss Sanbridge was flitting about, bright and beautiful as ever. Perhaps the faint blush at the sight of me made something of the good looks.

"Captain Dorvan in?" I asked.

"He left about an hour ago," she said. "I think he's gone back to Flampton."

"Wonder why he left?" I said, and just for the sake of something to say.

"I haven't any idea," she said. "Unless it was something to do with the man who called."

"Really?"

"I suppose I oughtn't to talk about it," she said, and gave a glance round. "But you're different."

I nodded mysteriously. I asked if the man was Tom Harris; a tall man wearing glasses.

"He wouldn't give any name," she said. "But he wasn't tall. And he didn't wear glasses. He was medium height and fat-faced. And he had one of those streaky moustaches like band-leaders have."

"Don't know him from Adam," I said unblushingly. "Suppose you don't know what happened?"

"Well. . . ." She moistened her lips. "You'll think I was listening, but I wasn't. I couldn't help hearing. They were making such a noise. It was the man, really. He was going on like anything. Then he and Captain Dorvan came out together, and this man was looking mad as a hatter. Absolutely blazing." She laughed. "When Captain Dorvan came back he treated it as a joke. He said it was a man he'd known, wanting him to give him a job."

"What time would this be?"

"When the man came?" The purple-painted nails drummed on her chin. "About four o'clock or so."

"I only asked," I said, "because I'd intended coming round to see Captain Dorvan yesterday afternoon myself. Then I found I couldn't make it."

I thanked her and said I might run down to Flampton myself.

"Any message from you?" was my arch farewell.

"You can make one up for yourself," she told me blushingly, and that was that.

I got on the telephone to Wharton at once.

"Yesterday afternoon at about four o'clock Sid Dorvan called on Bob at the Templemore. He wouldn't give Miss Sanbridge any name. In Bob's room they had a hell of a row. At least, Sid was his usual excited self. I rather guessed Bob did the placating. Then they left the hotel together. Bob's gone back to Flampton this morning early."

Wharton said that was good work and I might find ways and means to use it at Flampton.

"About Flatear," he said. "He went with Sid to Sid's flat. Sid had a camp-bed installed in his room. They haven't made an appearance yet."

We couldn't argue about that over the telephone, but as I pushed the car on towards my flat again, I was wondering just what it was of which Sid was afraid. Herbert Dorvan had gone and Netta had gone, but why should he expect his own turn to be next? Somehow it didn't make sense.

I drove to Flampton alone, and it was just after twelve o'clock when I walked into the Blue Boar. The landlady told me Captain Dorvan was out. As she was expecting him for lunch at one o'clock, I asked her if she could manage something for me too. Then I had a drink in the bar and watched a darts game, and stood a round and had another tankard myself, and then Dorvan came in. He wanted to stand me a third, but I stood him one instead.

I told him about lunch and he said we'd have it up in his room. I'd expected a far less genial reception, for he seemed quite pleased to see me. In the ten minutes before lunch he wrote a formal statement about Netta and signed it, and I told him he wouldn't be needed for the inquest.

The meal was quite good, as it happened to be a day for a joint. I told him how fit he was looking, and he said he'd been for a five-mile walk.

"That tip of mine do you any good?" he asked.

"All the good in the world," I said. "I wouldn't be surprised if they took me on for keeps."

"But you've got money of your own?"

I shook a dubious head, not knowing just how much he knew. Expenses were heavy, and what with income tax and this and that, things weren't too easy.

"Not that I can't just about manage," I said. "A regular job at the Yard, though, might make all the difference. That's why I'm damn grateful."

I chewed away for a moment or two, then came to a decision, or so I hoped he'd see.

"You've done me a pretty good turn," I said, "and I don't mind letting you know in confidence what's being done about all this business. I don't hear everything, mind you, but the police think Netta Bruff's death links up with your uncle's."

"Really?"

He was interested enough to pause in his eating. I nodded mysteriously.

"They think she was somehow mixed up in that murder, then had an idea we were getting pretty close."

"I wouldn't like to say," he said. "She was a tough baby. I'll say that for her."

More chewing, and then I asked if he'd ever listened to a Gerry Bruff Show.

"Oh, rather," he said. "I think they're pretty good. Anybody can do an impersonation or two. You can, perhaps?"

I said I could do Jimmy Durante and Horace Kenney.

"I used to do a few myself," he said, "but Gerry's got the whole of us beat—pros and all. I'll bet, if he was having this meal with us, he could get inside you, so to speak, and then go into that bedroom so that I'd swear it was you who was talking."

"He's good," I said. "He's got the gift."

He nodded, and that line of talk had petered out. I had to try another approach.

"Ever hear of a pal of your late uncle, named Peters?"

"Peters?"

I told him why I'd asked. I even showed him a copy of the telegram.

"Just a minute," he said. "Peters. . . . There was a little, stoutish, foreign-looking cove called Peters." He held up a finger as if for silence while he thought. "Where did I see him. At St. Leonards, that's where it was. One of those queer coves my uncle used to have down there. I'm sure his name was Peters. . . . Did I see him more than once, or didn't I?" He shook his head. "Can't remember, but I'm damn sure his name was Peters. What about asking Sid? He might know."

"That's an idea," I said, and then he was looking egg-bound with another theory.

"If this chap Peters was what I think he was, mightn't it be a good idea to apply to the Home Office? He might have been interned at the same time as my uncle."

I said that was a good idea, and it was.

"And what about the wording of the telegram? Does that convey anything to you?"

He had a good look, then folded the paper and handed it back.

"Nothing at all. Unless he was trying to get back into the Agency business—my uncle, I mean. That's where his heart always was."

The meal was then at an end. Dorvan said the coffee at the pub was filthy, but he always had a cup of tea after lunch.

I said that would suit me fine, so he hollered down the stairs for two cups instead of one. Then we got cigarettes going and I had to begin the conversation all over again.

"For God's sake don't ever let anything of this out," I said, "but the police are working on what they describe as a sealed envelope. Your uncle withdrew it from the solicitor's office a day or two before he was killed. I've got an idea they think it had something to do with those Fascist activities that landed him in clink. Which reminds me. Wasn't it you who gave me a hint that Sid was up to the neck in that business too?"

There was a tap at the door and a pleasant-faced, dumpy girl brought in the two cups of tea. She gave me a shy look, but she smiled at Dorvan.

"You seem well looked after here," I said.

"Not too bad," he told me. "But what was that you were saying about Sid?"

I mentioned that Fascist business again.

"I don't think there was any doubt about Sid being in it," he said. "But you people aren't making things retrospective, are you? I've no use for Sid, but I wouldn't have spoken if I'd thought the police might rake up any of that old stuff."

"Sid needn't worry," I said. "Have you seen him recently, by the way?"

"As a matter of fact I saw him only yesterday," he said. "He came round to the Templemore to see me, to tell the truth. In a filthy temper too."

"What on earth should he be in a temper with you about?"

"That Netta business. Reckoned I'd made trouble by poking my nose into her affairs and Gerry Bruff's. He as good as accused me of being responsible for her doing herself in."

"Sid's not too pleasant a piece of work," I said, and waited. But nothing else came. He asked if I'd have another cup of tea, and then began talking about the country around Flampton. When I knew there was never a hope of getting the talk unobtrusively back to where I'd hoped to get it, I suddenly realised how late it was. He walked with me to where the car was parked and saw me off.

"One thing I meant to ask your advice about," he said. "When's Netta's funeral?"

"I don't know," I said. "I do know that her husband is seeing to things. And I believe she's being cremated."

"Think I ought to turn up?"

"Well, that's up to you," I said. "I think Bruff would appreciate it."

He nodded and said he thought he'd go.

"So you got nothing out of him at all," Wharton said when he'd heard my report. "All you can say is that he was frank and apparently had nothing to conceal."

"You can't always back winners," I told him. "But you can't call that information about Peters nothing at all. You'll do something about that?"

"Most certainly I will." He waved an impatient hand. "But about this Bob Dorvan generally. Get any new ideas?"

"I rather like him better every time I run across him," I said. "He was perfectly open and above-board. He doesn't seem to have anything to hide. He doesn't like Sid, and he says so. He likes Gerry Bruff and he says so. The only possibly new thing I gathered was that he's not so keen on any detective business as he was. I think he's too full of his own affairs to worry about the murder of an uncle for whom he didn't care twopence, or very much about Netta Bruff for that matter."

"What's on his mind, then?"

"His leave with pay won't last for ever," I said. "He's got his living to worry about. Then there's that girl he's got an eye on." I added lamely, but definitely not apologetically, that I'd done my best with him, and that maybe Wharton, with a different approach, might have got more.

"Oh, I don't know," he told me graciously.

He hooked off those antiquated spectacles and began replacing them in the even more antiquated case. I guessed that something was coming.

"You want a sort of versatile mind in this game of ours," he told me, and then with an unctuous deprecation: "Not that I claim to see everything."

"Well, what *have* you seen?" I asked bluntly.

"Oh, nothing much," he said, but that was only a momentary annoyance at my having cut in. "I rather think you overlooked it yourself, though." Exasperatingly he hooked the spectacles on again and peered at me over their tops. "That money that Netta Bruff paid for the mink coat. Did that convey anything to you?"

"Only that there are mink coats and mink coats," I said, "and the one she bought wasn't off the top shelf."

"There you are," he said triumphantly. Then he leaned back. "Paid for it with two bundles of notes, didn't she?"

"So I was told," I said cautiously.

"Well, that set me thinking," he said. "While you were gone this afternoon I slipped along and saw Mrs. Cross. Then I had a private word with the manager of the bank. And what do you think I found out?"

"Can't say." I was almost tempted to say flippantly that the two were long-lost brother and sister.

"Those notes," he said. "Two bundles of a hundred each, and the wrappers round them. Like to see one?"

In his best conjuring manner he was holding a note beneath my nose.

"One of the old pre-war greens," I said.

"Exactly! Every single note was the same."

"Yes," I said slowly. "You don't see those notes too often nowadays. Two complete bundles can only mean one thing."

Chapter XIV
OUR MR. PETERS

I WAS RIGHT. There was only one answer. No bank in the country could nowadays hand out to a customer two complete packets of those pre-war green pound-notes. The money must have come from somewhere else, and, if only part of our suspicions were correct, then it must have come from some hoard or cache. Even a black-marketeer operating with five thousand in notes would have had his money circulating all the time, so if Sid Dorvan was not scared of having a flutter in that particular game and had received a hefty sum in notes, even then he couldn't conceivably have been paid in the old green ones. But the green notes that came from Netta's bag still had round them the bank wrappers, and though used were reasonably new.

As we saw it, it could only have been Sid who gave her that money. But from that point on, the logic led one down a mighty steep slope. If Sid gave her the money, then he'd found the cache. That meant he'd come into possession of the sealed envelope. That meant he'd killed his uncle. And that meant that his alibi was a fake.

"What about the fingerprints on the notes?" I said. "Nothing doing," Wharton told me. "Those packets had been split up. The bank hadn't more than twenty or so by the time I got there. Not one of them had Sid's prints." There was only one thing for it—to find a chink somewhere and get in levers and burst it wide open. So we settled down to a study of what we had against Sid. Suspicion and surmise were no use. What we wanted was actual fact, and all of that that we had was damned little. It seemed to be nothing but what I'd styled PHASE TWO of the overheard conversation.

> *Sid*: Dammit! It makes *all* the difference. Did he have it or didn't he have it?
>
> *Bob*: He had it. You bet he wouldn't part with it.
>
> *Sid*: Then how the hell are *we* going to get it? Tell me that.
>
> *Bob*: Why don't you go down there and have a look? You know the lay-out? Or don't you?
>
> *Sid*: Just what are you getting at?
>
> *Bob*: Sh! Want to broadcast all your business?

We'll cut out the discussion and come to the conclusions that Wharton and I drew from that.

> (a) The talk was about the sealed envelope.
>
> (b) Sid talked about *we*. Bob twice drew him back to *you* and *your*.
>
> (c) Therefore Bob had shown that he knew of the existence of the sealed envelope. Sid had tried to involve him in some way, but Bob wasn't having any.

Wharton rapped those notes with his knuckles.

"I still hold that Bob was trying to trip him up. If he could just get him to open his mouth a bit too far, then he'd know who killed his uncle. But he wasn't too tactful. Sid smelt a rat."

I agreed that that was all inherent in that PHASE TWO, and it was also plain that so far we hadn't made much progress. The only other peculiar fact we could find was Sid's employment of Flatear as a bodyguard.

"There's just one other thing," I said. "When you were questioning Sid about Netta, you asked him how she'd been the night before she quit. He started to tell you, and then he suddenly shut up. He realised something that knocked him all of a heap. He didn't even hear you when you spoke to him again."

But all that wasn't fact, and it was facts we were after. George said he might try to do something about Sid's banking account in case any large sum had been paid in, and including packets of green notes.

"You'll ask Sid about Peters?" I said.

"What's the point?" he told me annoyedly. "If there is a Peters and they were all in the swim together, then he'll swear like hell he never knew him."

"Then what *are* we to do?" I said. "Try the Midgley end again?"

"That line's stone dead. I had our man back today. Only wasting his time."

All he could think of was nobbling some old pal of Flatear and getting him to do some judicious pumping. And George himself admitted that that mightn't be worth the planning it'd take. Sid had hired Flatear, but the reasons he'd have given would be pretty far from the truth.

"You drop in at Sid's flat," he said, and I knew he was only marking time. "Make any excuse you like. See if Flatear's still there."

"You mean now?" I said.

"Of course I mean now," he told me with a glare. So off I went. And I had the idea that for some reason or other George had been trying to get rid of me.

* * * * *

Sid's flat was more of an office than a cosy nest. When I saw him, he was working at a huge flat-topped desk on which was a telephone and a typewriter. There was an enormous filing cabinet and a heavy safe. But that's getting on ahead.

I rang the bell and heard no sound. Just when I thought I'd ring again, the door opened about six inches and there was Flatear's face.

"Yeah?"

"The old story," I told him. "Mr. Dorvan in?"

The door closed in my face, but I heard the beginnings of what was probably, "Boss, it's that nose again." Then almost at once the door opened. "The boss'll see you," I was told, and in I went.

Flatear came behind.

"Beat it, Fred," Sid told him curtly, and I heard the door close behind me.

"Well, what is it this time?" asked Sid. He looked in a nasty mood and the sight of me wasn't doing him any good.

"Sorry to worry you again," I said, "but it's not my fault. Blame the Higher-ups. They'd like you to be more explicit about that alibi for Guy Fawkes Night."

He spread his palms and they trembled exasperatedly.

"Can't you ever leave me alone? Haven't I got enough troubles without you coming round here?"

"Troubles such as what?" I asked smoothly.

His eyes narrowed, then he got to his feet.

"Ah, what the hell! What is it you want to know?"

I told him, and at once he exploded again.

"Go where you like and ask what you damn-well like. Didn't I tell that Superintendent of yours so?" The hands were shaking again. He shrugged his shoulders helplessly and let the hands fall. "Go away and leave me alone. Go to the club. Ask who you like and what you like. Can I be more fair than that?"

"Sounds good enough to me," I said. "But why all the worry. The lads pay you a visit after all?"

"Look, Mr. Travers," he said patiently. "Can't you see I'm busy? Appeal against Income Tax assessment. Got to be in in two days' time. Or don't you know what Income Tax is?"

"I seem to have heard the word somewhere before," I told him. "But why not get your boy friend to help? He looks a sympathetic sort."

I hoped he lose his temper, but he didn't.

"Look," he said. "You go along to the club tonight and do as I said. All I ask is to be left alone."

So I left him alone. I didn't go straight back to the Yard, because there was no point in reporting nothing, so I stood myself a belated tea. When I did walk into George's room, he was studying something through his glass.

"Have a look at this," he said. "Straight from the Special Branch."

It was a dossier of a James Arthur Peters, and a photo-graph was attached. But something was wrong with some of the particulars, for this Peters wasn't a shortish fat man, but five foot eleven in height. I had been under the impression, falsely perhaps, that the Peters whom Bob Dorvan remembered was a man of mature age. This Peters was twenty-nine.

But he'd been a Fascist all right. There were extracts from speeches he'd made in public, and in 1939 he'd been concerned in a Jewish victimisation case, though he himself had swung clear. When the law had swooped on him in 1940 he had been living near Worthing. At the moment he was at a hamlet named Hendown, near Lewes, and working a smallholding. It didn't seem unreasonable to suppose that he had known old Herbert Dorvan.

"If everything's O.K., could you slip down and see him in the morning?" Wharton said.

I said I'd like nothing better, so it was left like that. He'd get in touch with the East Sussex police and make sure that Peters was still there. I said I'd ring Bob Dorvan and see if we could reconcile the difference in height between his Peters and ours.

I told him what had happened at Sid Dorvan's flat and naturally he had little to say. The Flatear business was as puzzling as ever, unless there had been some truth in Sid's implied admission that he was in bad with some of the boys. I left George to it and went back to the flat and tried to get Bob Dorvan. The landlady said she expected him at any minute, so I rang again in half an hour.

"Good," he said, when I told him about Peters. "I knew I was right."

When I told him about the height, he agreed that his man couldn't very well be mine. I said no other Peters had been detained.

"Maybe I'm wrong about the particular man," he said. "There was a Peters. I can swear to that. I must have got names mixed up."

There wasn't anything else to say. When Wharton rang later to say Peters was still at Hendown, everything was set. Just before eight o'clock the next morning I was on my way.

There's a text I often think of in connection with detection that you cannot tell which shall prosper, this or that. You assess something as a first-class clue, only to find it valueless. You pass over some obvious triviality and find you've missed a first-class clue. Take, for instance, those three factual happenings which were all that Wharton and I could associate with Sid Dorvan; the overheard talk, the Flatear business and the way he'd covered up over Netta's manner the night before her murder. Which of those would you assess as the most important? I'm open to bet you'd plump for the first, and you'd be wrong.

Take the day I was about to spend. Interesting enough for me, perhaps, and time wasted all the same. At least I was to think it wasted. If I'd known beforehand what I was going to see at Hendown, I'd have stayed in town and left the local police to handle things. And yet if I hadn't gone down, I'd never have discovered what I did. George and I once solved a murder case because a woman happened to rub her nose. It was the old, old story. Something sets going a train of thought, and, as Gerry Bruff might have said, Bob's your uncle. But to get on with what I did find at Hendown.

The tiny village lies just short of Lewes and to its right. When I enquired about a Mr. James Peters, I was told I'd passed his place half a mile back. I couldn't miss it, my informant said. It was the only bungalow on my left, and there were fowl houses and runs behind it. When I got back to it, I found there was also a rough track leading to a field, and I drew my car in there by the bungalow hedge. It was ten o'clock when I knocked at the front door.

Nobody seemed to be in, and that sent my spirits down to zero. Then I thought I'd have a look round, and when I went along a well-worn path and through a gate, I saw a man among the fowl-houses at the far side of the field. Three goats were tethered there too, and folded off like sheep were about a couple of score of geese.

"You Mr. Peters?" I said as I came up.

He was a gaunt-looking young fellow, hatless and wearing dungarees. For the last forty yards of my approach his eyes had been steadily on me.

"Yes," he said laconically, and waited.

I told him my name and showed him my Warrant Card. His eyes narrowed as he handed it back. It was rather disconcerting that he should say never a word.

"We want you to help us, Mr. Peters," I said. "This is a friendly visit and we shall regard ourselves as being under an obligation."

He still said nothing.

"It's connected," I said, "with the murder of a Mr. Herbert Dorvan. Perhaps you've read it in the papers."

"I might," he said curtly, but I knew that the name had conveyed more than that.

"Can't we go somewhere where we can sit and talk?" I said. "It might be quicker in the long run and I don't want to waste your time."

"You won't waste my time," he said. "I've got nothing to tell you."

I tried to laugh that one off.

"But you don't know what I want to ask you."

"This is Home Office business?"

"It's Police business," I said. "It's something arising out of a Scotland Yard enquiry."

"Same thing," he said. "I'm opening my mouth for no ruddy Government with Herbert Morrison in it. You can tell Herbert Morrison from me that he can . . ."

It doesn't matter what that particular advice was, except that if Herbert had followed it, he'd have been in an exceedingly uncomfortable position—forelock and all.

"Somebody steals some of these fowls of yours," I said. "What do you do? Go to the police."

"The police my ruddy foot," he said. "All I have to say to you is good day."

He picked up his tin and brush and went on with his creosoting.

"I think you're getting the wrong idea," I said. "I'm not concerned with that old Fascist business, neither are the police."

I might just as well not have been there.

"Look here, Mr. Peters," I went on, "I'm a working man like yourself. I've got my living to earn, and I've been sent down here to get a simple answer to just one simple, harmless question. It's not going to do me any good when I go back and say I couldn't get it."

The brush strokes had slowed a bit and I thought I'd touched his heart. But it was only to survey me quickly from shoes to hat, and then the brush went methodically on. Peters had evidently summed me up as a working man.

"Well, if you won't have it the easy way," I said, "you'll have to have it the hard. You'd better arrange for somebody to look after this stock of yours."

He shot me a look.

"Don't think I'm bluffing," I said. "I'm getting in touch at once with the local police and you'll be asked to accompany us. This is a murder enquiry and you're a material witness. How long we shall want you, I can't say."

I hadn't gone ten yards when he was calling.

"Hi, Mister!"

"What was that question you wanted to ask?" he said as I came back.

I handed him a copy of the telegram, and I told him a few things about it. He read it through at least three times.

"Handed in at the Strand," he said. "I haven't been to London for over a year. It's three years since I heard a word about Mr. Dorvan. Then I saw his name in the paper, about that murder."

He gave me the telegram copy back.

"There must be some other Peters," he said. "What should I send telegrams to Mr. Dorvan for?"

"But you knew him in the old days?"

"I don't like that *but*, Mister."

I hastily reassured him. No offence had been meant. And so that he wouldn't be troubled again, would he put his name to a simple statement that he knew nothing about the telegram?

We went back to the bungalow, but he wouldn't let me in. He wrote his statement inside and asked if it would do. I said it was just what we wanted, so he signed and I witnessed the signature. I told him we were grateful for his help.

"If you were once a friend of Dorvan's," I said, "you ought to be glad something's being done about getting the one who murdered him." I held out my hand and, to my surprise, he took it.

"You're just a hireling of the capitalist classes," he told me, nevertheless. "You're misguided. That's all that's wrong with you."

"You're probably right," I said. "But thanks again, all the same. I'll do that little job for you, by the way."

"Job? What job?"

"You know," I said. "If I run across Herbert Morrison I'll give him your message."

A dour smile came to his face. Before I'd gone a couple of yards he was calling again.

"If it interests you, I might tell you something. It's not to go any further, mind you."

"You needn't worry about anything you tell me, if it isn't in the signed statement," I said. "I'll give you my word as well, if you want it."

"I know the law," he said. "But about Mr. Dorvan. It was me who gave him the tip in 1940. I had a pal in the police, so I passed the tip on." The dour smile came again. "That's your police for you. And the funny thing was, it was me they had first."

"That's very interesting," I said, and thanked him again. There were plenty more questions I'd have liked to ask, but I didn't. In any case he was turning on his heel and making his way back to his creosoting.

It was only just after half-past ten. The sun was breaking through and, from that high ridge lane, there were views to take your breath away—sweeps of autumn colour and misty distances incredibly far away. I tell you that because it led to a decision, for as I drew the car up and looked across the great stretch of an open valley towards Hailsham, I suddenly told myself I'd be damned if I'd go hurrying back to town.

I remembered an occasion in the last war when I'd taken a party of men to Ireland, and, having conscientiously done my job and hurried back to England, had been greeted by the Adjutant with, "What are you doing here, Travers? We didn't expect you for a couple of days."

George wouldn't expect me back till the late afternoon, I told myself. So I'd take my time and treat myself to a respectable lunch on the way. Then I was suddenly asking myself why I shouldn't go back by Hastings and Porthaven. It'd be good to see that country again, and I could still be back in town before George expected me. As for Government petrol, I reckoned that they owed me a bit as it was.

It was just about midday when I was nearing Porthaven, and that shows how leisurely I took things. Then I naturally began to think about the last time I'd been there with Galley. That made me think of Wharton and I wondered what sort of an impression he'd made on the locals. I thought of Clare, for instance, and wondered what he'd thought of George, interested as Clare had said he was in his fellow men. That brought back to my mind the hour or so I had spent in Clare's office, and then suddenly I remembered something. In a moment or two I had drawn the car in to the kerb and I was polishing my glasses.

There I was, trying to recall a part of that conversation. Something like this, it went:

"That sealed envelope was one of the reasons why I'd told Dorvan he ought to make a will. In the event of his death, it would have to be handed over."

That was what Clare had said, and then he had hastily turned the talk aside. Even at the time it had struck me that he either didn't wish to mention some matter in connection with the envelope, or that he knew more about it than he was prepared to admit. And what he had said had been rather muddled. If Dorvan made a will, for instance, the sealed envelope would surely be mentioned specifically in that will. If he died intestate, as he did, then the envelope wouldn't have to be handed over. It would be merely a part of the estate and at the ultimate disposal of the beneficiaries.

In any case it seemed to me that Clare had been concealing something that he knew, so I told myself I'd see him again. But I went to work warily. At the Spaniards Hotel, where I found I could get lunch, I asked if they could make it two lunches if I brought a guest. Then I went along to Clare's office.

He was in, but engaged. Ten minutes later he came into the outer office escorting an old lady client. He recognised me and showed it, and when he came back he was taking me into his sanctum. I at once asked him to have lunch with me. He said he'd been in the habit recently of bringing sandwiches for midday, and leaving the office early, but it wasn't hard to see what he thought about sandwiches.

So we had lunch at the Spaniards, and I tried to do him well. Sherry before the meal, for instance; *à la carte* boiled fowl instead of the *table d'hôte*; some good ale during the meal and a glass of port after. At two o'clock we were still yarning before the smoking-room fire, and the topic happened to be our common interest in our fellow men. We were actually arguing about one of the waitresses. I said her accent was Birmingham; he put it as Cheshire.

"I expect you're right," I told him hypocritically. "You're a bit better at the game than I am. Where I might have you beaten is in listening to evidence and so on. Which reminds me of something. I meant to ask you confidentially before I went away but didn't get the chance. Nothing to do with that murder case, except perhaps very obliquely. You remember that sealed envelope of Dorvan's?"

"I certainly ought to," he told me feelingly.

I drew my chair in just a bit closer.

"Do you know, I had the idea—strictly between ourselves—that you had a very shrewd notion of what was in that envelope."

Heaven forbid that I should give myself a pat on the back. But the fact remains that he took the question in his stride.

"Well," he said, and he gave a little chuckling laugh. "There was a paper in it—I know that." He gave his Pickwickian squint up at the ceiling. "It might have been merely as a protection wrapped round what I happened to discover—purely accidentally, I assure you—*was* in it. It had been in my safe," he went on, "and something had stood on it and had caused a kind of impression. Naturally I couldn't help seeing it was some sort of a key."

CHAPTER XV
ZERO DAY

IT WAS LUCKY that Clare should say almost at once that he'd have to get back to the office. Five minutes later the bill was paid, my car shot out of the hotel yard like a bat out of hell, and I was on the way to Tonbridge. I was also doing some thinking, though I didn't need a lot of that.

There had been a key in Dorvan's envelope. He had hidden that key on the eve of his arrest and had recovered it on release, and then had deposited it with Clare for absolute safety. He had been murdered because of that key—the key to the safe or box in which he had placed his money just before the police had grabbed him. The murderer now had that key and the money as well. Netta Bruff had been given two hundred pounds of that money.

It was as simple as that. The rest of the details I left to the subconscious, for I was driving pretty fast. Just after three o'clock I was telephoning Wharton from the police-station.

"I think I'm on to something," I said.

"You've got Peters?" he was asking at once.

"Nothing doing," I said. "But I know what was in that sealed envelope of Dorvan's. It was a *key*."

"Can't hear you," he said. "Did you say *key*?"

"That's right," I said. "K for kitten, E for Ernie and Y for yourself. KEY."

He gave a grunt or two, then wanted to know when I'd be back.

"It doesn't matter about me," I said. "I want to put something up to you. Mightn't that key be to a safe-deposit box or something like it?"

"Yes," he said tentatively.

"Then why not get every available man on the job before the Safe-Deposit businesses close for the night?" I said.

"That's an idea," he said, and, "Right . . . I'll see what we can do. You get back here as soon as you can."

Then he rang off. There were at least two more things I'd wanted to say—two vital things, or so it seemed to me. Then I shrugged my shoulders. No use ringing George again. If I knew him he'd already be out of his room. And I'd be back in town in just over an hour. And tomorrow was another day. And George might have worked out for himself the very things I had been anxious to say.

I pushed on again. There was no fog, but the sun had gone in and patches of mist began to form. The roads were more tricky and I had bad luck with the traffic lights. It was half-past four when I went up to George's room, and he was out. Francis was sitting there at the telephone. I waited for half an hour and then said I'd slip out for a cup of tea. When I got back, Francis said Wharton had enquired for me over the telephone and had suggested that I should push off home. He'd drop in some time during the evening and tell me how things stood.

Bernice and I waited half an hour for dinner and then we had it. It was not till half-past eight that George turned up. All he would have was a beer.

"Nothing doing so far," he said. "It's a tricky business. Those Safe-Deposit Companies certainly run no risk of fraud. Worse than the bureaucrats. You can't move an inch without the Higher-ups."

"What name were you enquiring for?" I asked off-handedly, and I knew at once he'd missed the vital point.

"Dorvan, of course."

"A deposit in one name, or two?"

"What *is* this? What're you getting at?"

"I was just wondering," I said tactfully. "Remember that listening-in conversation? The mention of fake names?"

"But that didn't refer to what we are dealing with now?"

"Have another look," I said, and found my copy of the notes.

PHASE FOUR

Bob: All right. I'll tell you what we'll do. Grab your hat and we'll go round to Scotland Yard straightaway.

Sid: And benefit Bruff? You're balmy. And the fake names? How're you going to explain that away?

"Mind you," I said placatingly, "that conversation doesn't stick in your memory as it does in mine. You weren't there and I was. But doesn't that PHASE FOUR suggest that the deposit was made in two names? And they were false names? After all, Dorvan would have been taking chances by caching money—especially illegally acquired money—under his own name."

"Let me get this straight," George said, "and I'll quote this PHASE FOUR, as you call it. Bob wanted to go round to the Yard. Why?"

"As I see it, for this reason," I said. "The suggestion was a bluff. He was trying to force Sid to admit something. But leave that out and assume that it wasn't a bluff. Look at it the way Sid was supposed to look at it. In so many words Bob said this. 'The old man hid the money and you and he both had a key. You say you didn't commit the murder and so you haven't his key. All you've got is your own key. Someone's collared the old man's key and until we know who that someone is, you'll never get the money. So why not go round to the Yard and tell them all about it? They'll get the deposit-box open, and the money—they won't be able to prove whether or not it's legally acquired money—will go into the estate. Then all three of us will share.' Sid's retort was that the fact that the money was deposited under fake names would tell the police that it had been unlawfully acquired. And he was damned if he was going to benefit Bruff."

"That's clear enough," he said. "Except that Sid's real objections were that he was scared of further enquiry. But assuming all this is true. The names were fake ones. Then how can we possibly trace the deposit? You must have some name or other to go on."

"I suggest you try a long shot," I said. "Let me finish telling you what happened this morning with Peters."

"There we are then," I said. "Peters was the one who tipped Dorvan off. When Dorvan and Sid were ready to cache the money, and discussed what name or names it should be in, mightn't the name of Peters occur to them?"

"But he himself was collared later. The police were liable to enquire into any deposit he'd made."

"Not in this case," I said. "Peters got the tip from some pal in the know. He didn't expect to be arrested himself. But he was. All those arrests, except in the case of national figures, were secret. Dorvan didn't expect Peters to be arrested, and even when he was he didn't know it."

It was plain that George didn't have much faith in my arguments, but he didn't actually wax contemptuous about my theorising as he so often does. That's one of his little tricks, by the way. When a theory proves a dud, George reminds me of what he said about it; if it proves a winner, then suddenly it is George, and not myself, who was the begetter.

But he said that he'd get things going along the new lines first thing in the morning. There'd be no point in my loafing about the Yard. If anything happened he'd give me a ring.

So I had a comfortable morning in the flat. If anybody had told me when I opened my eyes that morning, that zero day had dawned, I'd have been highly sceptical. I also, in the hard light of day, was not so much in love with my own theories as I'd been overnight.

It was just like George to ring when he did. I was halfway through lunch when the telephone bell rang.

"That you?" he said, and without waiting for an answer; "I think we're on to something. You've got your car?"

I said I had.

"Then meet me at Cardinal Street—just off Moorgate Street, this end—as soon as you can. You needn't break your neck. You'll probably be there as soon as I am."

As a matter of fact I was there about a minute before he arrived. I was right about the unpretentious building we were due to enter—the Consolidated Safe Deposit Company. Wharton mentioned a name and we were taken up in the lift and shown straightaway into an office. It was quite a palatial one, and the urbane-looking gentleman who rose at our entry was evidently a director.

Wharton introduced himself and then me. The director's name was Quick. As I'd been given no explanations, I had to pick things up for myself as we went along.

"This is the book I thought you might like to see," Quick said. "Here's the original entry and the date. The end of June, 1940, as you thought."

"The name or names?"

"Peters. Thomas, Richard and Henry Peters."

So there were *three* names. I was only momentarily surprised. I should have guessed that old Herbert hadn't trusted Sid, and that Bob had been brought in as a safeguard. And that was why they'd had to wait till Bob got back from the Far East. But Wharton was giving a snort.

"Thomas, Richard and Henry, eh? That means Tom, Dick and Harry. Got anybody who can describe any one of them?"

Quick shook his head. Five years and more was a pretty long time. The staff had changed tremendously. The clerk in charge of the entries had been killed.

"I know how it is," Wharton said. "But what I thought was that a safe with three keys might have been something unusual."

"Oh dear no," Quick said. "We're an up-to-date firm. We have deposit boxes and lockers with up to six keys. The charges are in proportion, of course."

"And who kept up the payments?"

"The Richard Peters, for two years." He glanced at another book. "Sorry, no. For three years. Then the Thomas Peters paid."

"By cheque?"

He had another look at the book. Richard had paid by cheque and Thomas by money order.

"And now about procedure," Wharton said. "Suppose the wrong people get hold of a key?"

"There's safety in numbers," Quick said. "That's why in highly confidential matters people prefer double or treble key fitments. In the case of the ordinary one-lock fitment, the onus is on the holder. We're protected by the contract. It's the duty of the holder to see that his key doesn't get into the wrong hands."

"I get you," Wharton said. "And now may we see the man you told me about? The man who was on duty?—if that's the word."

A man named Sparks came in. He was a heavy-featured, Belcherian type, with a moustache the younger brother of Wharton's. He carried an old topper in his hand and was wearing some sort of uniform. Quick told him to take a seat and tell us all about that matter that had been discussed just before lunch.

"Well, it was like this, gentlemen," Sparks said. "All a matter of routine, you might say. I took the gentleman down in Number 2 lift. A fattish-faced gent, he was, with a dark moustache. He'd be about forty, now I come to think. Hair all going grey round his ears. He was wearing glasses and he had a handbag with him—though that's nothing unusual."

"What sized bag?" cut in Wharton.

"Oh, about two foot by one," he said. "About this size. Sort of bag you would have if you were going away. But as I was saying, sir, when we got to the vault I asked for his number again, and it was 771, so I stood by as usual while he went over to his box, and that was over to the left on the far side. In about a couple of minutes he was back and up we went, and when he got out he tipped me a bob."

"And what time was it?"

"About half-past one, sir."

That was all Wharton wanted to know.

"If you've got your master keys ready, we might as well go down," he told Quick.

Inside five minutes we were in that vault, and Quick was fitting three keys in the locks. He demonstrated that there was no movement of the door when two keys had been turned, and not till the third had been turned did the door open. Wharton had no need to look inside. The safe was empty.

"You think it's a case of robbery?" Quick asked anxiously.

"Not a bit of it," Wharton told him largely. "Set your mind at rest, Mr. Quick. Your Company won't be faced with any claim."

Outside on the pavement again Wharton suggested a quick coffee. The lunch rush was over and we found a table to ourselves in a little restaurant further along the street.

"Not a bad guess of ours about the name being Peters," he told me, and with never a blush. When the waiter came he remembered that he'd had no meal and took a chance on the *table d'hôte*. I had coffee.

"Who's your favourite for lifting the money?" I asked him.

"Don't know," he said. "Those three were all in town that morning. They're all about the same height. Sid wouldn't have needed plumpers, that's all. The rest of it—the moustache and the glasses and the white hair round the temples—anybody could have done."

"And the devil of it is," I said, "that a simple disguise like that is efficient and unobtrusive. Nothing to be gathered from the voice either, and the gent, as Sparks called him, kept his gloves on."

George wasn't listening. He wanted to know whose was the third key. When I told him why Bob Dorvan must have had it, he agreed, if with reservations. Bruff might just as well have owned it.

"He wasn't much more than a lad in 1940," I said.

"Lad, my Aunt Fanny!" he told me contemptuously. "But what's it matter? Sid had his own key, didn't he?"

I said he did.

"Then he's the central point," George said. "If he killed Herbert Dorvan as we think he did, then he had two keys. All he had to do was acquire the third by some trick or theft."

"If Bob had the third key, then his holding it might have been only as a kind of umpire," I said. "He mightn't have known what the key was for. Sid could have induced him to part with it. Or perhaps he parted with it just to see if Sid had the other two keys. In that way he'd know who killed his uncle."

"Theories, theories!" he snorted. "We've got a shortcut to everything. We'll get the truth out of Sid, and before this night's out—or my name's Robinson." Then he frowned. "I might report to the A.C. Nothing like putting the onus on the Big Bugs."

George knew that I loathed conferences, even those of an Assistant Commissioner, so what that virtually meant was that I'd stand by for later orders.

"That telegram still puzzles me," George was going on. "Sid sent it?"

"It's a hundred to one he did," I said. "Sid, you remember, was anxious about correspondence being found at Midgley, because he'd corresponded with his uncle about payments for the safe and what was to be done when Bob got home. He was the only one who knew the code word *Peters*. That name would be used by him and his uncle when their correspondence concerned the safe."

"All right," said Wharton. "Sid gets the old man up to London. Why? To try and get hold of his key?"

"I think so."

"But he didn't get the key. The old man saw through him and rang Bill Ellice's Agency."

He'd finished his meat course—if liver and bacon is meat—and was looking impatiently round for the waiter. When the sweet came, he didn't like the look of it, and asked for his bill.

"You going home now?" he asked me.

I said I thought I would.

"Don't expect an early call," he told me. "You mayn't be wanted till about six."

I parked my car at the garage and strolled back to the flat by Charing Cross Hospital. Something made me think of that A.C.'s conference, and George fuming inwardly at the chin-wagging and bursting to get on with the job. I hoped George wouldn't bring in his Aunt Fanny, and as I thought that I remembered an occasion when I'd had an Aunt Fanny too. That Porthaven doctor asking me why I'd killed Dorvan, and my somewhat footling reply. Galley and the doctor and I—all lads together and chuckling at anything that remotely resembled a joke.

And then suddenly my thoughts moved on. They switched incongruously to that telegram—a telegram which I knew by heart. There by the bus queues I was all at once polishing my glasses. I hooked them on again and I was telling myself something.

"My God, what a fool!" I said to myself. "Absolutely under our noses." I told myself a whole lot more.

And then I realised that if I was talking to myself, I was talking out loud. People were staring and a girl gave a giggle. As I moved on a copper came up.

"Not feeling well, sir?"

"Heavy thinking, not drinking," I told him, and showed my warrant card.

He handed it back, then asked for another look. As I crossed the road, I guessed that inside two minutes he'd be checking up on me at the Yard. But I didn't care what the hell he did. Maybe he'd report that I was tight. Maybe I was.

I made my way to the Southern Hotel and asked for the manager. Funny how people remember me. He didn't even ask to see my card, and when I'd described the clerk who'd been on duty the afternoon Herbert Dorvan had left, he had him brought to the office. He asked if he should stay himself.

"I should be glad if you would," I said. "You see, I don't want you to take any action against this young man because of anything that may arise out of what I hope he's going to tell me. Provided, that is, if he tells the truth. If I don't think he *is* telling the truth, I shall have to ask him to accompany me to Scotland Yard."

That seemed to have a good effect all round.

"What's your name?" I asked.

"Archer, sir."

"Tell me, Archer," I said, "what it was that Mr. Dorvan wanted you to do for him that afternoon of Guy Fawkes Day when he left this hotel? And while you're at it, tell me why. Tell me the whole story."

He shot a look at the manager and then back at me.

"Well, I didn't see anything wrong in it, sir."

"Don't let's argue about right and wrong," I said. "You tell me everything that happened."

This is the story, though not in the spasmodic way he told it. After Dorvan had found out about the train time, he went up to his room and had tea. At about five to four he came down to the desk and settled the bill which he'd taken up with him. Then he handed the clerk a letter for me, saying it was for a man he described.

"He wanted to do some business with me," he said, "but I've changed my mind. Later on I might, of course, but what I'd like to do is have a good look at him first. I shall go to the bookstall for a paper and I want you to tell him I've just gone, and bring him out to the platform so that I can judge what sort of a man he is. A goodish sum of money is involved."

Archer said he'd certainly do that for him, and Dorvan gave him a five-bob tip.

"That's all I want to know," I said, and smiled up at Archer. "Easy, wasn't it. Not half so bad as having a tooth out."

"You've told the truth?" the manager asked him, none too pleasantly.

"Oh, yes," I said. "He's told the truth. Mr. Dorvan had a good look at me. He even turned back on the platform and walked towards the barrier where I was standing, so that he could have a better look."

I got to my feet, shook hands with Archer by way of effect, and asked the manager if I could have tea.

"Certainly you can," he told me. "Here? In the lounge?"

I said I'd have it in the lounge. And by chance or hotel routine I had much the same tea that Herbert Dorvan had eaten—a hot-cross-bun kind of tea-cake, one sticky tart and a pot of tea. When I asked the waitress for the bill, she said it was paid for.

I looked at my watch. It was still only a quarter to four, so I sat on five minutes longer, then made my way to the barrier of Platform Five to reconnoitre. Then I bought a ticket to London Bridge. The barrier was open when I got back, and I went through to the platform and took up my stance about ten yards from it to the right, as if waiting for somebody.

You may have judged that I have a pretty good memory for faces, and yet I was far from hopeful as I waited. The man I wanted might have been making his one and only journey on that particular train. But I could console myself with the knowledge that even if my man didn't arrive, the case I hoped to build up would not be too prejudiced. So I had no despairs when the minutes went by and there was no sign of him. There was only the tiniest thrill when at last I saw him coming through the barrier.

I joined him as he strolled along, then coughed to attract his attention. There were only three minutes before the train was due to leave.

"Might I have a word with you?" I said, and was offering my credentials.

He raised his eyebrows as he handed the card back. Then he frowned.

"Haven't I seen you somewhere before?"

"You have," I said, "but let's get along to your seat. If there is one."

"Far too late for a seat now," he said, and he was right. So we stood in the corridor and hardly had we got settled there than the whistle blew.

"I was the man who looked into a certain compartment on Guy Fawkes Night," I said, "and asked if a seat was taken. Perhaps I didn't see the newspaper on it. It was a corridor seat and you told me it *had* been taken."

"I remember now," he said.

"The middle-aged gentleman whose seat it was," I went on. "How long was it before he came back. I rather gathered he was in the lavatory."

"I think he came back almost at once," he said. "I remember because, although he took his bag and left, he forgot his newspaper. I expect he caught sight of a pal in some other compartment and went to join him. They often do."

The train was slowing for Waterloo. I just had time to get his name and address and then out I got. He looked very surprised. Maybe he did a lot of thinking on his way to Orpington. I was doing a lot of thinking, too, as I made my way out of the station. Then I went through the main entrance and waited a few minutes till a telephone box was free.

"This is Travers, George," I said. "Has that conference been fixed yet?"

"Due in five minutes," he said. "Why?"

"Hold everything," I told him. "I've got something special. I know who did the murders and how they were done."

"My God, no!"

"You were right," I said. "It was a case of impersonation after all."

"Bruff!" he said. "Something told me all along that it must be Bruff. You're sure? This is none of your damned theorising?"

"Look, George, I'm not going to let you down. This is a certainty, but there's something you've got to do. Got paper handy?"

"I've got a head on me, haven't I?"

"Then do this," I said, "and treat it as urgent. Get hold of Bob Dorvan and tell him we're arresting Bruff tonight. We want certain comprehensive evidence which Bob can give. He's to be at Bruff's flat at nine o'clock sharp. If you can't get him at the Blue Boar, try that Colonel English's place. The number's in my notes."

"And what about Bruff? Suppose Bob warns him?"

"As soon as you've got Bob, then get Bruff," I said. "Tell him I'm coming round to see him at once. If you think fit you can warn Bob not to ring Bruff and tip him off."

"Anything else?"

"Not at the moment," I said. "I'll be with you inside an hour, all being well. One other important call to make."

And with that I hastily rang off.

Chapter XVI

ZERO NIGHT

In my callow days when I first began to work with George Wharton I was squeamish about telling lies even in the sacred name of justice. Today I am far from claiming to be as fluent and un-blushing a liar as George can be, but I have precious few qualms. Take, for instance, the matter of Gerry Bruff.

I tried to get him at his flat, but the line was dead. I tried the bureau, but all they could say was that he was out. I bought an evening paper, but he didn't appear to be on in any of the shows in town. Then I tried Broadcasting House and struck lucky. I guessed he was working on a script, and a young lady, with a highly cultured voice and the most Mayfair of vowels, assured me that Mr. Bruff would be given my message, which was that he should wait till I got there.

It was I who had the wait, if only for ten minutes. We walked towards Regent Street together and were nearly there before I told him why I wanted to see him.

"I'm warning you," I said, "that you're for the high jump if this gets out, but we're pulling in Sid tonight on a murder charge."

He halted in his tracks.

"He did it?"

"Amn't I telling you so?" I said. "But what Superintendent Wharton wants from you—you remember Wharton—is one little bit of evidence. I told him you'd co-operate."

"You're right, I'll co-operate," he said. "I'll be damn glad to co-operate. When do I go?"

"Get yourself some tea first," I said. "Five o'clock will be soon enough."

I said I had a job of work to do, but I'd be seeing him. Then I found a telephone kiosk and rang the Yard. I didn't want Wharton direct.

"Ludovic Travers speaking," I said. "Urgent message for Superintendent Wharton. Tell him Gerry Bruff should be at the Yard at five o'clock. Ask the Superintendent to hold him till I get back. . . . Repeat please."

I went in search of a taxi, and it was ten minutes before I could induce one to draw in at the kerb. Half-way to Sid's flat I saw another telephone booth, so I got out and tried to get him. The number was engaged, and that told me he was in. I wondered if Bob Dorvan was ringing him to tell him the news about Bruff.

In ten minutes we were at the block of flats. I told the taxi-driver to wait.

I rapped on Sid's door and there was the same old performance except that this time Flatear and I spoke together.

"Yeah?"

"The mixture as before."

In ten seconds I was in the room and Flatear was sliding out behind me. Sid was having a high tea. There was a pot of tea on the table, a loaf and a pound of what looked like honest-to-God country butter, and as fine a leg of ham as I'd seen for years.

"Looks pretty good," I said. "Like to tell me the name and address of your grocer?"

Nothing happened, so I asked how the Income Tax appeal was coming along.

"Can't grumble," he told me. He smoothed back that thin black line of moustache, or else made sure it was still there, and his eyes were on me all the time.

"I've got some news for you," I said, and something told me that he already knew it. "Not a word's to get out. You understand that?"

He said he understood.

"Then Bruff's being roped in tonight for murder," I said.

He nodded, eyes never leaving my face.

"No surprise?" I said.

He looked away.

"This is a free country, isn't it—or supposed to be. What if I guessed it beforehand?"

"You're thinking about your uncle's murder?"

That startled him.

"Was there another murder?"

"There was," I said. "His wife was murdered."

He stared, then slowly got to his feet.

"Why, the dirty bastard!"

"Sticks out a mile, doesn't it?"

"Yes," he said, and shook his head. "I hope to God I live to see him swing."

"Just what we wanted to hear," I said. "But there's one little bit of evidence Superintendent Wharton thinks you can give. At the Yard, at six o'clock, or six-thirty."

"Make it six-thirty."

"You'll be there?"

"You bet I'll be there."

"Right," I said. "You won't be kept long. If you like you can go straight on to the club."

"Suit me fine," he said.

I rose to go. He wanted me to have a drink.

"Some other time," I said. "Too many things to do at the moment."

He saw me off from the door.

"Just one little thing," I said. "You'll be safe enough at the Yard. You needn't bother to bring Boris Karloff." It took twenty minutes to get back to the Yard. When I entered Wharton's room a kind of free-and-easy conference was going on. The A.C. was there and a sergeant from the Special Branch. The A.C. gave me a nod and a grin which had a lot of questions behind it.

"A bit late, aren't you?" George said impatiently. "Bruff's been here a quarter of an hour."

"Couldn't be helped," I said. "Sid Dorvan's coming round too, but not till half-past six. That should give us plenty of time."

"Time?" he glared. "Time for what? Dammit, we don't even know yet what we're here for!"

"I know," I said as I took off my overcoat. "That's just what I meant."

It was eight o'clock that night by the time everything had been agreed on. What we proposed to do was rather like taking a short cut. If that short cut proved to be the same old long way round, then there'd be no harm done. It was true that at least one person would know just where he stood, but by then it would be too late to cover any tracks, and it would only be a matter of hours before we had the additional evidence we might need. If you don't see what I'm getting at, all I can add is that you won't remain very long in doubt.

When Wharton and I got round to Bruff's flat, the stage was already set. It was a curious scene, because there seemed to be no scene at all—no fuss, no activity, no noise. Everything was unnaturally quiet, with steps making no sound on that thick pile carpet in the lounge. Only half the concealed lighting was on, and one might have imagined that in the little dining-room where Wharton and I would wait, there was a coffin and the undertaker's men were due to arrive.

Wharton and I went over final arrangements, with who was to say this and who that. We were worried about Sid and whether he'd lose his nerve and depart from the script. We wondered what would break, and how. We hoped we weren't too confident.

"Well, we can't do more than what we've done," George told me, and I didn't somehow like the way he looked at me as that last word trailed off. It seemed to suggest that the whole scheme had been mine and he'd been against it from the start.

"That a bell?" he said, and cocked an ear.

It *was* a bell. Things began to happen. Francis came in with Bruff.

"You sit there, sir," Francis said quietly. Then he slipped the handcuffs on him and saw they were properly round the arm of the chair.

Sid Dorvan came in, eyes suspiciously round.

"Over there, Mr. Dorvan," Wharton said. "I'll be sitting facing you. And mind you stick to your script. You there, Mr. Travers."

I moved towards my chair and then George was lifting a hand for silence. Sergeant Jewle, a loose-limbed, awkward-looking six-footer, was coming in, and Bob Dorvan was with him.

"Here you are then," said Wharton, fussing forward. "Sorry to trouble, but we oughtn't to keep you long. Sit here, Captain Dorvan, will you?"

Bob Dorvan had a quick look round. Bruff, sitting dejectedly on that hard chair across the room, lifted his eyes and let them fall again. Sid didn't seem to notice the newcomer at all. I caught Bob Dorvan's eye and gave him a friendly nod, just to make him feel at home. He had what looked like a brand new overcoat over his lounge suit, and his shoulders were hunched as if he were still cold after the journey, and his hands were deep in the overcoat pockets.

"Sergeant Jewle?" called Wharton.

"Sir?"

"We shan't want you any longer," Wharton told him. "See Matthews at the Yard, will you, and get on with that job. Close the door."

Jewle gave a "Very good, sir" and left us. Wharton switched on the rest of the lighting and there we all were. The antiquated spectacles were duly adjusted. Wharton pulled out his notes, looked through them, then peered round over his spectacle tops. My heart, in spite of myself, began to beat a bit quickly. It was to Bob Dorvan that he addressed himself.

"Since we got in touch with you, Captain Dorvan, the situation has materially changed. Mr. Sidney Dorvan has come forward with a statement which we regard as highly important."

He broke off.

"You can take those cuffs off, Sergeant Francis. Mr. Bruff won't try to get away."

He watched that done, peered at his notes again, then leaned forward in his chair.

"Your stepbrother has been warned of the seriousness of the statement he's made, and since it involves several people—including yourself—I think you'd better hear him repeat

"That suits me," he said, but his eyes had narrowed and he sat more deeply in his chair.

"Very well then," said Wharton. "Mr. Dorvan, perhaps you'll repeat your statement. Take your time and begin at the beginning."

Sid didn't look at anyone, unless it was Wharton. Most of the time his eyes were on his own fidgeting fingers.

"Well, it was just before the fall of France, in 1940," he said. Wharton interrupted again.

"I'd like it to be plainly understood that I'm not prompting Mr. Dorvan. If I ask any questions, it will be for the sake of clarity. If anyone—you, Mr. Bruff, or you, Captain Dorvan—feels like interrupting or asking questions, then don't do it. Your turn will come when he's finished."

He wagged a finger to drive that home, and told Sid to carry on.

"As I was saying, all this took place when that Regulation 18B came in and they were rounding up what they called Fifth Columnists. My uncle had an idea he'd be for it, and then he got a private tip-off from a man named Peters, so he sent for Bob and me. Bob happened to be on leave. What my uncle told us was that he had a pretty large sum of money he didn't want the Government to know about, or get their hands on. It was about twenty thousand pounds in pound notes. He suggested it should go in a safe-deposit box with three keys, each of us to have one. If any of us died, we were to have made sure that particular key was left to one of the others, and if we were all alive after the war, then we could collect the money and share out. Or if one of us was dead, then the other two could collect because they'd have the three keys. And that's what we did. We went to the Consolidated Safe Deposit Company in Cardinal Street and signed the book and collected the keys. The same afternoon Bob and my uncle deposited the money. The reason I didn't go was because I'd sprained my ankle pretty badly in getting out of a taxi on the way back in the morning. Uncle Herbert had my key and he handed it back to me personally afterwards."

"I have a book here, loaned by the Company," Wharton said. "It bears the signatures of Thomas Peters, Richard Peters and Henry Peters. Perhaps you'd better look at the signatures and see if you recognise them."

"They look all right to me," Sid said. "The Richard one is mine. Uncle Herbert was Thomas. We practised beforehand so that we could reproduce the signatures if necessary."

"So far so good," Wharton said. "The money's deposited, you each have a key. What then?"

"The police collared my uncle and Bob was sent abroad," he said. "Two years ago we got word from him that he was in the hands of the Japs and not too badly treated. I'd done a bit of sweating before that news arrived for fear his key had been lost. Still, that didn't happen. Then Uncle Herbert was released and I saw him and he agreed to take over the payments to the Deposit Company. He and I paid one visit there, just to see what things were like. It was pretty lucky it hadn't been bombed. . . . Mind if I smoke?"

He lighted a cigarette. Wharton glanced at Bob with enquiring eyebrows. Bob grimly shook his head.

"Then we got news about the Jap collapse and prisoners coming home. We didn't hear anything from Bob, but we knew he'd come straight to me so that I could give him the dope on uncle. When he didn't turn up I began to get a bit worried. So was Uncle Herbert. Then my uncle was murdered and it struck me as a damn funny thing that I should hear from Bob almost immediately afterwards."

"What you thought isn't evidence," Wharton told him sharply. "It's no part of a statement unless it's given as a good and sufficient reason for subsequent action."

"Well, there wasn't any action," Sid said. "There wasn't anything I could do about it. It seemed to me it had to be tied up with that business of the three keys. And *I* hadn't killed him . . ."

"Let's get something elucidated," Wharton cut in. "Your duty was to go to the police and give information about those keys. You were questioned and you deliberately withheld information. You'd like to tell us why?"

Sid's hands rose, then fell. He shook his head.

"Then I'll tell you," Wharton said. Then his eyes bulged a bit. "Wait a moment, though. Why shouldn't Captain Dorvan tell us?"

"Delighted," he said, and his lip curled. "All we've heard up to the present is a lot of lies mixed up with what he thought would be just the right amount of truth to make it all sound convincing. He daren't tell you about that money. And why? Because it was probably German money—and Fascist money. He wouldn't have been able to account for the fake names. The Government would have collared the money, pending enquiry, and that was the last thing he wanted."

"What about you!"

That was Sid. Wharton let out a bellow.

"Wait till you're spoken to! I'm the one in charge here. I do the questioning. I'll tell you when to speak."

He gave a grunt or two and slowly let himself become pacified. A last breath was let out.

"Carry on, Captain Dorvan."

"We were all in it, as he said, but I didn't know the whole of it. I was only told so much. Later on I began to think. If that money wasn't crooked, why didn't my uncle deposit it himself? Then I saw the answer. He and Sid didn't trust each other. Rogues never do. I was only brought into it so that they didn't double-cross each other. That's why, when I got back home a few weeks ago, I decided to keep clear of that key business till one of them made a move. Then my uncle was murdered and I had to come forward."

"Well, that's clear enough," Wharton said. "Carry on now, Mr. Sidney Dorvan. You tell us what you did after your uncle was murdered."

"I couldn't do anything," he said. "Then Bob came round to see me at the club. He talked a lot of rot at first, about . . ."

He gave a quick look at Bruff.

"It doesn't matter what it was about. Then he got to the subject of the keys. What were we going to do about the third key. He had his and showed me it, and I showed him mine. Then we did a bit of sparring: him trying to make out he thought I'd done the murder and got the key, and I damn sure he must have done it and got the key. Then we talked over ways and means to find out if the key was still there somewhere, each of us knowing, of course, that there wasn't a hope, or else why had my uncle been done in. And that's how things went on, sort of drifting, till Netta did herself in."

He moistened his lips and gave another quick look at Bruff. Bruff's head dropped to his cupped hands.

"Then I suddenly thought of something," Sid went on. "Something that Netta had done the night before. She kidded me that she'd been listening at the door that night when Bob came round and had heard us talking or arguing about a key."

He paused. His tongue curled round his lips again.

"It isn't so easy to talk about all this, but she put on a sort of vamp act, though I didn't see through it at the time. I fell for it like a sucker. I was the big shot. I showed her the key—my key. 'What do you think that's worth?' I said. 'Looks worth about threepence to me,' she said. 'You used to buy 'em in Woolworth's.' 'Not this sort,' I said. 'This one's worth five thousand quid. Maybe ten.' 'My God!' she said. 'You're kidding me.' She was sitting on my knee and making us both drink out of the same glass. I gave her the key to look at, and she dropped it. She got down to look for it and it was a hell of a time before she found it. She wiped it with her handkerchief. Reckoned she'd trod on it."

He gave a look round at us as if we ought to know what all that meant.

"Carry on," said Wharton. "It's your ideas we want to hear."

"Well," he said, "as soon as I knew she was dead I began to think things out. It was when I was round at her flat, answering questions, that I thought it all out. The whole thing had been a plant. She'd had some wax or something handy and she'd taken an impression of that key. That's why she wiped it. 'And,' I said to myself, 'my God! Somebody's got my key, and that somebody has to be Bob. He did the murder and he's got the three keys, or as good as.' That's why I knew I'd have to have a showdown. The trouble was that now Netta was dead, I couldn't prove anything."

"So what did you do?"

"I went round and saw Bob at his hotel. I accused him to his face and he called me a bloody liar. If Netta had done what I said she'd done, then he knew nothing about it. So he said. Then we got arguing a bit more and he told me to go to hell. He said he had enough on me about that money to get me inside for three years or more. I could do as I bloody well pleased. If I liked to go to the police, I could. He'd had nothing to do with his uncle's murder and getting hold of his key, and the police knew it. Then we went outside and damned if he didn't accuse me of making the whole thing up! Reckoned that when I handled his key that night when he came round to the club, I'd worked that wax stunt, and now I'd made up that Netta story as a cover. He reckoned he ought to go to the police himself, sort of hinting that Netta hadn't committed suicide after all but that I'd put her out of the way."

"And is this where Flatear—Fred Jordan—comes in?" asked Wharton.

"Yes," Sid said and licked his lips again. "I'm not yellow, but I don't want to die with a knife in my back. I told myself that Uncle Herbert was dead and his key had gone. Netta was dead and my key had gone. Maybe the money had gone . . ."

"One moment," said Wharton, and turned to Bob. "I might tell you officially that the money *has* gone. We've had the safe opened by the Deposit Company."

Bob nodded—that's all. His eyes narrowed as he looked across at Sid. Wharton told Sid to carry on.

"Well, I thought the money might have gone too," Sid said. "So if I was to be bumped off under the guise of some nice little accident, who'd ever know that there'd ever been any keys at all? That's why I hired Flatear. I could only watch one way."

"I see all that," Wharton said. "Anything else you want to state, or is that the lot?"

"It sounds to me like plenty," Sid told him, and with the first sign of aggressiveness. "It's up to someone else to do the talking now."

Wharton gave a grunt that might have meant anything. He looked through the papers again, and again turned to Bob Dorvan.

"Any comments or questions, Captain Dorvan?"

"Plenty," he said curtly. "All these fantastic charges he makes stand or fall by one thing. Or two things, now I come to think of it." He smiled. "I haven't had time to think out fancy stories as he has. I'm telling you what I think now. Everything stands or falls on his word alone. He hasn't got a shred of proof. Everything he seems to think is proof simply turns against him if you twist it the other way. He accuses me and swears it's true. I say it's lies and accuse him."

He paused for a moment, nodding his head.

"This is the other thing. Everything stands or falls by Uncle Herbert's murder. If I did it, then he has a case against me. I'm going to find it very difficult to prove he's telling lies. Though what should I care? If I killed Uncle Herbert, then I'm for it. But I know I didn't, and the police know I didn't. Isn't that so?"

"That's so," Wharton told him.

"Very well then. By no possible stretch of the imagination could I have killed my uncle. But somebody killed him. Somebody must have got his key or else the money wouldn't be gone. There's only one living person besides me who knew about that key. We know who that person is. If that doesn't make logic and sense, then I never heard it."

"And what if Mr. Sidney Dorvan has an alibi also for that night?" Wharton asked.

Bob's lip curled.

"Then the gremlins did it."

Then he was looking quickly round. I was included in the stare.

"What's his alibi? It's only fair to me to tell me that. He's been making pretty sweeping accusations."

Well, said Wharton reluctantly, "he doesn't appear to have an alibi."

For half a minute the room had a heavy silence. My eye caught Wharton's and I cleared my throat. In the oppressiveness of that closed room it sounded like a rumble of thunder.

"We don't seem to be getting very far," I said, "or we've got to an *impasse*, if you prefer it that way. I'd like to make a suggestion, and about the murder of Herbert Dorvan. It seems to me by no means certain that he took that train from Charing Cross at four-ten on Guy Fawkes Night."

There was a sensation in court. As I looked at my notes I could almost feel the eyes that had suddenly turned on me.

"Come, come," said Wharton chaffingly. "Let's keep to facts. Murder's a serious subject, as somebody's due shortly to find out."

"That's why I'm treating it seriously," I said. "I say that someone might have impersonated Herbert Dorvan."

"Impersonated?" He gave a little snort. "You call that being serious?"

"Haven't we been forgetting one man who's in this room?" I said. "Impersonation's a mighty serious matter where Mr. Bruff is concerned."

Bruff spoke for the first time.

"Are you suggesting that I impersonated my uncle?"

"Did you?" I said. "Or let's put the question another way. A man calling himself Herbert Dorvan had his lunch in the Southern Hotel at twelve-thirty that Monday. That's beyond all doubt. Where were you, Mr. Bruff, at twelve-thirty that morning?"

He thought for the merest moment.

"At Broadcasting House, working with a couple of men on a script. I was there till one o'clock. I can give you their names and they can prove it."

"Excellent," I said. "But you may be interested to know that we've proved it already. And you, Mr. Dorvan. Where were you at twelve-thirty on that Monday?"

"I've already told you," Sid said. "I was with an Income Tax Inspector till after one o'clock."

Wharton made play with his notes, and murmured something about that being correct.

"Very well," I said. "What about you, Captain Dorvan? Where were you?"

"At Flampton," he said.

"That's curious," I said. "When we were enquiring into your movements it happened to be let drop at the Blue Boar that you'd left there the previous Sunday morning. You'd gone; car, luggage and all."

"Yes, of course," he said. "How silly of me! I'd gone to the Templemore Hotel."

"That's even more curious," I said. "When we were tracing your movements, we were told explicitly that you didn't arrive there till the Monday night. You signed the book to that effect."

"Sorry to contradict you," he said, "but there must be some mistake."

"We don't make mistakes," I told him. "It's our job to find out the facts and be certain of those facts. People hang or don't hang according to the facts we find."

His face suddenly flushed.

"You're not insinuating that I'm lying?"

"We don't insinuate," I told him provocatively. "We ask straight questions and say out bluntly what we know. And you'd be surprised how much we know." My wave of the hand had in it a touch of temper. "But leave all that for a minute. Let's get to that telegram that was sent to Herbert Dorvan on the Friday before his murder. You've all seen it. You, Mr. Bruff. Did you send that telegram?"

"I didn't," he said flatly. "I'd never seen it till I was shown it. Even then it was gibberish to me."

"And you, Mr. Dorvan?"

"The same here," Sid said. "I know nothing about a telegram."

"Then you, Captain Dorvan. Did you send it?"

"I've told you I know nothing about it."

"You're sure?"

"Of course I'm sure."

"I wonder if you'd mind having another look at this copy of it," I said, and passed it to Francis. Francis reached out and Bob Dorvan took it.

He looked at it carefully. He kept staring at it. Almost mechanically he folded it in two again. But he didn't hand it to Francis. He got to his feet as if to hand it to me direct. I held out my hand and leaned forward to take it, and then suddenly he halted in his tracks. Then he whipped round, back to the door.

A gun was in his hand. It didn't look a German gun to me. It looked more like an Army Webley, carrying a slug as big as the end of your thumb, and he held it low by his hip as a gangster holds a tommy-gun.

"Don't move," he said, and he was slowly backing towards the door. "The first move, and I shoot. And I *can* shoot."

The room had a deadly silence. His feet made no sound on the thick pile of the carpet as he shuffled steadily back to the door, and that gun was traversing slowly round. Then, across the room, Wharton got to his feet. What was in the wind I didn't know, but I rose too. Something was happening that hadn't been rehearsed. Maybe there was to be a concerted rush before Dorvan could get out of that door. I know that as that gun wavered between Wharton and myself, my forehead was suddenly cold as death with frozen sweat.

Dorvan backed and Wharton moved in time and then, like a flash, I knew what was in his mind. The gun was steady now, pointing only at Wharton, and then Dorvan's left hand went back and he wriggled the key clear from the lock. Wharton stood still, head forward, and eyes narrowing. Dorvan's left hand felt for the knob, and turned it and the door began to open as he moved sideways to the right. But his eyes were on Wharton only. That had been the reason for Wharton's madness.

For that was when Jewle had him. As his elbow pushed open the door and he backed through, Jewle's arm was round his throat and his knee in his back. A shot shattered the silence. Glass crashed and then tinkled as it fell. Francis and I were at the door together and through the door was a whirl of arms and legs. There was the click of the handcuffs and the bodies sorted themselves out. Jewle and Francis hauled Dorvan to his feet. Wharton was breathing a bit hard, and it was a moment or two before he spoke.

"Robert Dorvan, I arrest you for the murder of Herbert Dorvan. . . ."

I closed the door. Somehow, and I don't know why, I didn't want to hear the rest or watch that last tawdry scene. Sid Dorvan came across to me.

"My God, it came off!" he said. "Damn plucky of Wharton, wasn't it? Made my blood run cold."

I said nothing. I wasn't in the mood for Sid Dorvan, and suddenly I hated that face of his and the streak of moustache and the beautiful pearly teeth. Then as I moved across to Gerry Bruff, Wharton came in. But he wasn't bringing bouquets for Ludovic Travers.

"What the hell did *you* want to move for?" he was hurling at me. "Asking for a bullet in your guts?"

"Maybe," I said. "You were a bit of a bloody fool, too."

He snorted. "He'd never have had the pluck to fire. That sort never has."

Sid was at his elbow and the glare turned on him. "May I go now, Superintendent? I ought to have been round at my place half an hour ago."

"Yes," Wharton told him curtly. "And keep that mouth of yours shut. And don't forget, we shall want a statement from you tomorrow. A bit different from the one you made tonight."

His lip curled as he watched him to the door.

"Something about that oily customer makes me want to commit murder," he told me. Then he was glaring again. "What's the matter with you? Feeling all right?"

"Right as rain," I said.

"You ought to be damned pleased," he said, "the way things have turned out. You coming round to the Yard?"

"I don't think I will," I told him. "In the morning, perhaps, if you let me know the time."

He gave a nod—an uncommonly genial one for him—grunted something at Gerry Bruff and then went out. Bruff had got to his feet.

"A good job you people told me to keep my mouth shut, Mr. Travers. Half the time I didn't know what it was all about."

He was looking tired and drawn.

"You put up a damn good show," I said. "It isn't easy work sometimes, keeping your mouth shut."

"That telegram you showed him," he said. "Why'd he suddenly go all crazy when he read it? You know, whipping out that gun and all that?"

I took out my wallet and gave him a copy of the telegram that I'd passed across to Bob Dorvan.

SEEING YOU SUNDAY CONFIDENTIALLY. SUGGEST YOU HAVE READY K(nowledge) E(xpected) Y(ield). MEANWHILE AM B(uying) O(ut) B(usiness).

Chapter XVII

HOW IT WAS DONE

"It was a shock to me, Mr. Travers," Gerry Bruff told me. "Even when you and the Superintendent were telling me what we'd got to do tonight, I couldn't believe it."

He was looking years older than his age. I held no brief for Netta. Most of her had been gold-digger and trollop, but she still wasn't either to Gerry Bruff. If she'd still been alive and in spite of what he'd heard that night, I think he'd have crawled on his belly to have asked her to come back. And the following morning, as I remembered, was the cremation. Gerry, I told myself, wasn't going to have a good night's rest.

That was why I stayed on, and why—when he asked me—I told him most of what we knew. I could see he was longing for company; anything to shorten the time between then and the next day's light. I said I'd be delighted to have a drink. There was nothing I could do at the Yard that other people couldn't do better, and, if I was really wanted, they could call me at Gerry's place.

I'm not pretending, mind you, that what you're going to read is what I related that night in his flat. I'd had to go over the same ground in Wharton's room hours before, and so what is here set down is a kind of compromise, or a telescoping of two different accounts. You can judge for yourself what I told in Wharton's room and what was related to Gerry Bruff.

He'd said that the discoveries about Bob had been a tremendous shock. Why had Wharton told him he couldn't have done the murder, when all the time the police guessed he had?

"We've got to use duplicity of that sort sometimes," I said. "He thought he'd convinced me that he had an unbreakable alibi for Herbert Dorvan's murder, and so he had—till we broke it. But let's begin at the beginning.

"It started when he was coming home. There was a girl on board the boat, and he and this girl took to each other. He had nothing but what you might call a free-and-easy past, and the arrears of pay that would come to him. He didn't even know if he'd be likely to get a job—a job, that is, that would support that girl in the sort of way she might reasonably expect. She was class to the finger-tips. He wasn't. She had everything he hadn't got, including money, and probably the expectation of considerably more. I don't say she was a snob—I'm pretty sure she wasn't. She might have married him if he hadn't a cent, but that's not the point. Marriages in her circle don't go that way. There'd be her people to meet. Marriage settlements to arrange and so on. But what I'm getting at is that he'd have to prove just who he was and where he stood. And that was probably just what he couldn't do. I guess he'd done a bit of tall talking on that boat, trying to create an impression. When he went to Flampton Grange he knew his lies and bluffing had landed him in a mess—if he still wanted that girl, that is, and he certainly did. So there was only one way out. By hook or crook he had to have money, and quite a lot of it.

"I don't know if being a prisoner of the Japs and seeing the horrors he must have seen made him go cold-bloodedly into what he did. Perhaps his moral fibres were always weak. I don't know. I'm not trying justification. I'm merely trying to explain. What I do know is that he could be highly attractive in himself, especially to women. That girl at the Templemore fell for him like a ton of bricks. I rather think Netta fell for him. Even the country servant at the Blue Boar had a special smile for him.

"So he had to have money, and he thought of the three keys. Or he may have thought of them first. At any rate, there was the money if he could only get it. It would still be in that vault, for the simple reason that he still had his own key. All that was wanted then was the other two keys. So he began a preliminary reconnoitring. He approached you, Gerry, and got the family news, asking you to keep his visit confidential. I believe he went to Midgley. There's no reason why he shouldn't have done. Just a little elementary disguise—the kind he used when he drew the money from the safe—and he'd never have been spotted by his uncle. That's one of the enquiries we shall have to make—about strangers at local inns. If he did go to Midgley he'd have learnt everything about his uncle. He could have studied the lie of the land. He'd have learnt all about Midgley's programme for Guy Fawkes Night.

"But let's get on to facts. The things he did. The whole scheme was clear in his mind, and if you'll let me hark back for just a second, I shouldn't be surprised if he'd been thinking for months about schemes to get his hands on that money. But whether the scheme took a long time or a short to get into shape, get into shape it did. The opening gambit was to send a confidential telegram to his uncle. The word *Peters* would tell his uncle what that telegram was really about. And he expected his uncle to spot what the gibberish—as you called it—really meant.

And his uncle did. He was cleverer than the police were, perhaps because he knew what he was looking for. In any case, the telegram said that Bob was paying his uncle a confidential visit on the Sunday—confidential would mean that Sid wasn't to be told about it—and asked him to have his key ready. Herbert Dorvan followed the instructions.

"But he expected Bob for lunch, and Bob didn't arrive. The hot joint was put back in the pantry, and maybe he thought that if Bob came later, it could be the basis of a high tea. He expected Bob to stay at least a night and that's why he had the spare bed made up. When Bob did arrive—and that would almost certainly be in his car after dark—there was plenty to talk about. But as soon as Bob had got from his uncle all the things he wanted to know, he put a bullet in his head. It would be easy to deaden the sound, and that bungalow's not too near the road.

"Then he set to work. There was no fear of a caller, and he had plenty of time. He'd already booked a room at the Southern Hotel and it didn't matter much when he arrived. In fact, the later the better. A sleepy clerk isn't very observant. The lights mightn't be too much on.

"What were the things he had to do? Well, clear away the meal they'd had—just an ordinary tea after all—and remove every possible fingerprint. He'd brought two old bags with him, as near alike as possible, and he had to pack one with his uncle's belongings and leave it open on the bed to give the impression of a returned traveller. He had to study his uncle's handwriting and then destroy every bit of incriminating correspondence— any letters, for instance, that Sid had written. He had to leave a kind of quickly jotted-down note about times of Sunday trains and a fictitious Peters coming with a car.

"Maybe he didn't expect the police to find out about the telgram. But if they did, further reference to Peters would merely thicken the fog. Even if they traced a Peters who'd known Herbert Dorvan, it would merely have added to the mystery. He knew Sid would never dare own up to knowing anyone named Peters, so what was there to worry about? We can go even further and envisage every possibility, just as Bob Dorvan had to envisage it. Suppose, for instance, Sid was shown the telegram and guessed its secret. That would tell Sid who killed Herbert Dorvan, and still Sid would have had to keep his mouth shut, and for the simple reason that he was mixed up with the original spy or Fascist business for which he and others had been paid that money salted away in the vault. Sid did actually feel sure that Bob had killed his uncle, but what did he do about it? Go to the police? Not on your life. All he did was employ Flatear Fred when he knew he was the probable next on Bob's list.

"But going back to Peters. Bob didn't worry two hoots about owning up to a knowledge of a man of that name, when he wanted to curry favour with me. He was beginning to feel a bit safe, and he even suggested finding Peters through the Home Office. Even if we found that Peters, what connection would there be between that Peters and the murder? None at all. And there he was dead plumb right. It was pure chance, not the finding of Peters, that first showed us a spot of light.

"As for the other necessary jobs to be done before Bob Dorvan could leave the bungalow on that Sunday evening, there was the notice to put on the back door about milk and newspapers. He'd procured some squibs and he had to place them near the front door. There'd be many more things to do—things that I can't remember, but would be absolute proof that Herbert Dorvan had left Midgley on the morning of that Sunday and returned on the Monday evening.

"When everything at last seemed perfect, he drove back to town. Perhaps in his spare bag he had clothes actually belonging to his uncle. We may never know, and because we've no means of checking what clothes Herbert Dorvan actually possessed. My guess is that he garaged his car short of London—Bromley, for instance—and then did his changing in the lavatory of the train. Anything near enough to Herbert Dorvan would do temporarily. The perfect make-up could be done in the hotel bedroom before breakfast the next morning. And he wouldn't even then allow himself to be too closely inspected by whatever waiter brought in his meals.

"As the Herbert Dorvan whose voice had ordered the room, he arrived at the hotel and registered. He stayed in that room because he daren't risk his make-up in daylight, even though he had to take the risk when he came downstairs and sneaked out to the Station telephone boxes to ring up the Broad Street Detective Agency.

"But a word about his voice. When you, Gerry, are being George Robey—shall we say?—you are being Robey to people who know his voice as well as you do. You have to be perfect if you're to deceive. I imagine Bob Dorvan was pretty good at impersonations, but he didn't have to be perfect—at least, when talking to me. If his voice was near enough, then it'd be Herbert Dorvan's voice: a distinctive voice: a blurting, pompous kind of voice. In fact, when I came to enquire what sort of a voice Herbert Dorvan had had, I'd know it had been Herbert Dorvan's voice I'd heard.

"So I talk to Herbert Dorvan. He's scared. He thinks someone wants to kill him. He wants his trusty nephew found. Bob's a good lad—not like the others. Bob's genuine, straight as a gun-barrel. Bob will come to Midgley and look after his old uncle. And that was all he needed to say. He'd impressed Herbert Dorvan on my mind and prepossessed me in favour of Bob. I was to see him then at four o'clock *sharp*. That was essential. Not earlier or later, but on the dot. And I was to wait at the hotel bureau. And I had to describe myself so that his fears could be allayed. All so natural, wasn't it?

"So to the deliberate mistake about the time of the train. There was the letter which I was asked to burn. That letter made an appointment for the Wednesday, so that I ought to find the body. It was a very clever letter. It didn't want me at Midgley before the Wednesday, so it mentioned business with a lawyer on the Tuesday. It mentioned a will, but as he didn't know if there was a will or not, it was deliberately vague. But the main thing was that I had to have a good look at Herbert Dorvan before that, hence the arrangement with the hotel clerk. And Herbert Dorvan took every care, not that he should see me but that I should see him, though only at a safe distance. He showed himself in profile and he came back towards me for a further showing full face. Perhaps his bag wasn't a sufficiently good reproduction of the one we were to find in the bungalow, and that's why he had it taken on by a porter. The porter also reserved a corridor seat as requested, and stood by till Dorvan arrived. But Dorvan didn't stay in that seat to be inspected by the occupants of the compartment and possibly by myself. He left the compartment at once, with a newspaper to mark his seat, and as soon as the train was well on the move, he fetched his bag and dug himself well in the lavatory. There he became roughly Bob Dorvan again. At London Bridge—the last stop before Orpington—he got out. He may have taken a taxi or bus to Bromley and collected his car. At any rate, he reported early that evening at the Templemore Hotel. Further to establish his alibi he took Miss Sanbridge out for the night as he'd previously arranged.

"In everything he'd done there was never a flaw. We might ask questions: why, for instance, had Herbert Dorvan returned on the Monday instead of the Wednesday as arranged, but that would merely add to the mystery. Once we'd accepted the murder as having taken place on the Monday night, he was safe as Gibraltar's Rock. And there was no reason why we shouldn't so accept it, *provided* the medical evidence didn't bitch everything up.

"There he had to take a considerable risk. But my guess is that he knew that it's difficult to tie down the exact time of death for the period between, say, two and three days after that death. Provided that he could make it seem certain that death had occurred on the Monday, he was lessening that risk, especially as the examining doctor would be a country one and not a Yard specialist. I repeat that he probably knew all that. After all, he'd been a kind of medical assistant under the Japs. But he did take one precaution. He ate at the hotel the kind of tea that he and Herbert had eaten and he took care in the bungalow, before shooting his uncle, to let roughly the same time elapse so that the stomach content should agree. But he was also to have a bit of luck."

That was something I didn't tell Bruff. The way I put it to Wharton and the others was this. There was the old doctor, with never a murder case since the one we'd been concerned with two years before, and that particular case didn't require exact timing as to the moment of death. Galley had told the doctor about the man I saw on the train on the Monday night, and how I'd come to Midgley to find the same man dead. I, concerned with the case only as a possible witness, had to do some blethering. There the three of us were, as I said, old friends together again, and everything chatty and gay. In the face of all that, why should that doctor worry himself about niceties? He knew, for the simple reason that we'd told him so, that the dead man had been alive at four o'clock on the Monday afternoon. All he had to do was extract the bullet, look at the stomach content, and collect his fee. The time of death, as he knew, was somewhere about a couple of days before. So that was that.

Gerry had poured two more drinks. I tried to pull his leg about the quality of the whisky and the benefits of being in with the black market, but I couldn't raise a real smile. And that wasn't too good considering what had to follow.

"I don't reckon you'd better hear the rest, Gerry," I said. "It concerns you and Netta. Better forget it. Time I was getting along to the Yard, in any case."

"I'm not yellow," he said. "I can take it, Mr. Travers. I don't want to sit here after you've gone thinking things for myself. It's the truth I want to know. I'll feel better when I know the truth."

"Well, there isn't much that you don't already know," I said. "But let's get back to Bob. He had two keys and all he now wanted was one more. My hunch is that he'd arranged to fit in you and Netta all along. He kidded you that he was going to see Netta to try and induce her to come back here. My guess is that he double-crossed you from the start. He told her she was damn right to leave you. Then he set to work with the old personality. From the word go he concentrated on getting Netta just where he wanted her.

"Then he had to see Sid and get the lie of the land there. He let Sid know that he had few doubts that Sid had done the murder. He saw Sid's key. He bluffed a lot and saw a lot. The final upshot was that he induced Netta to work that scheme for getting an impression of Sid's key. All the while he was working his personality overtime. He was double-crossing you and making you think he'd only to talk to Netta just once more and he'd make her see sense."

I took a long pull at my drink. Then I slowly refilled my pipe. I was old enough to be Gerry Bruff's father, but suddenly I felt even older.

"Still want me to go on, Gerry?"

"Yes, Mr. Travers," he told me slowly. "I told you I could take it."

"Then I'll tell you what we think happened on the day Netta was murdered," I said. I had to look away as I waited.

I could feel his stare. Then I saw that the knuckles of the hand that held the glass were suddenly white, and I wondered if that glass would crush in his hand.

"You're sure of what you're saying?"

"Unofficially—yes. You'd still like me to go on?"

He nodded. But it was a moment or two before his eyes met mine again.

"Here's what we think happened that day," I said. "Netta had the impression of the key. She rang the Blue Boar—maybe overnight—and told him so. He agreed to meet her somewhere in town at, say, ten o'clock. He'd brought a bag with him and he'd parked that at a railway station cloak-room. He took the impressed wax or plasticine or whatever it was, and hurried off to some little key-cutting shop he'd marked down. He asked for urgency and was prepared to pay. Then he kept an appointment he'd made with a man from Broadcasting House and then he nipped back for his key. He told us he'd gone to the cinema. And so he had, but not on that particular day. He'd seen that picture and had carefully noted its timings beforehand.

"Next he met Netta by appointment. He'd been to the vault and extracted the money, and after he'd taken out two packets of notes, he deposited the bag in that cloak-room again or else in another. The search for it is going on now.

"Her stomach content shows that she had a substantial lunch and almost certainly therefore in town. He gave her the two hundred pounds as an earnest of more and asked when he could see her at the flat to give her the rest. She said at, say, four o'clock or a quarter to. But he didn't know what she wanted to do meanwhile. She'd known precisely what she was going to do with some of that money—buy a mink coat she'd seen advertised privately. And that's what she did. She blued the whole two hundred on that coat.

"She must have got back to the flat just before him. When she let him in, she'd be all dolled up in that mink coat. He'd slap his overcoat pocket and say he'd got the balance of the money. He'd tell her how well she'd done in pairing up with him. His line of patter would go something like this:

"'Tomorrow morning—or even tonight—we'll be away and gone as arranged. Next week you'll be making your first picture. I fixed it up this afternoon. What about writing a letter to Bruff and telling him and the others where they get off? What about something like this, just to make them sit up? You write and I'll dictate. . . . There, that's fine. Wait a minute, though. We're due for a celebration. See this? A bottle of special. Bought it for the occasion. Stuff called Versac. Damn good it is too. Bit too early for me, though. I think I'll have a tot of whisky.'

"His overcoat is on, remember, and his hands are gloved. Into her glass goes the cyanide and he brings the two glasses over. 'Here's health, then. Down she goes. No heel-taps.' And down the drinks went.

"And that's about all, Gerry," I said. I was talking at the back of his head, for that head was in his cupped hands. "Sorry you made me tell you all that."

His head shook and he looked up.

"That's all right, Mr. Travers. I asked for it. But what about him getting away from the flat. Didn't anyone see him?"

"It was dark by then," I said, "and foggy. He told us he'd taken a bus back to his car, and we couldn't disprove it, even if we'd suspected him, which we didn't. After he'd set the scene in the flat, he took the Underground and the Piccadilly Tube. Fog wouldn't affect that. What he did with the mink coat we don't yet know."

"You never suspected him at all?"

"Did you?" I said.

He shook his head.

"No," he said slowly, and then, "No," again.

"There *was* just one moment when I did suspect something," I said. "It was at the Blue Boar and I'd showed him a copy of that telegram. Not the one naturally that I showed him tonight. After he'd looked at it and said it conveyed nothing to him, he folded it up, and gave it me back. I said to myself, 'Why should he fold it like that instead of giving it back just as I gave it to him?' Then I thought no more about it. Now I know that the last thing he wanted me to do was to go on talking about that telegram. Folding it was an unconscious or even deliberate act of finality."

There was silence for a moment or two and then I began getting to my feet. He still sat on, and once more he was slowly shaking his head.

"Netta's being cremated tomorrow," he said quietly.

"I know," I said.

There was another silence. His thoughts must have been wandering.

"It was clever," he said, "the way he fixed it. Making it look like Bonfire Night. Those squibs and fireworks going off and everything."

I said nothing. He sort of nodded to himself.

"I'm glad you got him, Mr. Travers." Then he looked up. "He won't be able to wriggle out of all this, will he?"

"You bet he won't," I said. "In another forty-eight hours we'll have him tied up so tight that the devil himself couldn't prise him loose."

He gave himself another nod.

"I reckon Netta knows about all that," he said. "Guess she won't be sorry, no more than I am. Maybe she's thinking about me a bit different too."

You think that a bit turgid? Emotion's not in your line? Maybe you're the strong, silent type. Inoculated in your schooldays with a glandular injection of Kipling's *If*. But I wasn't feeling that way. I was doing some thinking too. I thought of that little Miss Sanbridge, and how her face had flushed when I'd mentioned a name. I thought of that girl at Flampton: the girl on the terrace, patting a dog and laughing up happily into the face of the man.

"I guess she is, Gerry," I said, and gently touched his shoulder. Then I heaved a sigh.

"I'll be pushing along now. Take a sleeping-tablet or two if you've got any. If not, there's an all-night chemist just along the road. Maybe I'll drop in for a moment in the morning."

He got to his feet. It was a long time since I'd seen that quiet smile on his face. For a moment he looked almost a boy again.

"You're a good sort, Mr. Travers. You're genuine, if you know what I mean."

"Forget it," I told him.

"Any show I'm in you've only got to ring me up and the best seat in the house is yours."

"Thanks, Gerry," I said. "That's mighty good of you. One of these fine days I'll be taking you at your word."

We parted at the door. I made my way down the carpeted stairs—the way Bob Dorvan had gone—and out to the concreted car-park and my car. It was well after midnight. The night had a kind of velvety blackness you could feel as you rubbed it in your bare fingers. Overhead, the sky was clear and the stars looked very large and uncannily near. In the distance across the Park was the faintest hum of traffic, like strange, distant bees across a meadow, and somehow the sounds were a background for the silence itself.

Then suddenly and from somewhere near was a sound. Some might have taken it for the crack of a gun. But I didn't even smile to myself as I knew it for the back-fire of a car. For a moment it had been Guy Fawkes Night again, and I had been in Midgley, and in the darkness there had been the sound of a squib.

THE END

www.ingramcontent.com/pod-product-compliance
Lightning Source LLC
Chambersburg PA
CBHW031014190726
48286CB00003BA/832